BURIED Secrets

RACHEL J. GOOD

REALMS

Most CHARISMA HOUSE BOOK GROUP products are available at special quantity discounts for bulk purchase for sales promotions, premiums, fund-raising, and educational needs. For details, write Charisma House Book Group, 600 Rinehart Road, Lake Mary, Florida 32746, or telephone (407) 333-0600.

BURIED SECRETS by Rachel J. Good
Published by Realms
Charisma Media/Charisma House Book Group
600 Rinehart Road
Lake Mary, Florida 32746
www.charismahouse.com

Cover design by Lisa Rae McClure
Design Director: Justin Evans

Visit the author's website at www.racheljgood.com.

This is a work of fiction. Names, characters, organizations, places, events, and incidents are either products of the author's imagination or are used fictitiously.

Library of Congress Cataloging-in-Publication Data:
An application to register this book for cataloging has been submitted to the Library of Congress.
International Standard Book Number: 978-1-62998-953-2
E-book ISBN: 978-1-62998-954-9

17 18 19 20 21 — 987654321
Printed in the United States of America

Chapter One

BUNDLED IN HER black wool cloak, Emma Esh knelt in the newly tilled garden, a flat of seedlings beside her. Once she would have danced with joy in the pale sunshine of early spring after being cooped indoors through the long, cold winter. But the past month had drained much of her exuberance.

So had the past three years of her life. She had no lingering physical aftereffects of the accident that had almost taken her life, other than the loss of her memory about the months before and after it happened. But her spirit had never healed. So she'd been happy to move to the Gratz area, more than an hour from Lancaster, to help her sister Lydia and brother-in-law, Caleb, before the birth of their twins. Perhaps once the *bopplis* arrived, Lydia would turn her mothering instincts to the newborns instead of worrying about Emma's every move. Her sister meant well, and Emma appreciated all Lydia, Caleb, and *Mammi* had done to nurse her back to health after her coma, but Lydia's hovering made her feel as if she were twelve instead of nineteen.

Emma concentrated on the plants beside her. Gardening soothed her, made her feel whole again. The spring sunshine warmed the ground and sent comforting rays through her cloak as she bent over the soft, moist earth. She lifted a seedling from its pot and inhaled the savory tomato-y aroma.

Then she pinched off the lower leaves, set it in the hole, and gently bent the stem before covering it with soil.

Whoosh. A heavy weight slammed her backward, smashing her head against the ground. Gasping, desperate to suck some air into her crushed lungs, Emma opened her eyes to find a furry face inches from her own. A huge mouth opened, revealing pointy white teeth. Then a wet pink tongue scraped across her cheek.

"Bolt," a deep male voice commanded, "off!"

A handsome stranger, black bangs hanging in front of his eyes, bent over her, his hand outstretched. *"Ach,* I'm so sorry. She slipped out the door again." He clamped his other hand on the Irish setter's collar and pulled the dog off Emma, leaving muddy paw prints across her skirt.

Still dazed, Emma lay where she'd fallen, gazing up at him, unsure whether the rapid pattering of her pulse was from her recent fright or from looking into the greenest eyes she'd ever seen.

"Are you all right?" Worry crinkled his brow.

"I–I'll be fine." Ignoring the hand he'd extended, she tried to sit but winced at the sharp jab in her side.

The stranger dropped to one knee beside her. "Don't get up if you're hurt. Is there someone I can fetch?"

"I don't need help." Heat flooded Emma's cheeks when her words came out sharply. "I'm sorry," she whispered. "Please forgive me." Then, pinching her lips together, she steeled herself to sit without assistance and without getting poked again by the straight pins. If only *Mamm* would let them use snaps instead of pins to secure their dress seams.

"There's nothing to forgive. I'm the one who let my dog escape." The words were barely out of his mouth when the

Irish setter twisted free and bounded off, crushing the rows of seedlings Emma had just planted.

"Oh, no!" The stranger dashed off after the dog, swerving to avoid the tomato plants the setter had crushed. Gasping for air, he made a desperate tackle, landing a few feet beyond the garden, the dog wriggling under him. With a firm grip on the Irish setter's collar, he stood, the front of his shirt, galluses, and black pants splattered with dog hair and dirt.

Emma suppressed the urge to giggle at his sheepish expression, the clod of mud clinging to his forehead, and the panting dog struggling to jerk free of his hold.

He pinched his lips together as he studied the mess. "I'm so sorry. Let me put Bolt in the house. Then I'll help clean up."

"Bolt?" Had he called the dog that earlier? Emma had been too distracted to pay attention. Now she couldn't hold in her mirth.

Rather than taking offense, the stranger glanced down with a rueful expression, then joined in her laughter. "*Jah*," he said between hearty chuckles. "Short for Lightning Bolt. She zigs and zags so fast I can't catch her sometimes." He waved a hand toward the disaster in the garden. "Like she did here. And now look at me."

Emma gazed at him, and her laughter ended in a sharp intake of breath. Then his eyes met hers, and she stopped breathing altogether. Part of her wished she could reach up and wipe that dirt from his forehead.

His cheeks flushed, the man lowered his gaze. "Well, I best get this troublemaker inside. I'll be back shortly."

Emma followed his progress to the back door as he cajoled Bolt along. She admired his patience with the unruly dog. Part of her hoped he'd hurry back, but another part warned her to finish repairing the garden before he returned. She knelt and hastily replanted a few of the undamaged plants, but the dog had destroyed most of them.

She was almost finished with the final row when he returned in fresh clothes. With a bit of disappointment, she noticed he'd washed the mud from his forehead, leaving his bangs damp.

"Sorry for taking so long. Please accept my apologies for the damage."

"*Ach*, no, don't blame yourself. Bolt can't help being lively." Emma chuckled, remembering him chasing the Irish setter.

A hint of a smile played across his lips. "I'm glad you can see the humor in it. Most people would be upset. I suppose I did look rather foolish chasing and tackling her."

"Not really." Actually he had looked athletic and strong, but Emma couldn't say that. When she was younger, she might have blurted that out. Over the past few years she'd learned to hold her tongue, but she couldn't control the laughter bubbling up inside. "It was the—" She dissolved into giggles and gestured helplessly to his forehead and shirtfront.

"The mud?" he finished. "I looked a sight, didn't I?"

Actually, except for the mud, he had been quite a sight. That thought was enough to quell the laughter. "I'm sorry. I shouldn't be making fun of you."

"I'm just grateful you aren't angry." His smile widened. "I'm afraid I never introduced myself."

"I don't think we had time."

"True. I'm Samuel Troyer. Sam." He motioned to the house next door. "I've come to help my *onkel* Eli with the planting and harvesting."

Emma felt awkward kneeling on the ground admiring the stranger towering over her. "Welcome to the neighborhood," she managed to answer. "I'm Emma Esh, and I'm new here myself. I came a month ago to stay with my sister Lydia and her husband, Caleb."

"It's nice to meet another newcomer. I've been here a week but haven't met many people yet. *Onkel* Eli keeps me busy." He rocked back on his heels and surveyed the garden. "I was sure she uprooted more plants than that. You've done a wonderful *gut* job of fixing the garden, but not all of those plants can be replanted, can they?"

He knelt beside her, close enough that the scent of soap wafted toward her. Although she wanted to lean closer and inhale the fresh smell, Emma resisted the urge. Sam's large tanned hand reached for the spade at the same time she did, and their fingers collided.

A hazy memory floated through her mind but disappeared before she could focus on it. If only she could grab the fleeting bits of the past and patch them together like the quilts *Mamm* made.

"Are you all right?"

Sam's voice came from a distance, cutting through the fuzziness.

"I–I'm fine." *I think.*

"You look dazed. You hit the ground rather hard."

"Don't worry, my skull's pretty thick. At least that's what my family always says. That I'm hardheaded."

Sam's deep laugh sent shock waves through her. "You have a great sense of humor."

Emma quirked one eyebrow. "My family never thought so. I'm afraid I was a lot like your pup when I was younger."

"That's good."

Good? Emma turned a puzzled gaze up to meet his but wished she hadn't. She found herself admiring the long lashes framing his eyes. She lowered her eyes and dug a hole for one of the last few seedlings, struggling to keep her mind on the conversation. "I doubt my family would agree with you on that. I had a habit of speaking and acting before thinking." Often she still did.

"That's called being spontaneous. It's a wonderful gift."

A gift? Emma almost choked. Not according to *Mamm* and Lydia, who'd spent much of their time trying to teach her to sit still, be patient, and stay silent.

She couldn't resist peeking up at him again to see if he was teasing or serious, and found Sam studying her closely.

"You look as if you don't believe me," he said.

"It's nice to hear my behavior called something other than troublemaking for a change."

Sam's eyes held compassion. "Many people don't appreciate the honesty that comes with speaking your mind. I've always found it refreshing."

Emma blinked back the moisture in her eyes. Ever since the accident, even simple kindnesses caused a sudden flood of tears. "*Ach*, if only my family believed that were true."

A seedling cupped in one hand, Sam tilted his head as if inviting a confidence.

Emma wished she hadn't said anything. Waving one hand dismissively, she said around the lump in her throat, "I was always the problem child." She couldn't look at Sam, so she concentrated on setting a seedling in the hole and patting dirt around it. "Breaking my exuberant spirit seemed to be everyone's mission."

"I'm so, so sorry."

"What?" Emma was sure she'd misheard him.

"As you can tell from my dog, I prefer exuberant spirits. I've always thought it a shame when parents force lively children to be docile and quiet." He pretended to glance over his shoulder. "I shouldn't let the bishop hear that. It's not always a popular view."

The crinkly smile lines around his eyes and the rueful twist of his lips intrigued Emma. It was a contrast to the dour frowns she'd endured most of her life.

Sam laughed. "I bet your family thought you were a lot of fun to have around."

"Not really. My earliest memories are of everyone—*Mamm*, *Dat*, my sister Lydia, the older women at church, even the bishop—glaring at me or pinching their lips in disapproval. Even worse was my *mammi*'s sad-eyed look of disappointment."

"That's such a shame." Sam's words sounded sincere.

Emma still wasn't sure if he was mocking her. "You seem calm now. Sedate even." Sam's face crinkled up in a mischievous grin. "Do you still break out and have fun? You know, like Bolt? *Do things* others don't approve of?"

"Not anymore."

Sam's gentle eyes promised acceptance, but her memories were too murky, and she shouldn't be criticizing her family to a stranger.

To deflect the feelings she was struggling to hide, she thrust his question back at him like a lance. "Do *you*?"

"I haven't for a while." His words held a hint of sadness. He stood, brushed off his hands, and dusted off his pants. "I should be getting back to work."

Emma wondered what had caused the light to disappear from his eyes. Once again she rued her words.

Sam held out a hand to help her to her feet. "And you should get out of the sun. Your cheeks almost match the tomatoes."

Thank heavens he attributed her flushed face to being outside. What would he think of her if he realized his touch, combined with his acceptance and kindness, had set her face ablaze?

When he let go of her hand, Emma's spirits dipped as if the day had gone from being sunny to overcast. "Wait." Emma reached for his hand again but stopped short. Hadn't she just told Sam she didn't act impulsively? She'd almost pulled on his sleeve to stop him from leaving.

Sam stood waiting, hands clutching his galluses, eyeing her quizzically.

"Umm, I thought..." What had she thought? She couldn't say that she wanted him to hold her hand again, stay and talk to her. But with Sam waiting patiently for her to finish her sentence, what could she say? "That is, I wondered, well, if you'd like a glass of root beer." She hoped he didn't detect the relief in her voice that she'd made a quick save.

When he looked at her, fingers plucking at his galluses, she regretted blurting out the invitation.

Sam looked regretful. "Much as I'd like to, I'd better leave for work. I told *Onkel* Eli I'd get there as soon as I could." One side of his lips rose in a crooked, but endearing, smile. "*Danke* for the thoughtful invitation."

Of course he had work to do. And he'd already been delayed by helping her. Still Emma couldn't help but feel disappointed. She forced herself to smile back. "I'm sorry to keep you from your *onkel*."

"You didn't delay me. It was my dog who caused the havoc."

Emma couldn't resist. "Well, you said you liked spontaneity."

"*Jah*, I did. And you have to admit, aside from the damaged plants, it was rather fun. After all, I got to meet you."

Emma wasn't sure how to respond. She wasn't used to compliments, although there was a time...The thought trailed off as she lost track of what had almost surfaced.

"I'm glad about that too. That I got to meet you, I mean. Not about the tomato plants. Oh—" Once again her tongue had tangled her in trouble. "Don't worry about them." She rushed her words out to cover the slip. "I didn't mind replanting them. Really I didn't."

"I regret that, but it was nice to spend some time with you." He shuffled and thrust his hands deeper into his pockets. "I should go, but I hope to see you around."

"Me too." Emma hoped she didn't sound overeager. She released a pent-up breath after Sam turned and walked away. But she lingered in the garden, taking her time gathering her tools and the flats, so she could watch him until he was out of sight. Then she carried the tools to the shed, her mind racing as fast as her pulse.

It had been a long time since she'd talked to a man around her age, and she regretted her lack of practice. Back at home, by the time she'd recovered from the car accident, other couples had already paired off. Even worse, conversations stopped abruptly when she approached, leaving her feeling self-conscious and left out. At least here at Lydia's no one knew of her accident or looked at her pityingly.

Emma shook off her gloom and concentrated on Sam. His smile. His closeness as they'd knelt in the garden. His kind words had soothed her and made her feel whole rather than broken. The thought of him smeared with dirt and dog hair made her smile. She tucked that image of him into her heart and her faulty memory bank.

Chapter Two

H ER LONG BLONDE hair still damp from the shower, Lydia brushed a few wayward strands from her face, supported herself against the kitchen counter, and reached for a glass in the upper cupboard. A twinge in her side made her catch her breath. She eased her arm down, set the cup beside the sink, where it wobbled a few seconds before settling, and then massaged just under her rib cage until the stitch ended. Even simple movements during her pregnancy often set off these odd spasms, so Lydia was grateful to have Emma's help with the chores.

At the same time, *Mamm* had been relieved to send Emma to Caleb's *daadi haus*, far from the gossip in their *g'may*. Lydia hoped that if Emma stayed in this new area, nothing would trigger memories of three years ago—the year Emma turned sixteen and started *Rumschpringe*. So far her younger sister hadn't remembered anything about those months or her time in the coma, for which they were all grateful.

As Lydia filled her water glass, she glanced out to the garden, where Emma was bending over the plants. Emma lifted her face to smile at someone beside her. Lydia scooched over until she had a clearer view. A dark-haired young man, who appeared to be in his early twenties, was squatting a row away from her sister, chatting as if the two of them were old friends. Who was he, and how had Emma met him without her and Caleb knowing? At least he was Amish rather than *Englisch*, but she and Caleb would have to find a way to keep Emma and this young man apart.

Hands cupped under her belly to ease some of the burden, Lydia waddled toward the back door. For now, she'd call Emma inside to help with a job. They could sort the baby clothes. That would keep them busy until Caleb got home. But before Lydia could reach the back door, Emma and the man stood. He tucked his hands into his galluses and looked uncomfortable as Emma spoke. Then he turned and left. Lydia exhaled in relief. Perhaps she had nothing to worry about—except for the fact that Emma stared after him for a long time after he left. Although Lydia couldn't see her sister's face, judging from Emma's stance, she'd definitely need to keep an eye on this situation.

As Emma picked up the tools and headed back toward the house, Lydia busied herself with filling her water glass. Should she speak to Emma about what she'd seen? *Mamm* had begged her to keep her younger sister out of trouble, but Emma often got prickly when Lydia made suggestions or expressed concern about her actions. They didn't need a repeat of three years ago, when Emma had fled her home and family, but blamed her rebellion on Lydia's interference. A heavy load of guilt caused Lydia to hold her peace and head for the nursery.

∽∞∽

Her thoughts still on Sam and their conversation in the garden, Emma wandered through the house searching for her sister. She found Lydia in the room they'd chosen for the nursery, sitting on the rocker, bending over to sort through some boxes on the floor.

"Are you all done planting the tomatoes?" Lydia's voice seemed a bit strained.

"Yes, I planted all the ones I could." For some reason Emma avoided telling her about Sam and the crushed plants. She wanted to keep that to herself for now.

Lydia stared at her intently, a tiny frown etching small creases on either side above her nose.

"*What?*" Emma said almost defensively.

Lydia shrugged. "You seem a little different. Almost as if…" She shook her head. "I guess planting made you smile like that?"

"*What?* I can't smile without it being odd?"

"I didn't mean that."

Emma held back the breath she wanted to huff out. Leave it to Lydia to dampen the joy she'd been feeling following her conversation with Sam. Lydia's expression made her want to snap, *What did you mean?* Instead she clenched her fists together and repressed her irritation. Lydia and Caleb had done so much for her, and her sister was extra sensitive now while she was pregnant, so Emma forced herself to ask, "What can I do to help?"

"I'm sorting through the boxes from cousin Hannah. We can wash the smallest baby clothes, and then we'll put the larger-sized ones in the attic."

Emma sat on the floor and drew one of the boxes toward her. They sorted in silence for a while, allowing her to replay her conversation with Sam. She pressed her lips together to hold back a giggle at the memory of Sam tackling Bolt, but a small snort escaped.

Her sister looked up, head tilted to one side, a questioning look in her eyes.

Emma sniffled a little and coughed, hoping Lydia would think it was a touch of hay fever from being outside. She should have known she couldn't fool Lydia. Her eagle eyes bored into Emma. Her sister's gaze always seemed to be judging her, making her feel inadequate, inferior.

All it took was a look, and once again Lydia had squashed Emma's happiness. To distract herself, Emma seized an outfit in the bottom of the box and held it up. "Oh, look at this. *Mamm* must have given it to Hannah."

Her sister's expression softened, and her eyes grew misty. "I remember when Zeke wore that."

The two sisters shared a smile at the thought of their youngest brother wearing that baby outfit. Emma could hardly believe he was nine already. The nostalgia eased some of the tension between them, and they sorted in companionable silence until they had all the baby clothes in piles for washing, storing, or mending. While Lydia leaned back in the chair, stretched, and massaged her back, Emma repacked the larger clothing into cartons.

"Are those too heavy for you to lift?" Lydia asked. "If they are, you can leave them for Caleb. If they're not, would you carry them to the attic?"

Emma bent and hefted one of the boxes. They were a bit heavy, but she was determined to move them. She schlepped up and down the steps, carrying the cardboard cartons until she was exhausted. While Lydia closed the lid on the last box, Emma opened the closet door.

"You have some bags in here, Lydia. Shall I pull them out for sorting?" Emma grasped the top of a bag and started to drag it out of the closet.

"What?" Lydia glanced up, and a look of alarm crossed her face. "Oh, no. No." She maneuvered herself out of the rocking chair and hurried over. She slammed the door and leaned against it, panting a little, her face flushed. "You've done enough hauling for one day."

"Are you all right?"

"Yes," Lydia said breathlessly. "Let's just leave those for Caleb."

"All right," Emma agreed, puzzled by Lydia's strange reaction. The bags were lighter than the boxes she'd been hauling to the attic.

"I–I'm hungry. Are you?" Lydia's chest rose and fell rapidly. "Why don't we have some lunch?"

"Um, sure. But maybe you should sit down for a while first."

Lydia shook her head. "I'm fine. Just a little winded. Why don't you go ahead and start lunch? I'll rest here for a few minutes and then come down."

Emma had no idea how Lydia planned to relax in that position, her back pressed against the door, her arms outstretched across it. The tight lines around her eyes and mouth revealed her strain. And Lydia seemed eager to get rid of her sister. Uncertainly Emma walked toward the door, but before she left the room, she turned to check on Lydia, who had her eyes closed. She was taking deep breaths and mumbling to herself. Something had upset her, but what?

◔◐◑

As soon as Emma padded down the hall, Lydia heaved a sigh of relief. She crossed the room, sank into the rocker, and tried to calm her racing heart. She'd forgotten they'd stored those bags in the closet. After everything they'd done to get Emma away from Lancaster, to help her forget, the last thing they needed was for her to find those clothes. Who knew what memories they would dredge up?

She had to keep Emma away from the closet until Caleb could dispose of the bags. She should have done that long ago. Originally she'd wanted to check with Emma first, but now that Emma was back in the faith, those clothes would not be needed. The sooner she got them out of the house, the better. Caleb rode to work with an *Englischer* who worked at the same hospital. Perhaps the man would know of a charity where they could donate the clothing.

Lydia only hoped her overreaction to the bags hadn't aroused her sister's suspicions. Knowing Emma, she might be tempted to peek inside. And staying up here so long would make her doubly curious. She needed to get downstairs.

Lydia maneuvered herself out of the rocking chair and shuffled down the hall. Then, clutching the railing with one hand, she tucked the other under her belly for support and eased herself down one step at a time. She was so big already, and she still had over two months to go. Carrying twins wasn't easy, but it would all be worth it if these *bopplis* were born alive and healthy. She tried to concentrate on that thought rather than the sadness that washed over her. *Danke, Lord, for keeping them safe so far. I pray Your blessings on both of these dear* bopplis.

By the time she reached the kitchen, Emma had made

Lebanon bologna and cheese sandwiches—two for Lydia and one for herself—and was setting out chow-chow and a pitcher of lemonade.

Emma glanced up and studied her. "I was just about to come upstairs to check on you. Are you sure you're all right?"

"Of course. Why wouldn't I be?" Lydia regretted her sharpness when hurt flickered in Emma's eyes.

Emma turned away and grabbed two glasses from the cupboard. "You didn't look fine when we were up in the room." Some of the old sullenness had returned to Emma's tone, and her words sounded disbelieving.

Lydia took a slow, calming breath. She needed to make peace with her sister. Emma had been concerned, and instead of responding with kindness, Lydia let her own worries drive a wedge between them. "I'm sorry, Emma. I didn't mean to sound so *grexy*. It's just that…" That what? *That I was scared you'd look in those bags and remember the past? That I feared my carelessness would cause you heartache?*

Lydia sank into her chair, but Emma stood beside the bench holding the cups as if waiting for Lydia to finish the sentence. "I'm tired," Lydia said, words that sounded lame to her own ears, and her conscience nagged at her. Not only had she told a lie—well, it wasn't really a lie; she truly was exhausted—but she'd also made excuses for her behavior, which was *hochmut*. A picture flashed through Lydia's mind of that long-ago argument when Emma had accused her of being prideful and self-righteous—an argument Emma might never remember, but one Lydia would never forget. And here she was proving Emma right.

Yet Emma surprised her by speaking gently. "Caleb

warned me not to let you do too much. I should have done the sorting myself and let you rest."

Lydia laughed. "If my husband had grown up in a big family, he'd know we're used to working hard. Instead he coddles me and wants me to take an afternoon rest." Not that she minded, and if she were truthful, she often needed the break. She felt guilty, though, letting Emma do so much of the work. And what would her parents think if they knew how lazy she was being? Their mother stayed busy from dawn until night. "Can you imagine *Mamm* ever taking a nap?"

"Nooo..." Emma said. "Most of the time we can't get her to rest even when she's sick."

"She does what needs doing in spite of how she's feeling. I told Caleb that, but if he had his way, he'd tuck me into bed and have people wait on me hand and foot the whole nine months."

Beside her, Emma frowned. "You should be grateful he wants to take care of you."

Lydia repressed a sigh. Emma assumed she was criticizing Caleb. Why did it seem she and Emma always talked at cross-purposes?

"I am grateful. It's only that—" There she went again, defending her motives. The truth was she didn't feel deserving of such pampering, and she struggled to accept help from others. As the oldest sister, she'd always looked after others. She still had trouble accepting all the attention Caleb showered on her.

Lydia's mouth curved into a smile at the thought of her husband's tenderness. After three years together, she loved him more than ever. Her heart overflowed with gratitude to God for giving her such a wonderful man.

Emma interrupted her thoughts. "We should eat so you can take your nap."

Her sister said it teasingly, but her tone had a slight bite of jealousy that added to Lydia's guilt. How could she be so blessed when her sister might never find true love?

She and Emma bowed their heads and said the Lord's Prayer silently. When Lydia looked up, Emma was nibbling at her lip rather than the sandwich. Should she ask what was wrong? Sometimes Emma resented her interference.

Before she could decide, Emma burst out, "You could think about Caleb's feelings sometimes, you know."

Lydia sat stunned at the hostility in her sister's voice. Just as she'd feared, Emma thought she'd been criticizing Caleb.

"He's lost so many people he loves. His parents. And then his *daadi* less than a year ago. No wonder he worries about you and the *bopplis*. Plus he blames himself for the miscarr—" Emma clapped a hand over her mouth, her eyes wide. "I forgot. Caleb warned me never to mention it."

"Caleb has no reason to feel responsible for what happened. Why would he think that?" Had he told Emma that, or had she jumped to her own conclusion?

"I don't know." Emma's sullen expression had returned. "He didn't tell me anything else, only that if he'd been here, it wouldn't have happened."

Oh, poor Caleb. He'd said he was sorry so many times, but she'd never realized he thought it was his fault. "It was an accident." Lydia shut her eyes, wishing she could block out the memory of that night. A sharp kick to her kidneys made her gasp.

Emma jumped up, almost knocking over the bench. "What's wrong?"

Lydia waved away her sister's concern but couldn't catch her breath. A tiny foot or elbow thumped again and again. She rubbed the side of her stomach, hoping to soothe the twin battering her insides.

"Are you in pain?"

"Good pain," Lydia wheezed out between kicks. An active *boppli* meant a healthy *boppli*, didn't it? When she could draw in a breath again, she thanked God for the kicks, which brought her back to the present moment and reminded her of His many blessings. "Don't worry, Emma. It was only one of the *bopplis*."

Her sister sat back down but kept a wary eye on her. Lydia picked up one of her sandwiches and took a bite, and Emma relaxed. They spent the rest of the meal discussing plans for fixing up the nursery. When they rose from the table, Emma cleared the dishes, while Lydia headed for the stairs to take her usual nap.

She paused in the doorway. "Oh, Emma, why don't you start on the mending? I'll put the pile on your bed." Although Lydia knew her sister disliked mending, she had to find a way to keep Emma out the nursery until Caleb had disposed of those bags.

Chapter Three

ENDING? EMMA ALMOST shrieked the word as Lydia turned and left the kitchen. Was her sister punishing her? Although she supposed she deserved it. She shouldn't have blurted out things Caleb had told her in private or reminded Lydia about the miscarriage. Caleb had asked her to keep Lydia's focus away from the sadness of the past, and he'd given her a long list of symptoms to watch for. His background in medicine along with his fear of losing another child made him overly cautious. Emma thought it was sweet that Caleb worried so much, but Lydia didn't seem to appreciate how lucky she was.

Their *mamm* and *dat* had a strong marriage, but she'd never seen her parents hug or kiss the way Caleb and Lydia did. At first whenever Emma was around, Lydia squirmed away, her cheeks pink. Lately she'd become more relaxed. Although Emma was happy for her sister, she had to admit she was jealous too. Part of her yearned to have a relationship like Lydia and Caleb's. Yet, at the same time, a strange sickish feeling churned in her stomach when she thought about dating. Someone like Sam might make her change her mind, though. They'd had a good time together that morning. She couldn't remember ever having that much fun with a guy, not since—Emma winced at the sharp pain in her temple. She'd almost remembered something, but when she tried to bring it into focus, the edges grew fuzzy and indistinct. Often these flashes led to migraines if she tried too hard to dredge up the memories, so she massaged her forehead and pictured Sam in the garden—his smile, the mud on his forehead, his kind words—until the shooting pains subsided.

Her headache threatened to return full force after she trudged upstairs to face the pile of baby clothing Lydia had left on her bed. She should mend the little dresses, but concentrating on tiny details made her impatient. And she despised sewing. Perhaps she could move those bags to the attic and scrub out the closet.

Emma tiptoed past Lydia's room and into the nursery. She eased open the closet door, grabbed the top of the first trash bag, and pulled it toward her. The bottom of the bag caught on the rough wood floor, so Emma tugged it harder. The bag came loose with a jerk, almost knocking her over. She managed to steady herself, but lost her grip on the bag. The top opened, and one of the garments inside tumbled to the floor.

Emma bent to pick it up. A green wool sweater. As soon as she touched it, her hand trembled, and fog curled around her brain. As she fingered the sleeve, a memory stirred deep in her mind. A hazy picture of her in a mirror wearing the emerald sweater danced before her eyes. Emma giggled. Ridiculous. She never would have worn *Englisch* clothes. Perhaps she had dreamed it? Or had she seen someone wearing it? Were these Lydia's clothes?

The harder she tried to remember her sister during *Rumschpringe*, the more her mind rebelled, dropping a thick black curtain over the past. Tight bands squeezed across her forehead, and pounding started behind her eyes. Emma rubbed her fingertips over her eyebrows to relieve the pressure building inside her scalp. Though it eased the tension slightly, a wave of grief washed over her.

She thrust the sweater back inside and twisted the tie to close the bag, but it had a huge hole in the bottom where it had caught on the floor. Emma tiptoed past Lydia's door again and went downstairs to the kitchen for a new trash bag, trying to shake off the tendrils of sadness squeezing her heart. Back in the nursery, when she lifted the torn bag and placed it inside the new one, the spiky heels of strappy red sandals poked through the opening. Emma laid them carefully in the bottom of the new bag but couldn't help wondering why Lydia had these clothes.

Before closing the new bag, she removed the emerald sweater. She wasn't sure why, but it felt as if this sweater held a clue to her shrouded past. She should ask Lydia about it, but for some reason she was reluctant to do so. She took the sweater and secreted it in her dresser drawer. Then she carted the bags to the attic.

By the time she finished scrubbing out the closet, the worst of the headache had eased. She closed the door with a sigh of relief and went to start supper. Lydia, groggy from napping, joined her in the kitchen. Several times as they prepared the meal, a question almost escaped Emma's lips, but each time something stopped her. After Lydia's reaction earlier that afternoon, Emma worried it might upset her sister to talk about the bags.

As usual, Caleb returned home around six o'clock. "Something smells delicious," he said when he walked into the kitchen. He made a beeline for Lydia and wrapped his arms around her.

Lydia darted a sideways glance in her direction, so Emma pretended to be absorbed in dishing out the potpie. The spark of jealousy she'd felt earlier flared into flames as Caleb extended the embrace with a lengthy kiss. Emma tried to tell herself she didn't do it on purpose, but the serving spoon clattered into the pot with such a loud clang that Lydia and Caleb jumped apart.

Lydia looked flustered, but Caleb smiled. "Sorry, Emma. I almost forgot you were here," he said. "This pretty lady makes me lose my head. I'm such a lucky man."

And Lydia was equally as lucky. Emma forced herself to smile and nod. She was happy for her sister; truly she was. But it was hard to watch their joy, knowing she might never marry. Couples in her *g'may* had already paired off, and she was unlikely to meet anyone in the short time she'd be here, especially since she attended church so infrequently. Seeing Sam that morning had given her hope for the future, which he'd dashed when he declined her invitation. Maybe he didn't want to come back to the house for a root beer because he was courting someone. And even if he didn't have a girlfriend, who'd want to marry someone with a missing memory?

As they sat at the table, Lydia's flushed cheeks and starry eyes reminded Emma of all she'd lost. For the past few years she'd wrestled with these longings and come to accept her lot in life as God's will, but meeting Sam had unleashed the old yearnings for a home and family and, most of all, someone to love.

The conversation drifted around her until Lydia said, "So Emma started the mending."

"Actually I didn't get to it yet." Emma took a deep breath.

Perhaps now was her opportunity to ask the question that had been bothering her. "I know you told me to leave those bags in the closet alone, Lydia, but I put them in the attic."

Her sister drew in a sharp breath.

"Did I do something wrong?" Emma set her fork down on her plate and looked from Lydia to Caleb and back again.

Caleb's brow furrowed in confusion. Lydia shook her head, but the panicked look in her eyes worried Emma.

She had to confess what had happened. "Actually, one of the bags split when I was dragging it. A few things spilled out—*Englisch* clothes. When I went to put them back, I saw a green sweater."

"A green sweater?" Lydia's voice turned sharp, panicky. "Did you see anything else?"

Maybe she shouldn't have started this conversation. "Just some red high heels."

Lydia blew out a breath. "Those were on top with the sweater?"

"No, they fell out of the bottom of the bag. I picked them up and put them all in a new trash bag." Well, that wasn't entirely true. She hadn't returned the sweater to the bag. But she would. Soon.

"I should have gotten rid of those."

"But why do you have *Englisch* clothes, Lydia?" Emma couldn't contain her curiosity.

"You have *Englisch* clothes?" Caleb echoed.

Oh no. Emma felt awful. Perhaps Lydia had not wanted Caleb to know.

Then Caleb's brow cleared. He glanced at Lydia. "Are those—?"

Lydia hushed him with a sharp, "Shh."

"Oh." Caleb swallowed hard. "Maybe we should ask her?"

Emma was totally confused. "Ask who, what?"

"Never mind." Lydia shot Caleb a warning glance, then turned to Emma and held out her plate. "I'd love another serving of potpie, if there's any still left." With an apologetic smile she waved at the almost empty serving dish. "After all, I'm eating for three."

Emma took the plate and serving dish, and jumped up. She filled both and hurried back to the table in time to see Lydia and Caleb, heads together, mouthing frantically to each other. What was going on? And why had those *Englisch* clothes caused such a stir? Whose were they?

Emma thumped the serving bowl onto the table, and her sister and Caleb stopped their silent communication. Then Emma handed Lydia her plate.

Caleb's serious look made Emma's stomach flutter. "Did I do something wrong?" She wanted to make things right. "If so, I'm very, very sorry."

Caleb took a deep breath, and ignoring Lydia's pleading look, he set a hand over Emma's. "Did you recognize any of the clothes?"

Emma shook her head. "No, why? Should I have?"

Lydia relaxed back into her chair.

"I suppose not." Caleb removed his hand with a sigh.

Yet Emma could tell that he wasn't satisfied with her answer. She tried again. "Well, the sweater has been bothering me."

Caleb leaned toward her, eagerness written in every line of his body. "Bothering you how?"

Emma gazed off into the distance. "I feel as if I've seen it before. But I can't remember who wore it or when. I don't have any *Englisch* friends, and I can't believe Lydia ever wore it. Unless she had a secret life we don't know about." Emma giggled, but it fell into a strange, vacant silence.

Both Caleb and Lydia stared at her with fearful, expectant eyes.

"*What?*" Emma felt as if she'd just exposed someone's deep, dark secret. Had Lydia—before she joined the church? "Oh, no, did I say something wrong? Lyddie, I'm sorry. Did you not want Caleb to know? Me and my big mouth. I must learn to curb my tongue."

Lydia waved as if to dismiss Emma's words, but her eyes held tears.

Emma plopped into her chair. "What's wrong? Tell me. What did I do?"

"Oh, Emma." The anguish in Lydia's words tore at Emma's heart. "I wish you'd never seen those clothes. Can you just forget them?"

Emma wasn't sure she could. And she'd brought the subject up because the sweater had been haunting her.

To make amends for whatever trouble she'd caused, Emma stacked the plates. "While I do the dishes, why don't the two of you go in the living room and relax? I can bring coffee and dessert out there later, if you'd like."

Following the end-of-meal prayer, Caleb helped Lydia from her chair. "*Danke*, Emma," he said. "It would be nice to spend time with my favorite lady."

"Emma might think she's not a favorite too," Lydia teased.

Caleb bowed in her direction. "Emma, my dear, forgive me. You certainly are a favorite of mine." He put an arm around Lydia. "But I have a special place in my heart for this gorgeous creature." He kissed the top of Lydia's head. "You do understand, don't you?"

Emma laughed. "Of course." She motioned them to the doorway. "Now scoot, and let me get the kitchen cleaned up." Tears pricked her eyes as Caleb pulled Lydia closer and led her down the hall. It had taken awhile to get used to Caleb's open expressions of love; he didn't care who was around when he cuddled Lydia. Perhaps that was because he'd grown up in the *Englisch* world, where feelings of love and affection were more openly expressed.

Lydia and Caleb whispered together as they walked down the hallway, and Emma thought she heard the words *green sweater*, but she wasn't positive. What had she started by finding it?

Once they were seated in the living room and out of Emma's hearing, Lydia relaxed a little, but the thought of her sister seeing the green sweater knotted her stomach. "What are we going to do? What if she remembers?"

Caleb's hand, large and warm, massaged her tense neck muscles. "If she does, it means her mind and spirit are ready to face the truth."

"I don't ever want to see that happen." Lydia's eyes brimmed with tears. "I can't even imagine how heartbreaking that will be for her." All her muscles tensed at the thought, and only the gentle pressure of Caleb's fingers released the tightness. Fretting about Emma seemed to be turning into a full-time job. "Oh, and there's one other thing. She met a young man today."

"That's nice. She hasn't had a chance to meet any *youngie* since she's been here."

"No, you don't understand. She already seems interested in him." Judging from the way Emma stared after him as he walked away, she was already smitten.

"Who is he, and how did they meet?"

Relieved that Caleb seemed to share her concern, Lydia relaxed a little. "I've never seen him before, but he headed across the yards toward"—Lydia choked on the next word—"Eli's." So many sad memories were tied up with their neighbor and his house. Lydia pushed them away to concentrate on Emma.

Caleb's hand stilled, and his eyes filled with sympathy. Wrapping an arm around her shoulders, he drew her close. "I wonder if it's his nephew. One of the men at church mentioned he was coming to help Eli farm this summer."

Lydia suspected Caleb was right. If this nephew lived right next door, how would she be able to keep him and Emma apart? "What will we do if they decide to date?"

Caleb looked thoughtful. "We'll have to trust God for guidance."

"I am. I mean…" At Caleb's probing look, she hung her head. "I guess I'm not trusting if I'm worrying."

Caleb tilted her chin up. "You're worrying because you care." With gentle fingers he smoothed the wrinkles in her forehead. "It's hard not to worry when you're the oldest."

How true. And Caleb had even more to worry about than she did. As guardian of his younger brother, Caleb had spent many hours in prayer for Kyle's soul. But Kyle, now in his third year of premed at Duke, had turned his back on Caleb, his extended family, and especially on God. He wanted nothing to do with the Amish faith and refused to visit his brother.

"I can't believe Kyle will be turning twenty-one in a few weeks. I figured I'd see him then because he'd want me to sign the papers to turn over his trust fund, but…" Caleb's eyes reflected his sorrow.

Lydia reached for her husband's hand and squeezed. He had tried so hard to connect with Kyle.

"He called the hospital before my shift started this morning"—Caleb's jaw clenched—"when he knew I wouldn't be there. He left a message. A lawyer told him it can all be done by mail."

"Oh, Caleb." Lydia snuggled closer. "Maybe it's for the best, though, with Emma here."

"I'd invited him here for spring break before I knew she was coming." Some of the tightness around Caleb's eyes eased. "I suppose for her sake it's good that he refused, but it still hurts. He's all I have left."

"You have me." Lydia laid her head against his chest.

Caleb's arm tightened around her. "Oh, sweetie, I didn't mean it like that. You and the babies mean the world to me."

"I know," Lydia said as he kissed the top of her head.

"Kyle is all I have left of my childhood family. With Mom and Dad gone, and now *Daadi*…"

"You don't have to explain. I understood what you meant." Caleb had lost his parents in a car accident when he was in college. He'd dropped out to care for Kyle, who seemed to have no appreciation for his older brother's sacrifice. And Caleb had only recently met his Amish family. Losing his grandfather had been difficult.

They sat in silence for a few minutes before Caleb said,

"But back to Emma. I was hoping when she mentioned the green sweater, it meant her memory was returning." He sighed. "I guess not."

"I consider that a blessing." Unlike Caleb, Lydia hoped Emma's memory would never return. She never wanted her sister to have to face her painful past—a past that held so many buried secrets.

*

Emma dawdled doing the dishes to give Caleb and Lydia some time together, but she also found herself daydreaming about Sam. The kitchen windows provided a view of their driveway and Sam's, which ran side by side. His house sat several yards from the driveway. Back when she was the star pitcher in her *g'may*, she might have been able to lob a base-ball and hit their side window. She pretended to wind up and throw, imagining Sam's startled face appearing to see what had banged into the glass. With her luck lately, though, she'd probably shatter the window.

Emma turned her attention back to the dishes, but kept glancing up, hoping Sam might come out to walk the dog. Or that he would do some work in the fields behind the house. When she could delay no longer, Emma headed for the living room. She hated to barge in on Lydia and Caleb, but she'd promised to bring them dessert, so she padded down the hall in her stocking feet and paused to listen. If they were talking, she'd pop her head into the room to see if they were ready. If they were silent, she'd give them their privacy.

Emma truly wasn't trying to eavesdrop, but she couldn't

help overhearing Lydia's question. "You don't think Kyle would come to see the babies, do you?"

"I doubt it." The wistfulness in Caleb's voice made it clear he wished his brother would show up.

Poor Caleb, Emma thought. Kyle was his younger brother, but for the life of her, Emma couldn't remember ever meeting him, and he didn't visit. She'd heard Lydia and Caleb mention his name once, when they were planning their wedding, but they stopped talking when she entered the room, so she couldn't ask any more about him. Perhaps Kyle was upset that his brother had joined the Amish and left him to face the *Englisch* world on his own.

She couldn't imagine being estranged from her sisters that way. *Jah*, she and Lydia annoyed each other sometimes, but deep down they loved each other. She hoped Caleb and his brother would soon make their peace. It was sad when family members held grudges; they needed each other.

Emma didn't hear Caleb's murmured response, nor did she want them to know she'd been eavesdropping, so she slipped back into the kitchen and loaded a tray with slices of chocolate mayonnaise cake and cups of coffee. Then she banged a few cupboard doors open and shut before calling out, "Ready for dessert?"

In spite of all the noise, she still surprised them with guilty looks on their faces when she came through the doorway holding the tray.

Caleb rapidly smoothed his expression into a welcoming smile. "That looks delicious, doesn't it, Lydia?"

Lydia stared in Emma's direction, an absentminded frown crinkling her forehead. The corners of her lips twitched as if she were attempting to curve them upward but the rest of her facial muscles were fighting it.

"Lydia?" Caleb repeated.

Emma's sister shook herself as if waking from a nightmare. "What?"

"The cake," he said as Emma handed him a generous slice. "This is one of my favorite kinds."

"Oh, yes, it looks good." Lydia's words came out expressionless, but she held out a hand for the dessert plate. Her "Thanks, Em" sounded strangled.

Emma wasn't certain, but she thought she glimpsed a flash of pity in her sister's eyes. What was going on?

Chapter Four

As Sam and his *onkel* headed back to the house after milking the cows the next morning, Sam's mind was still on the previous day's incident in the neighbor's garden. "*Onkel* Eli, is there a place nearby where I could buy some tomato seedlings?"

Onkel Eli stopped and tugged on his beard as he eyed Sam. "You fixing to plant a garden?"

"No, it's just that"—Sam's face heated—"Bolt trampled the neighbor's garden yesterday."

"Told you that dog would be trouble, boy." He looked Sam up and down, mumbling something about problems with neighbors.

"What's that? You've had difficulties with the neighbors? They seem nice enough." Granted, he'd only met one of them, but she seemed friendly.

Harrumph. *Onkel* Eli cleared his throat and studied Sam's face. "I saw you with that girl yesterday. Be neighborly, but don't go getting tangled like that pup with his leash. Not worth it," he muttered. "You love 'em, and then they die."

Aunt Martha died last fall, and *Onkel* Eli had been grieving so much he'd barely been able to get out of bed in the mornings. Sam's mother had insisted he keep his *onkel* company on the farm this year. Not that Sam minded getting away. It was easier not seeing Leah Rabin—no, Leah

Stoltzfus now—every day. His heart still ached from her betrayal.

"Yer not pining after that other girl, are ya?" *Onkel* Eli's features settled into a deep frown. "While yer here, best stay away from trouble. And the pain."

Sam had to agree. "I'm not in the market for a wife," he assured his *onkel*. "But I do need to replace those damaged plants."

"*Jah, jah.* That would be the right thing." *Onkel* Eli waved toward the turnoff beyond the next farm. "Follow that road toward Gratz, and there'll be a market on the left. They should have seedlings."

"I'll join you as soon as I've walked the dog and taken care of the garden," Sam said.

For the past few days *Onkel* Eli had been building a stone wall for one of the *Englischers* a mile down the road. Sam was assisting, but he didn't have his *onkel*'s gift for masonry.

The minute Sam lifted Bolt's leash from the wall peg, the setter bounded over, tail wagging. She wriggled so much, Sam could barely clip the leash to her collar. He hadn't been prepared for a dog, but when this stray turned up, dirty and bedraggled, ribs showing, a few weeks before he left for his *onkel*'s farm, he'd taken her in and cared for her. But he hadn't realized how many challenges an overactive animal would present—although even if he had, he still would've adopted the Irish setter. One look into those eyes was all it took.

His thoughts drifted to Emma. Even while she smiled and laughed, she had a hint of sadness in her eyes, as if she'd been badly hurt. A fear, a holding back, a slight hesitancy to engage. He'd seen the same apprehension in Bolt's eyes when he'd brought the shivering dog inside. Beneath that, though, Sam could see the free spirit Emma said she once was. If only there were a way to unlock it. His *mamm* had warned him about collecting strays. He wondered if she'd classify Emma as one of his "reclamation projects," as she called them.

Sam shook his head. No, planting tomatoes was as far as it would go. He had enough trouble with one stray; he didn't need another.

Lydia and Emma were just finishing a midmorning snack when someone knocked at the door. Lydia struggled to get up from the chair.

Emma waved her back into her seat. "I'll get it." She hurried down the hall and pulled open the door.

Sam stood on the doorstep, a flat of tomato seedlings in his arms. "I wanted to replace the plants Bolt destroyed."

Emma hesitated before answering to prevent an effusive welcome from slipping out. "*Danke*, but you didn't need to do that."

Sam's slightly crooked grin warmed Emma's heart. He seemed almost nervous, but surely she wasn't that intimidating.

"I certainly did. Your garden's only half planted because of my dog. I wanted to ask permission before digging in your yard, though."

Emma had been about to refuse the seedlings, but if she did, he'd plant them himself. "Don't be silly. I can put them in myself. Like I said, you didn't need to get them." She reached for the container, but he stepped back and held it out of reach.

"I'll do it, but I wouldn't mind some company, if the day's not too chilly for you."

"I intend to help. Just let me get a warm coat."

Sam nodded. "I'll meet you around back."

Emma pulled her cloak off the wooden peg by the front door. She headed through the kitchen, where Lydia was nibbling on her slice of coffee cake.

Lydia glanced up questioningly. "Who was that?"

"Umm...your next-door neighbor."

"What's the matter? You have such a strange look on your face. And you're wearing your coat. Is something wrong?"

No, something's right. For once. Emma tried to mask her excitement. "Everything's fine. He brought tomatoes because his dog ran through the garden yesterday and uprooted some."

"That was thoughtful. But why don't you sit down and finish your tea? The tomatoes will wait."

Ah, Lydia, ever the practical one. "He's out back, intending to plant them. I can't let him do that."

"Of course not. Eli is getting too old to stoop and kneel. But...wait. You said dog. Eli doesn't have a dog."

"Not Eli. His nephew, Sam, owns the dog."

"So you've met his nephew? You never mentioned it."

The odd expression on Lydia's face made Emma nervous. Was there something wrong with her meeting Sam? Or did Lydia know something bad about Sam? Emma didn't have time to find out. She needed to get outside before Sam planted all the tomatoes. *Sure,* her conscience needled her, *you only want to prevent him from doing too much work.*

"I met him yesterday when his dog got loose." Inside she was wriggling with impatience, but she balled her hands into fists and hid them under her cloak. She had to hide her eagerness from Lydia. Emma didn't want her sister to get the wrong idea. "Sam feels guilty about what his dog did."

Hoping she'd said enough to satisfy Lydia's curiosity, Emma forced herself to turn and walk toward the door casually enough to dispel Lydia's suspicions.

The chilly spring wind slapped her in the face as she closed the door behind her. Heavy gray clouds blocked the pale sun, making Emma shiver. Or was it the sight of Sam kneeling in the garden, his back to her? Hoping Lydia wasn't watching from the window, Emma rushed toward him.

"Hi," she called out, but then wished she hadn't. Her greeting sounded breathless and overeager.

Sam turned, and the smile that lit his face erased the cloudy sky, and sunshine spilled over her, warming her until she overflowed with joy. Before she could stop them, her lips responded, returning the smile with such enthusiasm her cheeks ached.

Although Emma wished she could keep staring at him, she lowered her gaze.

"*Gude mariye*," he said. "You didn't have to come out and help."

Emma tried not to let her hurt show. Didn't he want her there? She'd been so eager to be with him; perhaps she'd misunderstood his teasing earlier.

But Sam dispelled her gloom when he added, "Not that I don't want your company. I only meant planting these should be my responsibility."

"I'm happy to help." Emma reached over and gently removed the seedling he was practically crushing.

"I'm sorry." His cheeks reddened. "I should have been paying more attention."

Emma sighed inwardly. Why did she do things without thinking? Better to have a squashed tomato plant than to hurt someone's feelings.

His lips set, Sam picked up the spade and jabbed it into the ground. Was he upset with her for embarrassing him? Or frustrated with gardening?

"Sam? You don't need to plant them. I can do it."

He glanced up. "I'll do it." His teasing smile returned. "Unless you're afraid I'll mess this up too. I actually do know how to dig holes. I've been doing that since I was three."

He flipped the soil over, and Emma relaxed. Maybe she hadn't offended him after all. "You must be an expert at it then. Why don't I plant the tomatoes after you dig the holes?"

"*Gut* idea." Sam started on the second hole. "I'm sure the tomato plants will be grateful they're in your hands rather than mine."

Emma giggled and knelt by the first hole, but then wished she'd waited. Sam was so close, his arm brushed hers, setting off a swarm of bees buzzing in her stomach and zooming along her nerves. Though she longed to lean closer, she forced herself to stay in place as he moved to the next spot, and then she waited until he moved on before putting in the next plant.

At the end of the row, Sam rubbed his back, stretched, and took a deep breath. "Ahh, it smells like plowing time."

Emma inhaled the warm, moist scent of freshly turned earth, a comforting, familiar smell. Spring flowers lightly perfumed the breeze. "My *dat* always sniffs the air and crumbles the soil between his fingers to tell when to begin tilling the fields."

"He doesn't rely on the *grundsau* then?"

"Of course he does," Emma teased. "The *Englisch* aren't the only ones who watch to see if the groundhog will see its shadow."

"*Jah*, I know. Even *The Budget* mentioned Groundhog Day this year."

"That's because the *grundsau* didn't see its shadow, so everyone thought we'd have an early spring. Last year at this time we had two feet of snow. It's hard to believe it's warm enough for planting already."

Sam sighed as he turned over another pile of fresh dirt. "I wish I could convince *Onkel* Eli to start the farming. I prefer being in the fields; I don't think I'm much help when he's repairing stone walls. Except for carrying rocks."

"I'm sure he's happy to have your assistance."

"Perhaps, but I'm mainly here to keep him company. I'm not sure I'm successful at that either. He barely eats or speaks. *Aenti* Martha's been gone since last fall, but he still misses her something fierce."

"I'm sorry. I'm sure she was a wonderful woman."

"She was. She loved children but never had any of her own, so every summer she invited one of my brothers or me to stay with them, and my sisters took turns too. We helped *Onkel* Eli on the farm, and *Aenti* Martha took care of us, fed us, and made us laugh."

"She sounds lovely."

"*Jah*, that she was. I suspect that's why *Onkel* Eli's avoiding the tilling. *Aenti* Martha always helped him in the fields."

"That would be hard."

Sam nodded. "I understand how he feels. I just hope he doesn't put it off until it's too late."

"Most people have already started." Tractor motors growled in the distance as their *Englisch* neighbors plowed and planted, but Emma preferred the Amish way of horses pulling the plows. "Caleb doesn't farm his *daadi*'s land; his cousins do. They began a few weeks ago. If they knew your *onkel* needed help, I'm sure they'd be happy to do his fields too." The fields stretched behind both of their houses with only a rail fence between them.

"I'd be happy to do the work, but *Onkel* Eli insists he needs me for the masonry work. I hope I can convince him differently." Sam stood and moved to the next row. "So you're here to help your sister? And will you be staying for a while?"

"I'll stay as long as Lydia needs me."

"Do you miss your family? That's been the hardest part for me. I'm grateful *Mamm* writes several times a week." Sam cleared his throat. "But it's not the same as being home."

"I know what you mean. I miss *Mammi* and Sarah the most." Emma rarely felt judged around them, and *Mammi* had cared for her after the accident, strengthening the bond between her and her grandmother. "It's also hard being away from *Mamm* and the boys. But *Dat*..." She stared off into the distance.

After a few moments, Sam prompted, "And your *dat*?"

Emma's chest tightened until it was as constricted as her heart, and the lump in her throat blocked her air passages. Neither would let words escape. She could only shake her head to let Sam know. The sympathy on his face and understanding in his eyes released the tears she'd been blinking back. She tried to brush them from her cheeks with the backs of her hands, but the dirt on her fingers mingled with tears to form muddy streaks on her hands. Mud she was probably smearing across her face.

That reminded her of Sam with the clump of mud on his forehead and his chase after Bolt. A laugh bubbled up, releasing the block in her throat. She tried to stop her chuckle, but it pushed its way out until she was laughing through her tears.

Sam's brow furrowed, and his expression switched rapidly from compassion to concern. But she couldn't catch her breath to explain.

"I'm...all...right," she managed to wheeze out, but he didn't look convinced. "I was just...remembering...you chasing...your dog."

Sam smiled, but his eyes remained wary as if he were worried she was edging toward hysteria.

Emma pinched her lips together to contain her laughter, but giggles exploded from her. "I'm...fine. You...and Bolt."

The tension around Sam's eyes eased into smile lines.

Worrying she may have hurt Sam's feelings, Emma choked off her laughter. "I'm sorry. I wasn't laughing at you."

"I know. I imagine it was hilarious, me chasing the dog. And I was a mess after tackling her."

"Like I am now," Emma said, holding out her dirty hands. "Picturing streaks of mud on my face reminded me of that."

"Hold still a minute." Sam steadied her chin with the fingertips of one hand and drew a handkerchief from his pocket. He wiped the tears from her cheeks, creating muddy stains on the soft cotton. Then he tilted her face from one side to the other, studying it from every angle. After taking one more swipe, he balled up the handkerchief, dirty side in, and released her chin.

Emma closed her eyes, wishing he hadn't let go. The warmth of his fingertips remained imprinted on her skin. After taking a deep breath, she said, "Before I started laughing, you asked about my *dat.*" She concentrated on lifting another seedling from the flat and placing it in the ground. "When I was young, I was *Dat*'s favorite. I preferred doing chores with him, while Lydia and Sarah stayed indoors with *Mamm.* I milked the cows with him until my younger brothers were old enough to take my place. I also helped him with farming, except at harvest time, when everyone worked together."

Sam had rocked back onto his heels and was listening intently. His gentle smile encouraged her to continue.

"*Dat* and I stayed close, and I went to work in his cabinet business when I finished eighth grade. But a few years after that"—her lower lip trembled—"everything changed." She clenched her fists and stared at the ground. "Now it's like he can't stand to look at me. And…and I don't know why."

"I'm so sorry. That must be hard."

"It is. When I get homesick, I remember that, and it makes it easier to stay here. And I also think about—" Emma broke off before she confessed her loneliness around the other *youngie* of the *g'may.*

Sam's raised eyebrow invited her to continue, but Emma didn't want to admit the truth. How the others had ignored her, how everyone her age had already paired off, leaving her an old maid.

With a shrug she brushed it off with a quick "It was

nothing." But the lie turned her stomach as sour as the time she'd eaten too many green apples.

"I'm glad you're here. It's nice to have someone else who understands the homesickness. Most of the *g'may* have lived here all of their lives."

His heartfelt smile chased away the sting of past snubs, but it couldn't erase the pain of *Dat*'s rejection. To keep her tears in check, she turned her full attention to Sam's welcoming face. Maybe as newcomers they could support each other, become friends, and perhaps in time she and Sam could become something more to each other. But why did that thought fill her with as much fear as exhilaration?

Chapter Five

YESTERDAY'S GRAY CLOUDS had massed into dark, stormy skies. Outside the windows, rain gushed in torrents and splashed from the gutters in waterfalls as Emma pulled the breakfast casserole from the oven. The aroma of sizzling onions, bacon, and cheese filled the steamy kitchen.

Milk containers clanked on the back porch, and then Caleb banged through the back door. He turned, shook the dripping black umbrella, and thrust it into the holder near the door. A blast of cold air seeped from the open door, making Emma shiver.

She hurried over to take the basket of eggs. "Thanks for gathering these for me."

"No need for both of us to get soaked." Caleb handed over the basket before returning to the porch for the milk. As he removed his galoshes, he sniffed the air. "Breakfast smells delicious. I'll see if Lydia's ready to eat." He hung his wet coat on the peg by the door, washed his hands in the sink, and headed upstairs.

He returned a short while later, his arm around Lydia, who was already dressed for church. He helped her into her chair and bent to kiss the top of her head. Emma should have averted her eyes and allowed them their private moment, but she couldn't help watching and wishing that someday a man would treat her with that much caring. Sam, perhaps?

When Caleb cleared his throat, Emma jumped. She'd been standing there staring, lost in daydreams. Pushing away the fantasies, she picked up the pot holders and carried the casserole to the table.

After they'd bowed their heads and said the Lord's Prayer in silence, Emma served the casserole, being sure to serve Lydia an extra-large portion. Lydia smiled and thanked her, and Caleb added his own grateful smile. They ate a few bites, and then Caleb turned toward Lydia.

"I was thinking it might be best if you stayed home from church today. It's windy and pouring out there, so you might catch a chill."

The tenderness in his eyes touched Emma's heart and again made her long for someone who cared for her that deeply. She'd gaze at him as adoringly as her sister was gazing at Caleb.

Lydia's gentle words matched the sweetness of her smile. "I'm sure I'll be fine. I'm healthy, and I've always gone to church in all kinds of weather."

"Still, I'm worried about you and about the babies."

"If it bothers you that much, I'll stay home." She patted his hand.

Emma hid her own smile at the thought of Lydia being coddled. Lydia had always been the hardest worker in the family and the least delicate. She'd milked cows, worked in the fields, carried in wood, and done chores in all kinds of weather. *Dat* had shielded *Mamm* and the girls from some of the heavier chores, but when he wasn't around, as the eldest, Lydia took over those duties.

"I'd rather not take that chance."

By the time breakfast was over, though, the cloudburst had let up. A light drizzle fell, streaking the glass and pattering lightly on the porch roof. While Emma gathered the dishes, Lydia and Caleb whispered together. She overheard her name, but the clatter of silverware and dishes blocked out the rest. When she returned to the table, Caleb had just pushed back his chair.

"I'll get ready for church, and then we'll see. If the rain slows more and you bundle up, I think it will be all right for you to go." He turned to Emma, and his face sobered. "I don't suppose you'd consider going? The Schrocks' house is only two or three miles away."

Emma snatched up the last of the dishes and backed away. Her hands trembled so violently that the stoneware chattered in her hands. She hurried to the sink and set down the plates. Her back to him and her breathing ragged, she said, "If you give me directions, maybe I could walk." It made her nervous to think of walking in a strange area alone and possibly losing her way, but the idea of being in a vehicle on the road brought up pure terror.

Caleb sighed. "You shouldn't walk in this weather. With the way the wind's blowing, you'd be soaked by the time you got there."

The disappointment in his eyes added to her shame, igniting a flare of anger. Why did he keep pushing her to ride in a buggy when he knew her reluctance to do so? It didn't matter if it was two miles or twenty. After her accident she'd developed a deep aversion to riding in anything, buggy or car. Sometimes even thinking about roads or crossing busy streets brought on panic attacks. As much as she longed to go to church, she couldn't. Not unless she walked.

∽

Leaving Emma behind on church Sundays filled Lydia with guilt. She blamed herself for her sister's accident. If she hadn't begged Emma to come home that night...If she hadn't chased her around during *Rumschpringe*...If she'd been less self-righteous...

"Lydia?" Caleb took her arm to help her into the buggy. With his other hand he sheltered her with an umbrella.

Tears pricked at her eyes. She didn't deserve such loving-kindness when she'd made such a mess of her sister's life.

"Are you all right?" A tiny frown puckered Caleb's forehead. "Are you in pain or anything?"

Lydia forced herself to smile. "I'm fine. The babies are fine. I was worrying about Emma. I wish..." Her voice trailed off.

"I know. We need to find a way to help her get over her fears. She's curled up in the living room, reading her Bible, but it would be nice if she could attend church."

That hadn't been what Lydia was concerned about, but if she confessed what she'd really been thinking, Caleb would only remind her it wasn't her fault. Just as she'd once assured him that it wasn't his fault that his brother's reckless driving had caused the accident. Both of them still believed they were responsible for what happened to their younger siblings.

Caleb went around the buggy and climbed in the other side; then he flicked the reins, and the horse trotted off. "Emma's mention of that sweater got me thinking. She tries not to let it show, but it's obvious she's not only afraid to get in vehicles, but she's also deathly afraid of the dark. I wonder if knowing the truth about the past would help her get over some of her irrational fears."

Lydia sucked in a breath. "Oh, Caleb, no. Don't ever tell her about that, please."

"But what if it helped her heal?"

"How would knowing about the past help her? She's better off never knowing what happened."

Caleb held the reins lightly in one hand and stroked his beard with the other. "I'm not so sure."

Lydia leaned over and gripped his arm. "No, please. Promise me you'll never tell her."

Caleb pulled to the side of the road to allow several cars to speed past them. The cars splashed muddy water, which splattered the side of the buggy. He turned to face her. "I'm not sure that's the right choice."

Lydia squirmed under Caleb's probing gaze. He was her husband, and she'd need to abide by his decision. When she lowered her head, he chuckled.

"Giving in to me, eh? I'm not sure I'll ever get used to that aspect of Amish life. Too many years as an *Englischer* run through my veins."

Lydia peeped up through her lashes at his heartwarming smile, but she kept silent. She trusted her husband's judgment. He was always fair and kind.

Before he pulled back onto the road, Caleb took her hand. "We'll do it your way for now, but if it seems she'd be better off knowing the truth, we'll discuss what to tell her, and we'll do it together."

"*Danke,*" Lydia breathed, grateful to have such an understanding husband.

Letting go of her hand, Caleb watched for a lull in traffic and then steered the buggy back onto the road. "I'm surprised she's never asked any questions."

"I'm thankful for that. I'm not sure she wants to know."

"You may be right."

"But that makes me even more concerned about the situation with Sam. Emma has no idea she shouldn't date. What are we going to do about that?"

"Why don't we trust God to work things out?"

Of course, Caleb was right. He'd reminded her of their need to trust God before. Lydia wished she could surrender her worries as easily as he did.

After they pulled into the Schrocks' driveway, Caleb helped Lydia into the house and gave her elbow a quick squeeze before she joined the women in the kitchen. She missed Caleb's warmth and support before and during the service, although he always kept an eye on her and raised a questioning eyebrow to be sure she was all right. She smiled and nodded each time he checked.

The nearest crowd of women shifted to let her join their circle, and they greeted one another with a kiss. Lydia answered all their questions about how she was feeling. Her mind still on Emma, though, Lydia let most of the conversation drift around her until several women mentioned Sam's name.

"Samuel Troyer? Is that Eli's nephew?" she asked. "I haven't had a chance to meet him yet."

"*Jah,*" Annie Fisher replied. "He's here to help his *onkel* with the farming, although they haven't gotten much plowing done far as I can see. Sam helped out on the farm when he was younger, but the past few years his brothers have each taken a turn. Last summer his brother said he was courting the bishop's daughter, so I expected him to be married by now." A gleam entered her eye. "He's such a fine young man, though, I can't help hoping he's available."

With six daughters, the Fishers would be happy to have another eligible bachelor in the neighborhood. Annie would see to it that Sam paid attention to her girls. Evidently Annie and her daughters weren't the only ones interested. Several other mothers sounded equally intrigued. Lydia relaxed a little. With so much competition for Sam's attention, maybe she didn't have to worry about Emma after all.

By the time Emma started washing the dishes that evening, the grays of dusk had darkened into shadowy gloom. Caleb and Lydia had arrived back from the church service in the late afternoon, so Lydia napped much later than usual. After a supper of soup and sandwiches, they'd gone up to the nursery to discuss painting the room, leaving Emma alone in the kitchen. With darkness pressing in on all sides and only a small circle of light to illuminate the sink, her nerves grew tauter and tauter.

When someone rapped on the front door, the plate she was cleaning almost slipped from her hand. Her teeth clenched, she clutched at the soapy stoneware to keep it from crashing into the sink. Who would come calling now? Emma dreaded opening the door at this time of night, but Caleb and Lydia were upstairs. Whispering a prayer for courage, she let the plate slide back into the dishwater and dried her hands. Then she forced her feet down the hall to the door, one slow step at a time.

Taking a deep breath, she clicked the latch and inched open the door. It took a moment before the silhouette on the doorstep became distinct from the vast blackness beyond.

"Sam?" She breathed his name, both startled and pleased. She assured herself the fluttering of her pulse was from fear of the dark, but then Sam smiled, tripling her heart rate.

"Hi, Emma. I noticed you weren't at church today. I was hoping you weren't ill."

"No, no." Her hasty reply came from her constricted throat. "I–I never go to church when..." Her voice trailed off. "Never mind."

He hesitated as if waiting for more of an explanation, but when she remained silent, he asked, "So you're not sick?"

"Nooo." But she soon might be. The darkness behind Sam was pressing in, making her chest tighten. Her hand gripped the doorknob until it almost cut off her circulation.

Sam's words rushed out. "*Onkel* Eli suggested I go to the hymn sing tonight at Zooks'. I get nervous when"—Sam plucked at his galluses—"I have to talk to strangers. It's been years since I've been to a hymn sing at this *g'may*. I thought maybe..." He stuttered to a stop.

Emma bit her lower lip, and her hand trembled. The cold cuts from dinner congealed in her stomach.

"I have the buggy out and thought...maybe you'd like to go with me?" Sam gestured toward his horse, waiting patiently in his driveway.

Emma's eyes widened. "In your buggy?" Her voice squeaked, then grew hoarse as she blurted out, "No. Oh, no."

Wooziness closed over her. *No, no, no*…She pitched forward, slamming the door.

Stunned and shell-shocked, she collapsed against the closed door, shivering. Sam's invitation had stirred up a whirlwind of fear and pain. Terror swirled around her, and the trembling increased until she was shaking uncontrollably. Anguish rose from deep inside, constricting her lungs and throat, closing off her breathing.

Her legs wobbly, Emma crashed to the floor. The memory of peering out into the pitch-black night sent tremors coursing through her, and dread pooled in her stomach.

A night ride in a buggy? No, no, a thousand times no. Pressing shaky hands to her face, she shuddered. Although she had no recollection of the night of the accident, she had a deathly fear of getting near a vehicle of any kind. And the dark only magnified her terror.

Since her recovery, she'd been in a vehicle only once—on her trip to Caleb and Lydia's house. Only God and concern for her sister had helped her endure the white-knuckled ride here in Andy's car, praying whenever she was coherent enough to form words, but afterward she spent two days in bed with a migraine. Much of the ride, she fought the swirling blackness that threatened to engulf her, the same murkiness closing over her now.

Lydia had offered to help with dishes after supper, but both Caleb and Emma shooed her out of the kitchen. It went against her nature to be idle and leave someone else with the chores, but at Caleb's insistence she settled in the nursery rocker. Caleb sat cross-legged on the floor, his back against the sides of the used crib he'd be assembling later that week.

Lydia pointed toward the two cans of paint. "That's the leftover paint John dropped off yesterday. One's half empty, but it should be enough, don't you think?"

Caleb nodded. "Should be. That was nice of him."

"When Mary heard I wanted to paint the nursery sage green, she said they'd bought too much for their kitchen and had him bring it over."

"I love how the community is always helping each other. I hope I can help others that way."

Lydia beamed at her husband. "You already do. You shoveled Eli's snow all winter and helped with the Zooks' barn raising and..."

Caleb waved his hand to stop her. "Anyone would have done that."

A knock on the door downstairs startled them. Lydia clasped her hands to her chest to calm her fluttering heart. "Who's that?" Ever since the night of Emma's accident she panicked whenever someone knocked on the door. Especially at night.

"I'm sure everything's fine, honey." Caleb knelt by the chair and took both her hands in his. "Relax."

The warmth of his hands soothed her, but her nerves remained on alert as the murmur of voices rose from below. Although she couldn't distinguish words, she recognized Emma's tones. When a man replied, Lydia's pulse raced. In her mind she heard the police officer on the porch three years ago, telling them Emma had been in an accident.

Please, God, don't let anyone be hurt.

Lydia jerked one hand from Caleb's and clutched at his sleeve. "Should we go down?"

"Emma will call us if she needs help."

But Lydia's anxiety increased as the conversation lengthened. Suddenly the door slammed, followed by a loud thud. She tried to jump up from the chair, but Caleb was already on his feet, pressing his hands on her shoulders to keep her in place.

"I'll go. Why don't you stay here."

But Lydia couldn't stay upstairs wondering what had happened. She followed Caleb through the hall. He pounded down the stairs ahead of her.

Lydia wanted to hurry, but the *bopplis*...She had to take care not to slip. That night in the kitchen. She couldn't bear to lose these *bopplis* too. Clinging to the railing, she waddled down the steps as fast as she could.

Below her, Caleb scooped Emma into his arms and carried her to the couch. "Hold your breath," he commanded.

"What's wrong?" The shrillness of Lydia's voice echoed around the room.

"It's only a panic attack, honey. Don't worry."

Only a panic attack?

While Lydia stood by helplessly, Caleb continued issuing orders as he laid Emma on the couch. "Again. Hold your breath longer now."

Emma's chest rose and stayed still for a short while.

"Good. You're doing fine, Emma." Caleb's voice softened. "One more time."

He squatted on the floor beside her and took one of her hands. "Now take a deep breath. You're okay. Try that again." Then he repeated over and over, "You are safe. Breathe.

Exhale," until Emma's breathing returned to a slower rhythm and her eyes fluttered open.

Only then did Lydia realize she'd been holding her own breath. She exhaled loudly, and Caleb glanced up at her.

"Are you all right?" When she nodded, he explained, "Emma was hyperventilating. Her rapid breathing caused too little carbon dioxide in her blood, so I had her hold her breath to let it build up."

"I'm so grateful you knew what to do." Lydia turned to her sister. Who was the visitor, and what had caused Emma to respond so violently?

She had a good guess at the answer to the first question: *Sam.*

If Sam had developed an interest in Emma, all the match-making *mamms* in the world were not likely to make a whit of difference.

Dread pooled in her stomach. *What are we going to do?*

Emma gazed around the room, her eyes frightened and unfocused. When they settled on Caleb, she shuddered.

Her chest ached, and she could barely drag in a breath. From a distance Lydia's question "What happened?" penetrated the waves of terror overwhelming her, but Emma's reply came out as a croak.

Breathe. Exhale. I am safe. I am safe, Emma repeated over and over. She inhaled deeply to calm her quivering limbs one after the other until her heart stopped pounding in her ears. Caleb's face came into focus—his encouraging smile, his familiar blond beard and bangs, his gentle eyes. A few moments ago his face had morphed into someone else's. Someone who upset her, who scared her. Someone who was angry with her. Someone who had hurt her.

Slowly she unclenched her fists. But her throat remained too tight to answer her sister.

Lydia's voice grew even more shrill. "Emma? Who was at the door? Is everything all right?"

No, everything was not all right. It would never be all right.

Her breathing still uneven, Emma forced herself to choke out, "It–it was Sam."

"Sam? What did he want? Did something happen to Eli?" Lydia's voice, high-pitched and tight, signaled her anxiety.

Caleb sent Lydia an *everything's-going-to-be-all-right* glance, and Emma hastened to reassure her. "Nothing's wrong." Her hoarse, shaky words would do little to calm her sister. "Sam just wanted to..." Now what did she say? Lydia would misunderstand Sam's offer to take her to the hymn sing.

And Sam. Oh no. What must he think of her? He was being thoughtful and friendly, and she'd said no and then the door slammed in his face. She'd have to make amends.

"He–he was just being neighborly, asking if I was ill because he didn't see me in church."

"So why didn't you invite him in?" Lydia's brow creased, and she examined Emma closely.

Emma wished she had invited him in instead of leaving him on the porch, but she bristled at her sister's nosiness. Lydia had always been overprotective, and the accident had made it worse. Somehow Lydia always managed to make Emma feel weak and inadequate. And now Lydia was staring at her, waiting for an answer. "He left." As hard as she tried, Emma couldn't keep the quaver from her voice.

"Oh, that's too bad. I'd been hoping to get a chance to talk to him. I barely had time to greet him today after church." The disappointment in Caleb's voice matched that in Emma's heart. Sam had been so kind to her, and she'd repaid his friendliness with rudeness. Worse than rudeness. Harshness. Cruelty.

If it weren't dark out, she'd yank open the door and run after him to apologize, beg for forgiveness. No one deserved that kind of treatment, especially not Sam. How would she ever make it right?

"But what happened to cause the panic attack?" Lydia asked.

Emma didn't want them to think Sam had caused her panic attack. Well, he had. But not intentionally. "It started when I opened the door. It was so dark out..."

Lydia's eyes filled with concern. "Oh, Emma."

The anguish in Lydia's voice added to Emma's distress. She'd already hurt Sam; she didn't want to upset her sister or the babies. Caleb had stressed how important it was to stay positive and upbeat, and now his questioning gaze made it clear he suspected she had more to tell.

Forcing a stiff smile, Emma said, "Everything's fine. Sam just wanted to..."

"Wanted to what?" Lydia's worried expression spurred Emma to tell the whole truth.

"He asked if I wanted to go to the hymn sing tonight."

"The hymn sing?" A look of surprise crossed Caleb's face. "You and Sam? I didn't realize you knew him well enough to be dating."

"No, no. He only meant as friends." Emma's breathlessness contradicted her words. Lydia and Caleb would both misread that as attraction to Sam. Although Emma couldn't deny she was attracted. But after the way she'd reacted, she'd have little chance of even being friends with him.

"He doesn't know anyone around here that well. He was just being neighborly." Her words sounded defensive and unconvincing.

"I assume you said no?"

The sympathy in Caleb's voice increased Emma's humiliation. She hung her head, and her voice came out muffled. "Of course I did. It was dark outside. Besides, I can't ride..." Again, the look in Sam's eyes floated before her eyes. How could she ever explain?

Lydia walked across the room and took her hand. "I'm so sorry you still have these fears. Although I must admit, my stomach still clenches whenever there's a knock on the door late at night."

At the distress in her voice, Caleb came to stand beside Lydia, and slipping his arm around her, he kissed her cheek. Then a covert look passed between the two of them, a secret understanding that excluded Emma, leaving her outside in the cold, alone. She'd seen that look often over the last few years. At first she'd thought nothing of it, figuring it was a newlywed couple's way of communicating. But since she'd arrived to stay with them, it happened more and more often, adding to her unease. It was as if they were deliberately hiding something from her, a deep, dark secret. One they couldn't tell her.

And now she had an additional worry. Memories of Sam's face haunted her—the surprise, the shock, the hurt. She had to apologize to him and explain why she'd reacted like that. But how would she get up enough nerve to confess her deep-seated fears?

❧

As Emma pulled herself to her feet, clinging to the couch arm to steady herself, Lydia's heart contracted. She wished she could erase all the pain from her sister's face.

"The dishes still need doing," Emma said in a shaky voice. "I'll finish them and then go to bed."

"Leave the dishes," Caleb told her. "I'll take care of them."

Lydia waited until Emma had mounted the stairs before turning to Caleb. "She still looks pale and shaky. That's why I think it's best not to remind her of the past." How would Emma face knowing the truth?

"I'm not so sure. Remembering might put some of those fears to rest."

"Oh, Caleb, you can't think knowing what happened would be good for her."

"It might be better than having this blank space. When— or if—her memory comes back, it could be traumatic. I wish there were a gentle way to help her remember things gradually."

Having her sister recall that year was the last thing Lydia wanted. If only there were a way to wipe away that part of the past.

"I worried that seeing the green sweater would trigger memories of the time Emma and I were together." Lydia sank onto the couch and buried her face in her hands. "How upset she was at me. She yelled at me for interfering in her life."

Caleb sat beside her, reached for her hand, and entwined his fingers with hers. He always seemed to know just what she needed.

"Since she's been here, I've tried so hard to give her freedom to be herself, but even my suggestions must come out bossy. At least it seems so from the resentment on Emma's face."

"Honey, give her a little time. She'll come to see how much you love her."

Lydia sighed. "I wish we could be close, yet everything I do seems to push her further away."

The gentle pressure of Caleb's fingers assured her he understood.

"It's not just that," Lydia confessed. "I know it's selfish, but I'm afraid if she regains her memory, she'll remember how much she resented me—even hated me."

Caleb wrapped his arms around her. "She's grown up a lot since then. She'll realize you did it because you wanted to protect her."

Lydia wasn't so sure. Although the warmth of her husband's arms comforted her, nothing could erase the cold fear inside. Someday Emma might remember the past. And when she did, would their relationship survive?

Chapter Six

NEAR DAYBREAK THE next morning Sam and his *onkel* took off in the farm wagon for the long ride beyond Valley View, where *Onkel* Eli was restoring an old stone springhouse overgrown with brush. Usually Sam's spirits rose when the sun peeked over the horizon, but that day he swung the scythe harder than he needed to, mowing down a huge swath of the weeds *Onkel* Eli had asked him to clear.

"Are you all right?" *Onkel* Eli asked.

"Fine." Sam bit off the word, then regretted his brusqueness. "I'm sorry to sound so *grexy*. It is not you but myself that I am impatient with."

His *onkel* raised an eyebrow as if inviting an explanation.

Sam squirmed and stared down at his boots, dusty and covered with bits of chaff. "I, um, asked Emma Esh to go to the hymn sing with me last night."

Onkel Eli snorted. "Thought you didn't plan to do any courting."

"I didn't mean it that way. I thought with it being so long since I've been here and with her being new, we could go together as friends." But had he explained that to Emma? He couldn't remember. All he remembered was his unsettled stomach and the bang of the door.

"And she turned you down?" Uncle Eli stepped closer and

slapped Sam on the back. "Don't take it too hard, boy. Not sure what's wrong with her. She don't attend church regular, that girl." He shrugged. "If yer looking for a girl to court, the Zook girl has a sweet disposition."

"I don't want to date anyone." Sam emphasized each word. And Emma had made it quite clear about not spending time with him. But her rejection reminded him of—

Sam blotted out those memories. He refused to speak or think her name again. He intended to do the same with thoughts of Emma.

Emma slipped out of the house extra early with the egg basket and headed for the chicken house, hoping to see Sam before he left for the fields. Although the sun was barely peeking over the horizon, enough light dispelled the gloom before dawn to allay her fears. The grayness of morning didn't scare her the way dusk did, maybe because the day would keep getting lighter. If she didn't time it right, though, dusk meant getting caught in the dark. Just thinking about the blackness of the night sky made Emma's stomach twist.

She'd only gathered a few eggs before Eli's old farm wagon rattled out of the barn. She rushed to the door, but the wagon was already at the end of the driveway. They'd left earlier than usual, and she'd missed them. With Eli sitting beside Sam, Emma didn't want to call out to stop them. Her shoulders drooped. Now she'd have to go through the day imagining the hurt on Sam's face.

When she reentered the coop, the sharp ammonia smell of chicken droppings stung her nose and eyes, or was it because she'd failed to talk to Sam? Disappointed, she finished collecting the eggs and replaced the dirty straw. Then she trudged back to the house to start breakfast, but the disappointment stayed with her as she did the chores.

With the exception of weeding and cooking, Emma spent the day helping Lydia mend the baby clothes, do the washing, and fill drawers with blankets, diapers, and clothing. Her mind wandered to Sam so often during the sewing that she pricked her finger with the needle several times and once absentmindedly stitched part of a hem to her own skirt. She sighed as she unpicked the stitches.

Lydia looked up from the treadle machine. "Is something wrong?"

Not wanting to admit her mistake, Emma answered crossly, "I've never been good at needlework." She waved the tiny garment in the air, and her needle flew off the thread and landed on the rag rug.

"I'm sorry," Lydia said. "Maybe you'd like to take a break or do something different."

"Never mind. I'm sorry for being so out of sorts." Emma knelt on the hardwood floor at the edge of the rag rug, searching for the needle, which seemed to have buried itself in the variegated blue coils. One of the straight pins holding her dress together poked her in the side, and Emma grumbled under her breath as she swept her hand across the hills and valleys of the tightly woven coils.

"Ouch!" She'd found the needle. She picked it up with her left hand and sucked at the tiny drop of blood on the forefinger of her other hand.

One thing she'd often noticed was that whenever she felt guilty, all the small things in life seemed to go wrong. It was as if she were punishing herself. She needed to find a way to talk to Sam before those little things turned into big ones.

The day went from bad to worse. As the sun sank below the distant hills, Emma sloshed dishwater over that evening's dirty supper dishes and avoided looking out the window when hooves crunched along the driveway next door. Of course, Sam had arrived home after sunset.

The next few nights, Sam and his *onkel* stayed out until dusk. With night closing in, Emma couldn't walk the short distance to Eli's back door.

Late Thursday afternoon as she scrubbed vegetables for dinner, a wagon rattled up the driveway and into the barn next door. Sam was home! And darkness hadn't fallen yet. Emma dropped the carrot and scrub brush in the sink, and hurried to put on her shoes. Impatience made her clumsy, and the laces tangled in her hands. After several tries she finally managed to tie her shoes.

When she stepped onto the back porch, the chilly air raised goose bumps on her arms. But she didn't want to wait to pull on her cloak. She had to tell Sam the truth. And do it now, before the sun slipped any closer to the horizon. She crossed their lawn and the two driveways into Sam's backyard.

She hesitated for a moment on Eli's back porch and sucked in a breath for courage. She tried never to talk about or think about her accident. Most of it was only a blur of jumbled images mixed with terror. But Sam deserved to know why she'd slammed the door in his face.

When she knocked, Emma was surprised not to hear Bolt's bark. She expected the pup to skitter to greet visitors. Emma had once been like that, racing her siblings to be the first to meet guests. All the more reason to apologize for the way she'd treated Sam. Not only had she been unwelcoming, but she'd been downright rude.

When the door snicked open, the roiling in her stomach increased. What would she say to Sam? How could she explain? Lydia would have thought out her words ahead of time, planned a proper apology and explanation instead of racing over here with no idea what she was going to say.

At least Emma could say the words she'd repeated the whole way over here: "I'm so sorr..." Her voice trailed off when she glanced up to see Eli in front of her. She should have expected that. "*Gut-n-Owed*, Eli. I, um, came to see Sam."

"*Ach, vell*," Eli said. "Sam's not here now."

"He's not?" She stood there staring dumbly at him. She'd come over as quickly as she could. Then it dawned on her that she'd only heard the wagon, not seen if Sam was in it. And she hadn't even introduced herself. "Oh, I'm Emma Esh, Lydia's sister."

"I know." From Eli's unfriendly expression, Emma guessed Sam must have told his uncle about her behavior Sunday night.

"Do you know when he'll be back?"

Scratching his white beard, Eli stared at the ground, not meeting her eyes. "I couldn't say."

"Is he out walking the dog? Maybe I could catch him there. Do you know which way he went?"

Eli only shook his head. "Won't catch him out there. He's gone out in the buggy."

Emma's feet twitched, wanting to run back to Lydia's. Much as she longed to flee, she forced them to stillness.

Before Eli could shut the door in her face, she blurted out, "I wanted to invite you both for dinner tomorrow night."

Eli looked as startled as she felt. She hadn't come over with any such intention, and she should have checked with Lydia and Caleb first. Now that the words were out of her mouth, she regretted them. Having both of them for dinner wouldn't give her a chance to explain to Sam.

Eli shook his head. "I don't think…"

Now that she'd made the invitation, she wasn't going to back down. "I know it's not easy cooking after farming all day." Even if she couldn't talk to Sam privately, maybe he'd see this as her way of apologizing. And perhaps she could ask him to meet her later for a talk.

When Eli still hesitated, she blurted out, "Lydia and Caleb would love to have you." At least she hoped they would.

His head cocked to one side, Eli studied her. "Would they now?"

Emma squirmed inside at the half-truths she was telling. But surely Lydia would be happy to host her neighbors for dinner. Eli's questioning gaze and her own conscience made her uncomfortable.

Eli sighed as if pained. "Guess it wouldn't be neighborly to decline then." Every line in his face sagged. "I don't go out much since…"

Once again Emma had thought only of her own needs. In her eagerness to make things right with Sam, she hadn't considered how Eli might feel. Now that she'd issued the invitation, he'd be obligated to come and also to reciprocate.

"You don't have to come." Oh, no, that sounded even worse. Like she was uninviting him. "I mean—"

Eli held up a hand to stop her rush of words. "I know

exactly what you meant. You're right. I can stay here and let Sam go alone. That's what you're really wanting."

The sadness coloring Eli's tone increased Emma's guilt because the truth of it was, she had wanted only Sam to come. Not that she didn't want Eli. Her thoughts spun faster than the weather vane on the barn. "No, no, you misunderstood." Emma clapped a hand over her mouth. She had just contradicted an elder. First, she insulted him—well, actually, she hadn't been trying to do that—and now she was telling him he was wrong.

She hung her head. "I'm sorry. My tongue sometimes— well, actually, often—gallops away like an unruly horse. I meant to say we'd love to have both you and Sam. If you'd even consider it after my bad manners."

Eli plucked at his galluses, a gesture that reminded Emma of Sam. "Tell Lydia and Caleb we'll come to dinner tomorrow night as soon as we get in from the fields." Shoulders bowed, he turned and shuffled back inside.

Emma left the house, her conscience a storm of emotions— joy warring with shame. As she neared the front porch, another worry joined the melee. Now she had to confess to Lydia and hope her sister wouldn't be too upset about having unexpected dinner guests. If Lydia or Caleb said no, she wasn't sure she'd have the courage to uninvite Eli. And she'd lose her chance of making up with Sam.

Heading across the lawn and into the kitchen, Emma dragged her feet. She wasn't looking forward to telling her sister.

Lydia was beside the sink, one hand pressing against the small of her back, the other gripping the counter.

Emma rushed to her. "Are you all right?"

Her face pale and contorted with pain, Lydia said through gritted teeth, "I'm fine." She hissed out a breath and loosened her grip on the counter.

Emma put an arm around Lydia's shoulders and led her to the table. "Come sit down. What were you doing washing the vegetables?"

Lydia massaged her back with both hands, and her face relaxed. Color flooded into her cheeks. "Stop fussing. I only had a sudden spasm in my back. It's pretty much gone now."

"You're supposed to be taking it easy. That's why I'm here."

"But you weren't here, and someone needed to start dinner."

Guilt piled up faster than weeds overtook a garden. "I was just..." Maybe now wasn't the time to give Lydia the news that they'd be having dinner guests tomorrow. "Never mind. I'm here now, and I'll take care of dinner. Why don't you lie down upstairs or at least stretch out on the couch."

But Lydia stared at her with an *I'm-not-moving-until-you-explain* look on her face. Emma's attempt to deflect Lydia's curiosity obviously wasn't going to work.

Emma picked up the scrub brush. It would be easier to explain if she didn't have to see Lydia's reactions. "Sorry I'm late. I stopped next door."

"At Eli's? Whatever for?" Then Lydia's eyes narrowed. "You went to visit his nephew? Oh, Emma."

Emma gritted her teeth. The tone of that *Oh, Emma* echoed in her mind, a remnant from childhood. How many times had Lydia scolded her that way? And *Mamm* and *Dat*. They frequently scowled at her, disappointment in their eyes, when she danced, teased, or had fun. She thought she'd grown past that now and tried hard to curb her impulses and her tongue.

"It's not what you think," she said, but her defensiveness couldn't cover up the fact she had—once again—let her tongue loose. She needed to own up to what she'd done. "I only spoke to Eli."

Lydia's tense expression relaxed slightly, but her eyes widened after Emma explained she'd invited Eli and Sam to dinner. Her sister winced, but then sat motionless, sadness flitting across her face. Then sucking in a shaky breath, she asked, "Eli accepted?"

Emma could be honest about this part. "He seemed reluctant at first, but he agreed when I told him the invitation was from you." She ducked her head to hide her flaming cheeks. That wasn't the only untruth she'd told.

Lydia closed her eyes and massaged her temples.

"What's wrong?" Emma bent over her sister. "Are you all right?"

Lydia didn't answer, just waved Emma away. After a few seconds, she said, "Maybe it's for the best. It's time we put it all behind us."

"I don't understand."

"No, you wouldn't. It happened before you were here."

Lydia slumped in her chair, the memories of that night weighing her down with grief. The sharp pain in her back paled in comparison to the one in her heart. The emptiness, the agony of the night and the days that followed, closed over her.

"Lyddie, what's wrong?"

Lydia waved a hand to stave off Emma's barrage of

questions. Questions she didn't have the strength to answer. Questions that might crumble the barrier she'd erected to hide her heartache.

Knowing that Eli was coming to dinner, that he'd be here in their kitchen, had already dislodged a piece of that barrier, and anguish threatened to overwhelm her.

Please, God, help me get through this. And Eli too.

She couldn't believe Eli had accepted the invitation. He'd avoided her ever since that night. The night his wife died. The night she'd lost the babies.

A hand clamped on her shoulder, shaking her, brought her back to the present. To the oak cabinets lining the walls, to the white porcelain sink filled with vegetables to scrub, to Emma bent close to her.

"Lydia, you're scaring me. Are you all right? Is something wrong with the *bopplis*?"

Lydia groaned. Nothing was wrong with these *bopplis*. At least as far as she knew, but the word *boppli* brought the memories rushing back.

She forced herself to concentrate on Emma's face. The lines of strain around her sister's mouth and the fear in her eyes. Lydia had to explain, but how could she put into words all the misery rushing through her? Emma deserved an explanation; she needed to know all the undercurrents she'd stirred up by issuing that dinner invitation.

Lydia swallowed back the ache in her throat and pushed the words past her lips. "I haven't talked to Eli since...since last autumn..."

Emma leaned closer to hear Lydia's choked whisper.

"I went over to help Eli the day his wife died. I slipped on his kitchen floor, had a bad fall, and—"

Lydia's words were barely audible, and they sounded as if she were pushing them through a throat clogged with tears. "That was when I had the miscarriage."

"Oh, Lyddie, I'm sorry. I didn't realize…" Emma laid a hand on her sister's shoulder and squeezed her eyes shut, aching inside for her sister's loss. *If only I'd known.* She'd been so focused on making things right with Sam, she never questioned why Eli hadn't visited. Her self-centeredness had brought heartache to her sister. And to Eli.

Lydia lifted her head, her eyes damp with tears, her lips pinched into a tight line. After a few seconds, she spoke. "Eli avoids being around me. When he sees me at church, he averts his eyes or scurries away. It's too painful for him. Not only do I remind him of the day his wife died, but he also blames himself for my fall."

Emma pressed a fist to her mouth to stop her own tears. No wonder Eli had reacted so strangely to her invitation. She assumed he'd been protecting Sam from further humiliation, but he'd also been wrestling with his own painful memories.

"I tried telling him it wasn't his fault, but I'm not sure he's ever forgiven himself. Plus he associates me with Martha's death, so I've tried to stay out of his way as much as possible until he's had time to heal."

"I wish I'd known. I never would have invited him." Emma set her hand over her sister's, and the two of them sat lost in their own thoughts for a while.

Once again she had rushed in and caused a disaster. Her impulsivity hurt so many people. The night before it had been Sam. Today, Lydia and Eli. It seemed she was always making amends for her *spontaneity*, as Sam had called it, but Emma was inclined to call it *troublemaking*. And the catastrophes she'd created were not easily fixed or forgotten.

"Lydia, can you ever forgive me?"

Her sister glanced at her with tear-filled eyes. Empty seconds stretched between them as Lydia, her mouth quivering, took several deep breaths. When a barely audible *yes* came from her lips, one burden tumbled from Emma's soul.

"I'm so, so sorry. I wish I could take back the invitation."

Lydia sighed and slid her hand from underneath Emma's. "What's done is done. God must have a reason for this. If Eli accepted, it must mean he's healing." With both hands on the edge of the table, she pushed back her chair and stretched out her legs. Placing one hand on her belly, she said with an effort, "We have much to be grateful for. Not one *boppli* on the way, but two. God is good. I pray Eli will find peace and happiness as well."

Emma did too. She also prayed that the next night's dinner wouldn't open all the old wounds. What she'd done to make up with Sam had now rippled out to affect everyone else.

Dear God, please take my mistake and use it for healing everyone's hearts. And help me learn to think before I act.

She rose from the table. "I'd better finish preparing the dinner before Caleb gets home."

Lydia's voice was still a bit shaky when she responded, "I feel so useless. I should be doing all these chores myself."

"Absolutely not." Pretending to frown, Emma shook a

finger at her sister. "Your job is to rest and stay healthy." *And please, God, keep her and the* bopplis *safe.*

"I know you're right, but it's hard to watch other people doing the jobs that should be mine."

Emma tried to lighten the mood. "Look at it this way. I'm paying you back for nursing me all those months after the accident. *And* for all those chores of mine you had to redo when I was little."

Lydia looked thoughtful for a moment, and her lips curved into a half-smile. "In that case, I can easily sit here for months. Or years even."

The tight bands inside Emma relaxed at her sister's teasing tone. Lines remained around Lydia's misty eyes, but her mouth and jaw had lost their earlier grimness. Emma inhaled, loosening the tension constricting her own breathing.

As Emma picked up the vegetable brush and a carrot from the sink, Lydia said, "I'm curious. What in the world made you decide to ask the neighbors for dinner?"

Emma attempted to deflect the question. "It must be hard to work in the fields all day and then come home and cook."

"Very thoughtful of you." The overly exaggerated sarcasm lacing Lydia's words made it clear she doubted Emma's motive for the invitation. "You've been here for more than a month now and never once expressed concern for Eli's long hours."

"Planting season only began recently." Emma scrubbed at the carrot harder than she needed to.

Lydia only stared at her, obviously waiting for the real reason.

"All right, all right." Emma set the carrots on the cutting

board and whacked them into rounds for stew. "I went over to apologize to Sam. He wasn't home, so I ended up inviting them both for dinner."

From the look in Lydia's eye, the inquisition wasn't over. "Apologize? For what?"

Emma sighed and, with the knife blade, swept the carrots into the stew pot. "I wasn't very polite when he stopped by on Sunday night and offered to take me to the hymn sing." To avoid Lydia's gaze boring into her, she picked up a potato and concentrated on peeling it.

The silence between them grew uncomfortable, with questions looming unasked until Emma could no longer stand it.

"I was already frightened by the dark, and then when he asked about riding in the buggy..." The paring knife clattered from her fingers, which were trembling at the memory. "I–I slammed the door in his face."

"Oh, Emma." This *Oh, Emma* held less censure than the previous one, but it cut much more deeply. This time Lydia's tone combined sorrow, pity, and distress.

And it heaped more guilt onto Emma's already overloaded conscience. Was there anyone she hadn't disappointed lately? She'd hoped to escape her father's aversion by coming to Lydia's house, but now she'd managed to upset everyone here too.

She whispered a quick prayer that God would heal all the hurts she'd caused. She needed to trust Him to correct the blunders she'd made. It would be nice, though, to make fewer mistakes.

Chapter Seven

E VERY TIME LYDIA entered the kitchen to help with
dinner the next evening, Emma shooed her out.

"Quit worrying. I have everything under control,"
Emma said.

But that wasn't what Lydia was concerned about. She
needed something to do to occupy her mind so she wouldn't
have to think about the company coming for dinner. Being
told to go and rest only added to her anxiety. She also wondered if Emma was working hard to impress this Sam, and
that added to her worries, but other fears overshadowed that
possibility.

Would she be able to carry on a normal conversation
with Eli? Just seeing him and sitting across from him at the
dinner table would release a flood of memories she'd kept
suppressed. Caleb had promised to get home earlier than
usual if he could, but he hadn't arrived yet. Either he was
caught in traffic coming up the river from the city, or Bob,
the *Englischer* who drove him to work each day, hadn't been
able to leave early.

She paced from the living room window to the kitchen
and back again until Emma barked that she was driving
her crazy. Emma seemed almost as nervous as Lydia was,
and Emma had already apologized several times for inviting

tonight's company even after Lydia assured her she was forgiven.

On Lydia's next pass through the hall, the door opened, and Caleb hurried in. "Sorry I'm so late. A fender bender slowed traffic on Route 225." He blew her a kiss. "I'll go get cleaned up."

Though she longed for a hug, Lydia had to wait. Caleb worried he might bring germs home from the hospital. As a hospital receptionist, he spent most of the day around sick people, so he wouldn't go near Lydia and the *bopplis* until he'd washed and changed clothes.

She stood impatiently at the bottom of the stairs until Caleb bounded down the steps. Then he swept her into his arms and kissed her thoroughly. In his embrace she almost forgot the fears that had paralyzed her all day.

"Honey, I know this won't be easy for you, but it may be best for everyone. I've been praying for you and Eli all day."

Too choked up to speak, Lydia could only nod. She'd been praying all day as well, but getting through dinner wouldn't be easy. She hoped she could keep her distress from showing on her face. Hand in hand they went to the kitchen to wait.

Emma wished Lydia and Caleb would wait in the living room rather than out here in the kitchen. She was nervous enough without Lydia scrutinizing her every move. Although the scalloped potatoes were bubbling in the oven next to the meat loaf, which was filling the air with the homey scent of tomato and onion, Emma feared a meal disaster. Or maybe it was the thought of facing Sam that had her so tense.

Caleb insisted on setting the table, and as he set Lydia's plate to the left of his, he said, "We can seat Eli at the other end of the table."

Lydia's dazzling smile was for Caleb alone. "*Danke*," she whispered.

Emma's stomach, already upset over the upcoming dinner and seeing Sam again, churned even more as she saw the tension on Lydia's face. She promised herself she'd try harder not to be so impulsive. And she whispered a prayer that the evening would go smoothly for Lydia and Eli.

The sun was low on the horizon when Eli arrived at the back door in his work clothes. He removed his mud-caked boots on the porch and, hat in hand, entered the kitchen. As he'd promised, he'd come straight from work. Sam had somehow found time to change into a fresh blue shirt and black pants and looked as if he had recently washed up. Whereas Eli's hair was wet with sweat, Sam's damp bangs smelled of soap, and his clothes had the fresh scent of laundry dried in the sun—a scent that drew Emma nearer until she realized she was leaning toward him as he stepped through the door. She straightened quickly, but not before Eli directed a sour glance her way.

Too discomfited to speak, she was grateful when Caleb stepped over to greet them. "*Gut-n-Owed*, Eli." He shook the older man's hand vigorously as Lydia half-hid behind him.

Eli kept his gaze on Caleb. "This is my nephew Sam," he said, his voice gruff.

"Hi, Sam." Caleb reached out to shake his hand as Emma hovered in the background. "We met at church last Sunday, but you were surrounded by so many new faces, I'm sure you don't remember me."

Sam smiled. "Actually, I do. It's nice to see you again."

"This is my wife, Lydia." Caleb clasped Lydia's hand and drew her forward. "She was at church last Sunday too." He motioned behind him. "And I believe you've met Emma."

"*Jah*, I have." Sam's words sounded strangled.

"*Gut-n-Owed*," Emma said to both Sam and Eli, and received only stilted *good evenings* in return. Though she understood the reason for Eli's brusqueness and Sam's standoffishness, it still cut her deeply. She had to find a way to let them both know she hadn't meant to hurt either of them. She wasn't sure how she could let Eli know without bringing up a sadness best forgotten. Sam deserved an apology, though. She had to find a way to talk to him after dinner. For now, she'd have to endure his coldness.

She took a deep breath and invited them to the table. "*Kumm esse*," she said and motioned for them to take a seat, while Caleb helped Lydia onto the bench beside him.

Eli inclined his head in Lydia's direction. "*Danke* for inviting us for dinner."

"I didn't..." The crimson that stained Lydia's cheeks matched the red beet eggs at the center of the table. "I mean, I'm glad you agreed to come."

Eli acknowledged her comment with a brief nod and downcast eyes as if he were offering an apology of his own.

Caleb smiled at both guests. "Have a seat. We're happy you both could join us."

Sam returned Caleb's smile and took the seat he indicated across from Emma, but glanced at Lydia. "Everything smells delicious."

Lydia gestured toward Emma. "*Danke*, but my sister deserves the credit for the meal."

Emma's heart pounded as Sam turned toward her. When he looked at her, she hoped she could convey how sorry she was.

Sam gave a brief, impersonal nod in her direction, never meeting her eyes. Instead he directed his remark to Lydia. "It was wonderful *gut* of you to share your meal with us. *Onkel* Eli and I both appreciate it. I'm glad not to have to cook, and I expect he's grateful not to eat my attempts."

Lydia's tense forehead relaxed in the warmth of Sam's friendliness. "A man shouldn't have to make meals after working in the fields all day. I'm glad this will give you a chance to relax."

Her hopes dashed, Emma turned her back to the room to hide her trembling lips. How could she let Sam know how she felt if he wouldn't even look at her? She sliced the meat loaf with shaky hands, then pasted on a smile before she carried the platter over.

Caleb settled into the chair beside Lydia. "I'm guessing you won't be making meals for long, Sam. Once all the unattached girls in the *g'may* discover you're here, mothers will be knocking on your door every night, bringing casseroles and single daughters."

Lydia chuckled, and Eli wheezed out a laugh. Sam's polite smile, though, seemed a bit pained. Emma tried to keep her forced smile, but her lips refused to cooperate.

"Nothing like a single young man in the house to attract attention and dinner invitations." Eli shot a pointed look at Emma, the slight curl of his lip conveying his disdain. "Once Sam starts going to the hymn sings and meeting more of the *youngie*, the line of girls and their *mamm*s will stretch down the road."

Thinking of other girls flocking to Sam, Emma clenched her jaw. She focused on setting the meat platter beside the creamed corn and scalloped potatoes so Eli couldn't see the hurt in her eyes. But his remark made her shrivel inside, and she wished she'd never issued the dinner invitation. Now Eli would classify her as one in that long line of hopefuls.

With a sly glance at Emma, Eli continued, "Only to be expected when there's a handsome *youngie* about."

Sam brushed away the compliment as if swatting at flies. "I doubt anyone will be coming to see me."

"Oh, they'll come all right. You'll have to be choosy about which ones you pay attention to." The daggers in Eli's eyes pointed right at Emma; there was no mistaking their message.

Emma had no doubts now that Sam had told his *onkel* about her reaction to his hymn sing invitation. Evidently Eli didn't take kindly toward females who hurt his nephew. Between his barbed comments and Sam's ignoring her, not to mention Lydia's nervousness, all Emma wanted was to escape to her bedroom and shut the door. But she had to explain, had to get Sam alone somehow. Meanwhile she hoped that Lydia and Eli could endure the time together.

Following the silent prayer, conversation became stiff and awkward. For once, words deserted Emma. Her heart cried out for Sam to make eye contact so she could convey an apology. But he saved his warm, friendly smiles for Lydia and Caleb, and avoided glancing in her direction. After Emma tried several times to get his attention, her hope ebbed, and she concentrated on her meal.

Eli sat, head bowed over his plate, pushing food around. Emma worried that the meat loaf tasted as dry and flavorless to him as it did to her. She struggled to choke it down but needed most of her glass of milk to wash it past the lump in her throat.

The conversation had lagged, and she should have said something, but instead she pretended to nibble at her scalloped potatoes. She'd used *Mammi*'s recipe, which usually turned out creamy and tangy with pepper and cheese, but that night the potato slices tasted like cardboard. Between Eli's barbs and the uncomfortable tension between her and Sam, Emma remained tongue-tied.

She glanced around the table. Sam and his *onkel* Eli were engrossed in their meals. Although Eli seemed to be picking at his food rather than eating, Sam was eating with gusto. He forked a bite of scalloped potatoes into his mouth and closed his eyes as if they were as tender and tasty as usual. At least he didn't seem to find the food as unappetizing as she and Eli did.

Seated at the head of the table, Caleb was staring at Lydia with concern, and she returned his look with grateful eyes, although her face was drawn and tense, and it appeared she'd eaten little of her meal.

Across from her, Sam picked up his knife to cut his meat loaf; then he laughed and set it down. "I'm so used to cutting my own rock-hard meat loaf, I thought I'd need a knife. But this one's so tender I can cut it with a fork."

Emma glowed until Eli, jaw set, eyed her and shook his head.

To her relief Caleb chimed in. "Lydia and Emma come from a long line of good cooks. You should taste their *mammi*'s cooking. It's out of this world. She's the one who taught them to make these dishes."

Sam's expression was rueful. "I wish I could learn to cook like that. I haven't attempted scalloped potatoes, although *Mamm* sent her recipe. Slicing all those potatoes and making the sauce takes a lot of work. And with my tendency to burn things"—Sam sent an apologetic smile his *onkel*'s way—"I can understand why *Onkel* Eli only picks at his food."

Eli shook his head. "It ain't your cooking, son. It's just that I haven't had much of an appetite since—" He swallowed hard, and moisture glinted in his eyes. He dipped his head again.

Lydia paled. Her fork clattered to the plate, and she pinched her lips together as if holding back tears. "I'm sorry," she said in a shaky voice barely above a whisper. "I should have thought to send meals over to you. It's only that..."

Caleb, who had been buttering a roll, clenched his knife as tightly as his jaw. His eyes, filled with sympathy and pain, met Lydia's.

Sam looked from Lydia to Caleb, then back to his uncle, a puzzled expression on his face. If Lydia hadn't explained the situation to her the day before, Emma would have been equally as startled.

Eli's back stiffened, and then he lowered his head and mumbled, "I didn't mean to stir up bad memories. I only meant to thank you for this." Head bowed, he gestured toward the small pile of scalloped potatoes, his partially eaten meat loaf covered with a congealing puddle of gravy, and the creamed corn oozing milkiness across his plate. "I certainly never expected a meal from you. Not after what happened."

"Still..." Lydia's eyes brimmed with tears. "I should have thought of it."

"I was fine," he said through tense lips. "Many other people brought meals. Not that I ate much back then. Still don't, as my nephew here can tell you." He pointed his fork in Sam's direction.

Emma's heart went out to Lydia, whose head remained down. Was her sister fighting back tears? This was all her fault.

His full attention on Lydia, Caleb sat frozen in place, his white-knuckled grip on his utensils the only sign of his distress. He reached across the table as if to touch her hand, which was clenched around her water glass. "Honey, don't be so hard on yourself. You weren't able to cook."

Eli kept his head bent over his plate and occupied himself by sliding bits of meat loaf through the gravy, bites of food he never lifted to his mouth.

Sam, his brow furrowed, looked from one to the other. For the first time, his gaze met Emma's. She wished she could explain, but her skin flushed hot at the thought. It wouldn't be proper to talk about Lydia's condition with men. Glancing around the table, she hoped someone else would change the subject.

When she looked back at Sam, his eyes were shuttered. He was fiddling with his silverware, and although his mouth opened and closed several times as if he were struggling to restart the conversation, it was obvious he wasn't sure what land mines he needed to avoid.

Emma longed to help him by coming up with a conversation starter, although she was at as much of a loss for neutral topics as he was. If only she could get him alone to explain and, even more importantly, to apologize.

Eli choked, and Sam slid down the bench to pound him

on the back. Spluttering and coughing brought tears to Eli's eyes that he dashed away with the back of his sleeve. Emma wondered if he'd done it on purpose to cover up watery eyes. Sam still appeared confused about why everyone around him seemed so tense. He eyed Lydia warily and studied his *onkel*'s hunched form. Emma wanted to reassure him none of it was his fault. Perhaps if she could find a way to talk to him privately after dinner, she'd tell him about the situation, once she'd had a chance to apologize.

He shook his head slightly and went back to his meal. When Caleb turned the talk to planting and harvests, he interjected comments but spent most of his time eating a second helping of everything. At least he liked her cooking.

When Emma collected the plates, Sam's smile was genuine, but once again he avoided her eyes. "*Danke.* That was delicious."

Caleb over-praised the apple pie she served for dessert, and Emma wondered if he did it to fill in the conversational gaps. Sam agreed with all the comments, and Eli grunted twice, which Emma assumed was a sign of approval. He even deigned to eat several bites.

After the end-of-meal prayer, though, he rose immediately. "We should be getting home. *Danke* for having us."

Emma jumped up, hoping to catch Sam's attention. They wouldn't have any privacy with everyone crammed into the kitchen, but maybe she could give him a secret look to convey her apology and—

Before she could reach Sam, Caleb ushered him and Eli to the kitchen door, and after a flurry of thanks and good nights, they headed across the backyard to their house without once turning in her direction.

Shoulders slumped, she headed to the sink to wash the dishes.

Caleb closed the back door. Then he stacked the dessert plates and brought them over to the sink. "Would you like some help?"

Her throat tight with unshed tears, Emma could only shake her head.

"I'm happy to help. I know how many more dishes there are when company comes."

She appreciated his kindness, and any other night would have taken him up on his offer, but now all she wanted was to be alone. "It's all right," she managed. "You and Lydia should spend some time together. Besides, you did them on Sunday."

Caleb hesitated. "If you're sure."

"I'm sure."

After Caleb and Lydia left the kitchen, Emma sank into the nearest chair—the one Eli had occupied during dinner—and cupped her face in her hands. She should have been starting the dishes, but all she could think of was Sam.

Daydreaming doesn't get chores done, as *Mammi* liked to say. Emma shook herself, stood, and cleared the glasses from the table. After plunging her hands into the dishwater, she scrubbed each cup and plate, wishing she could wipe away the memories of last Sunday's cruelty and this night's awkwardness.

When she finished drying the dishes, she wiped the counters and table slowly, delaying the time until she had to turn out the light, leaving only the battery-powered lantern to light her way through the darkness and to her room upstairs.

As she passed the living room, she was surprised that

Caleb and Lydia were still deep in conversation. She didn't want to interrupt them, so she tiptoed past and started mounting the stairs. She stopped abruptly when she heard Sam's name.

Lydia's voice drifted up from the room below. "Well, I'm glad I finally got to meet Sam. I must admit I was concerned about him and Emma."

Caleb answered, "From what I could see, he didn't seem that enamored by her. He avoided her eyes, was overly polite, and seemed uncomfortable around her. And Eli made it clear that there will be other girls in the picture. For all we know, he might have a girlfriend at home. Might be best just to wait. No point in worrying needlessly."

Emma turned to head back down, determined to ask Lydia why she was worried about her and Sam. She didn't want to admit she'd been eavesdropping, but she had to know the reason.

"You're right. We can deal with it when or if it becomes a problem." Lydia's sigh dragged with it a heavy burden.

Emma froze in place. That sigh echoed in the far-off recesses of her brain. She'd heard her sister's pained exhale before. Many times. Sadness coupled with the certainty of being a terrible burden to her sister closed over her. If only she could fan away this fog to bring the vague memories into focus. The more she tried to concentrate, the faster they turned to wisps of smoke and disappeared. Disoriented, she stood there as they swirled off into nothingness.

Then she yanked herself back to reality. One step at time, she descended until she could peek over the railing into the living room. Her question about Sam died on her lips at the sight of Lydia, feet tucked up on the couch, cuddling close to

Caleb. His arm encircled her, and he pressed his lips to the top of her head. They were so engrossed in each other, they hadn't noticed her.

She slipped back upstairs, struggling to douse the flames of jealousy in her heart. Lydia had everything Emma dreamed of having—a loving husband, *bopplis* on the way, and a happy home life. Emma had never even dated. By the time she recovered from the accident, most of the boys her age in the *g'may* had paired off. Many had already married. The few unmarried older ones avoided her as if she had a disease.

Sam had been the first to look at her with a spark in his eyes. Yet Caleb was right about two things. Sam most likely had a girlfriend at home. If he didn't, he soon would, with all the girls lining up. But Caleb's other point had cut more deeply. Sam had barely looked at her. He'd made it obvious he had no interest in her. Not anymore. She'd hurt him too badly. Maybe that would change when she had a chance to apologize. But finding a chance to speak to him alone seemed almost impossible—especially if he stayed in the fields until sundown. And she couldn't—wouldn't—go out after dark.

Emma's heart was heavy. Not about Caleb and Lydia's worries. Right now the only opinion she cared about was Sam's, and he had already rejected her.

Chapter Eight

E MMA WAS FINISHING her Saturday morning chores when Lydia exclaimed from the living room, "Oh, that looks like Sam. What a gorgeous dog. Is it an Irish setter?"

Sam? Outside walking the dog? Emma dropped the washrag into the sink and rushed for the front door.

"I'll be right back," she said as she flew past the living room, where Lydia sat with her feet propped up.

"Emma!" Lydia's rebuke followed Emma as she yanked open the door and dashed toward the street.

"Sam!" Emma yelled as she barreled toward him. At his distant expression, she skidded to a stop.

Bolt, though, didn't follow Sam's lead. The dog turned and licked Emma's hand. Emma knelt and hugged the Irish setter, part of her wishing she were free to do the same to the dog's owner. *Emma Esh, what are you thinking?* Her cheeks heated, and she avoided looking at Sam as she stood; she wouldn't want him to read that in her eyes.

"Is it all right if I walk with you? I–I need to explain about…"

His posture stiff and unyielding, Sam didn't respond for a few seconds, and Emma regretted running after him. Only now did she realize what that looked like to the neighbors, not to mention Lydia, and her cheeks grew even more fiery.

"I understand if you don't want anything more to do with me after the other night. But please at least let me apologize. I've been sick about it ever since. I invited you to dinner so I could explain…" She glanced up at Sam, and the remoteness in his eyes reflected deep hurt. "I'm so sorry," she babbled, unable to remember what she'd planned to tell him. "Will you forgive me?"

Her plea hung on the air between them until Sam cleared his throat. "Certainly."

But Emma didn't want the rote forgiveness their faith commanded; she wanted a deeper forgiveness and understanding, and even more, she wanted to erase the pain and sadness in his eyes.

Bolt, who had been sniffing the ground at their feet, lifted her head and yanked on the leash, pulling Sam away from Emma.

"Wait, don't go." Realizing how desperate that sounded, Emma pressed her fist to her mouth. "I mean," she mumbled, "I'd like to talk to you. I need to tell you something."

Sam looked as though he couldn't get away from her fast enough, and Bolt, who was straining at her leash, kept propelling him along. Emma hop-skipped to keep pace with them, her heart thumping in time to her brisk movement. Whether her rapid pulse was from hurrying after them or from her nearness to Sam she didn't want to examine too closely.

"Please, Sam, I need to explain."

"No need." Sam's tone was formal. "I'm sorry I bothered you. I only meant to be neighborly." With each frosted word, he seemed to grow more distant. "I won't trouble you again."

"You didn't bother me." Emma puffed out the words

between breaths. Chasing Sam and Bolt had winded her. "I mean, you did, but it wasn't your fault. Maybe if you had asked me earlier…" Was she telling him how to ask her out on a date? *Great, Emma, way to put your foot in your mouth.*

"I'll keep that in mind," Sam said dryly.

Was he laughing at her? Emma glanced up to see a twinkle in Sam's eye.

"You've forgiven me?"

"I said I had."

"I wasn't sure you really meant it. And I haven't even told you why I—"

"Slammed the door in my face?" Hurt still flickered in the back of his eyes, but the laugh lines on his face deepened. "I'm sure you had your reasons."

"*Jah*, but they didn't have anything to do with you. I mean, I didn't say *no* because I didn't want to go with *you*." Emma's gut clenched. Getting the words out was harder than she'd expected. "It was the darkness."

Sam tugged at Bolt's leash and brought the dog to a halt. Then he turned and stared at Emma, a frown creasing his brow. "The darkness?"

Emma couldn't meet his eyes. "I'm afraid of the dark." She peeked up at him to gauge his reaction. One of his brows quirked in puzzlement, so she hastened to explain. "Three years ago I was in an accident at night." Her breathing constricted, and she sucked in a breath to control the fear rushing through her veins. "Since then I've had this deathly fear. Of night. Of riding in buggies. And of being on busy roads. That's why I didn't go to church on Sunday, and that's why I panicked when…"

"When I asked you to ride in a buggy at night," Sam murmured.

"You didn't know. But there's more." Now that she'd started, she might as well tell him everything. The story poured out in staccato bursts, her chest rising and falling in the same sharp rhythm as she gasped for breath between each phrase.

Sam's kind expression encouraged her to go on, so she confessed something that nobody but her family knew. "Anyway, I was in a coma for months, and when I came to, I didn't remember anything. Nothing about the months before the accident, and nothing for months after. I've lost almost all my memories of my sixteenth year."

Sam's eyes widened. "Oh, Emma, I never would have asked you to the hymn sing if I'd known." Bolt danced at the leash, but Sam pulled her back. "Quiet, girl. We'll walk soon." He bent down to pet her until she calmed but kept his gaze on Emma.

"It's not your fault." If Sam's eyes had shown pity, she never would have continued, but his face and posture reflected only understanding. "I had to relearn to walk and feed myself and...Well, it was a struggle, but I recovered. Except for the fear. I get terrible migraines and have panic attacks even thinking about getting into a vehicle."

"Panic attacks?"

At Sam's puzzled look, Emma explained, "My heart races, I get short of breath, I get dizzy, and...and...I get this overwhelming feeling that I'm going to die. Caleb says there's nothing physically wrong with me, that it's related to the accident, but understanding it doesn't make the attacks go away."

"I'm so sorry."

"No, no, no. *You're* not supposed to be apologizing to *me*." Emma clapped a hand over her mouth. Now Sam would think she was bossy—if he didn't already. "*I'm* supposed to be apologizing to *you*."

Sam's chuckle stopped her rapid flow of words. "I think you already did." Then he sobered. "I'm sorry about your accident and that I caused a panic attack."

Somehow this had all gotten turned around, with Sam apologizing to her instead of the other way around, but before she could speak, Bolt spotted a squirrel and dashed in circles around them, barking and twisting the two of them in her leash. Each revolution tightened the leash around them, and Emma stumbled against Sam's chest. He reached out a hand to steady her but instead wrapped his arm around her and drew her closer. With his other hand, he fumbled for a tighter grip on Bolt's leash and tugged hard to slow the dog's frantic darting.

"Stop!" Sam's sharp command had no effect on Bolt.

Emma wished he could command her heart to slow as well. Being this close to him was affecting her breathing too. She stared up at him, and he met her gaze, his eyes gentle, lips parted, and for a fleeting moment, she dreamed he was about to kiss her.

Then he broke eye contact and concentrated on getting his excited pup under control. Maybe she'd only imagined it. Her family often laughed at her flights of fancy.

"I'm so sorry," Sam said after he'd calmed Bolt and started to untangle them from the leash.

Emma was sorry too. Sorry to lose this chance to be close to him. By the time he stepped out of the final loop and unwound it from around her feet, the desire to be back in his arms had increased rather than decreased. She clamped her teeth on her lower lip to prevent herself from blurting out how she was feeling.

Still on the ground, trying to straighten Bolt's leash, Sam rocked back on his heels and pointed to her damp, grass-stained stocking feet. "You ran all the way out here without shoes?"

Emma hung her head. "I couldn't let you go on thinking I'd slammed that door because I didn't like you. Because I do." Oh no. She couldn't believe she'd said that aloud. Her face burned, and she hurried to correct herself. "As a friend," she stammered. Although if she were honest—

Sam's left hand curled into a fist around one of his galluses, and he clenched Bolt's leash tightly. "I know what you mean," he said gently. "I like you too. As a friend."

The way he emphasized the word *friend* made it clear he intended to keep his distance, but Emma was overjoyed he'd forgiven her and still wanted to be friends. She wanted to dance through the grass, but instead she clutched her hands together in front of her and tried to act ladylike.

"I appreciate you telling me all this." Sam's smile poured over Emma like sunshine, bathing her soul in warmth. "I'm sure it wasn't easy to do."

"No, it wasn't, but I'm glad I did. I feel so much better."

"Emma?" Lydia called from across the street. She managed to make her question sound more like a rebuke.

"I'm sorry," Sam said. "I think I may have gotten you in trouble with your sister."

"It's not your fault. Lydia's probably upset about the neighbors seeing me chase after you and then, well, get tangled…"

She stopped before the breathlessness of her words gave her away.

Sam's face creased into a smile. "I'm glad we straightened things out. And I apologize for my unruly dog. I hope your sister didn't think we, um, I"—his face flushed, he looked down at his feet—"did that on purpose."

Emma wished it had been on purpose. She tilted her chin. "I don't care what anyone thinks as long as I've made things right with you." With a quick wave to Sam and Bolt, she turned toward the house, where Lydia stood in the doorway, glowering. She thought she'd outgrown Lydia's lectures about her behavior, but no doubt from her sister's point of view, she needed one now. Although it would make Lydia even more upset, Emma couldn't help stopping to watch Sam continue down the street with Bolt.

"Emma!"

At Lydia's barked command, Emma tore her gaze from Sam and quit dawdling. No sense in provoking her sister more. Yet Emma's heart soared at the memory of Sam's smile and the brief time they spent tangled in the leash, and it gave her feet wings. She scurried toward the house, trying to erase the smile curving her lips.

"Emma, what were you thinking?" Lydia stood in the doorway, hands on her hips. "I certainly don't think your behavior is anything to smile about."

Emma hung her head and stared at her dirty, torn stockings, more to hide her smile than out of guilt. "I know it may have looked bad, but I owed Sam an apology."

"Making things right is important, but not at the expense of your reputation. I'd hoped we'd never have to deal with anything like this." Lydia sounded ready to cry. "I promised *Mamm* and *Dat* I'd keep an eye on you."

Emma gritted her teeth. That was so unfair. Lydia was talking as if Emma were a child. She was old enough to look after herself. Most girls her age were already married. And the whole time she'd been here, she'd done her best to be docile and agreeable, to act decorously, to curb her tongue. Except for a few slipups with Sam, she'd managed to keep her exuberance under control. Until today.

"I have no idea what to do." A few tears slipped down Lydia's cheeks. "I'm so tired, and I can't go chasing after you anymore."

"You don't need to chase me." Though Emma wanted to snap at her sister, she forced herself to use a gentle tone. Her whole purpose in being here was to help and support Lydia. Instead she'd become a burden. "I'm sorry I made you cry."

A half-gulp, half-cry escaped from Lydia's lips. "That's not your fault. Ever since I've been expecting, I cry about everything." She brushed the tears from her cheeks.

Upset because she'd caused Lydia such distress, Emma reached out and hugged her. After standing stiffly for a few moments, Lydia relaxed into the hug and even patted Emma's back.

Their family had never been much for hugging, but Caleb, with his *Englisch* background, showed his affection freely. None of the married couples Emma had been around hugged or kissed like that around others, but deep in her heart, Emma yearned for a man who would be as openly affectionate as Caleb, one who wouldn't mind her giving him spontaneous hugs. Sam had seemed comfortable being close to her. He'd even held her. Although, if she were honest, he'd had little choice.

"I'm sorry I didn't think about how it would look before I ran after Sam." Emma pictured herself as Lydia and the neighbors must have seen her, and her stomach became even more unsettled than it had been when she was in Sam's arms. "I only wanted to ask his forgiveness. I'd hoped to do that last night at dinner but never had a chance."

"Oh, Emma." Lydia's tone made Emma feel like a small child who deserved a spanking.

"If the dog hadn't gone wild about the squirrel, it wouldn't have looked quite so bad," Emma said defensively. Although her chasing after Sam certainly hadn't appeared innocent, and if anyone had been close enough to see the look in her eyes...

Lydia only shook her head. "One thing that concerns me is your interest in Sam. Last night I assumed he didn't share it, but now I'm wondering. I'm sure most of the neighbors are too."

Emma stiffened. Why should Lydia worry if Sam and she were interested in each other? Didn't Lydia want her to court and marry? But she kept her voice even. "Don't worry. Sam and I are only friends, and we intend to keep it that way. He made that very clear." It pained Emma to say those words, but Sam's phrase *as a friend* ran through her mind. That seemed to be a warning to keep her distance. Yet his eyes when he held her conveyed a different message, although she might have been misinterpreting.

"We'll discuss this more once Caleb gets in for lunch."

The ominous ring of Lydia's words set Emma's stomach roiling. They wouldn't send her home, would they? Lydia needed her help. Unless they planned to replace her with her younger sister, Sarah. Emma couldn't go back, not when *Dat* acted so...so distant. If only she knew what had caused him to dislike her so much. Sometimes she wondered if she had done something before the accident that had offended him, but try as she might to remember what that would be, she couldn't recall anything. Since she graduated from eighth grade she'd done the bookkeeping in his business, and *Dat* enjoyed having her there. During her recovery, though, cousin Ben had replaced her, and he still worked in the business with *Dat*.

Lydia headed to the kitchen. "I'll make sure lunch is ready."

"No, no," Emma rushed past her. "You sit down. I'll take care of lunch." If Lydia believed she didn't need help, no telling what would happen after the talk with Caleb.

As Emma headed for the kitchen, Lydia rubbed her forehead. She'd come off as her old critical self, scolding and criticizing Emma. If Emma rebelled again and chased after Sam just to defy her, what would she do? When she'd agreed to have Emma's help with the twins, worries like this hadn't crossed her mind. She'd been hoping the baby would bridge the rift between them. Instead, she'd gone back to her old habits of snapping at Emma as her concerns about her sister's behavior multiplied.

A few minutes later Caleb walked through the door for lunch but stopped short in the doorway of the living room.

"What's the matter, honey? You look upset." He came and sat beside her on the couch.

"Oh, Caleb, I'm worried about Emma, and I made some big mistakes in handling it." Lydia was so *ferhoodled*, she wasn't sure what to tell him first.

Caleb made it easy for her. "So what about Emma?"

Lydia launched into an account of Emma's encounter with Sam and ended by saying, "I couldn't see Sam's face from this distance, but he didn't seem in any hurry to untangle the leash."

"Obviously I wasn't there, but is it possible he was still off balance or he wanted to be sure Emma was steady on her feet before he let go?"

"I suppose." Lydia loved her husband, but she'd rather he weren't always so logical. He liked to consider everyone's side before he made a decision; she was more apt to judge and repent later. "But Emma was standing in plain view of all the neighbors. And she's interested in Sam, I can tell. What are we going to do?" Her voice sounded too shrill, especially in comparison with Caleb's measured tones.

Caleb stroked his beard and looked thoughtful. "Didn't we agree last night that Sam seemed disinterested?"

"So you think I'm overreacting?"

Patting her hand, Caleb said, "Perhaps you're making too much of something that sounds like an accident."

The accident part wasn't what upset her. It was Emma's and Sam's obvious reluctance to move apart. Or had that only been Emma? She had seemed reluctant to let go. Lydia sighed.

"You're not upset with me, are you?" Caleb asked when she didn't respond.

Lydia shook her head. Not with him.

"Promise you won't hit me?" he asked in a teasing tone, pretending to cower. "Some of your worries might be hormones."

"I know, I know. That's what you keep telling me." She playfully swatted his arm. "You and your med school talk."

Regret flickered in his eyes but disappeared so quickly Lydia wondered if she'd imagined it. Why had she reminded him of such a painful time in his life?

"If you're really concerned, I can talk to her," Caleb offered.

"Would you?" That would be such a relief. Emma listened to and respected Caleb.

"Lunch is ready," Emma called.

Caleb stood and held out a hand for Lydia, and together they headed for the kitchen.

Emma had set two ham and cheese sandwiches on Caleb's and Lydia's plates, along with a large handful of potato chips. When her sister and Caleb entered the kitchen, she unscrewed the lid of a jar of refrigerator pickles, inhaling the sharp vinegary scent. After placing a small portion on each plate, she set the jar on the table. Lydia might want more.

Caleb greeted Emma, helped Lydia into her chair, and took his seat for the silent prayer. When they finished, he looked up. "How was your day so far?" he asked.

Emma shrank lower in her chair, waiting for Lydia to tell about her morning's escapade.

Instead Lydia smiled at Caleb and said, "Let's talk about this after we eat so we can enjoy our meal."

With an inward sigh of relief, Emma let her shoulders relax. She bit into her sandwich, forcing herself to taste the tang of mustard blended with smoky, salty slices of ham and letting the conversation flow around her until everyone's plate was empty.

Then Caleb cleared his throat. "So I hear Sam was out walking his dog today."

"*Jah*, he was," Emma said. Was Caleb baiting her? Expecting her to confess? Getting ready to lecture her? "I went out to talk to him."

"Talk to him?"

Lydia's tone irritated Emma, so she replied with sarcasm, "*Jah*, Lydia, *talk* to him."

"It didn't look as if the two of you were doing much talking. When I looked out, you were in each other's arms—"

"—because we got tangled in the dog's leash."

Lydia opened her mouth to say something but closed it when Caleb shook his head.

"Sam was here last night. You couldn't have talked to him then?" Caleb's question sounded curious rather than critical.

"I asked him to dinner to make amends, but we never had a chance to talk. And I could tell by the way he behaved last night, I'd hurt his feelings. So I wanted to explain my behavior and ask his forgiveness."

"Forgiveness?"

Emma lowered her head and plucked at her apron. "I told you he offered to take me to the hymn sing last Sunday, but I didn't tell you I was so frightened, I slammed the door in his face."

Caleb leaned forward, elbows on the table, chin in hand. "I see." His eyes twinkled. "Next time please keep a safe distance between you. You wouldn't want a dog leash to damage your reputation."

That was it? That was all he intended to say? Emma turned grateful eyes in his direction.

Lydia *rutsched* in her seat as if struggling to get comfortable. "But what if someone saw them together like that?"

Caleb sent her a reassuring look. "I don't think we need to worry. For all we know, you were the only one. If that's the case, there'll be no gossip."

"I hope you're right."

The two of them exchanged glances. Once again, they'd shut her out, yet Emma had the distinct impression they were communicating silently about her.

What was going on? Why didn't they want her to see or be seen with Sam? Did they know something about him? Something that made them worry when she was with him?

To chase the troublesome thoughts away, Emma stood and began clearing the table. She'd keep her questions to herself for now. No point in alarming her sister and Caleb by expressing curiosity about Sam.

Chapter Nine

ALL WEEK LONG as he and his *onkel* tilled and planted from dawn until late into the evening, Sam's thoughts kept returning to Emma's fears. On Saturday morning he woke with an idea, one he mulled over all morning. He'd helped Bolt overcome her skittishness; perhaps he could help Emma with hers. That made him smile. Of course, he'd have to use a different method. Bones and dog treats wouldn't do the trick, but getting Emma to face her fears in tiny increments might work. He could hardly wait to ask her.

He clipped on Bolt's leash and headed toward the house next door. Before he knocked on the front door, he hesitated. What if he offended Emma by asking his question? What if she thought his idea was crazy? What if his offer triggered another panic attack?

His doubts piled up faster than cow plops in the barn. Getting rid of negative thoughts was like mucking out the stalls. With a quick prayer he shoveled them up and discarded them. Right now he'd just see if she'd like to walk the dog together. Then he'd wait for an opening in the conversation. If it came, he'd know asking her was the right thing to do.

Swallowing hard, he knocked on the door. Bolt danced

on the porch, pulling on the leash, eager to be off. "Calm down, girl. You'll get your chance in a few minutes."

Emma peeked out, her cheeks flushed, a few strands of hair escaping from her kerchief, a kerchief like the ones his *mamm* and sisters wore when they did the chores. And it was obvious Emma had been busy. A smudge of flour dotted her nose, and a sprinkling coated the front of her apron. "Sam?" Her eyes widened, and she pulled the door open. "Come in."

"I'd better not." He motioned toward the dog, but when he jingled the leash, Bolt took Emma up on the offer, barking excitedly and racing toward her.

Emma stepped back, but not quickly enough. Bolt leaped on her and licked her face. Emma staggered backward under the dog's weight and nearly toppled over. She clung to the edge of the door for balance.

Sam reached for Bolt's collar and wrestled her off Emma. "I'm so sorry," he said, his chest heaving as rapidly as the Irish setter's sides. He knelt beside the dog, an arm wrapped around her, his other hand stroking her silky coat to calm her. He looked up at Emma with a rueful smile. "I know I told you I like exuberance, but sometimes she's a bit much even for me."

He patted the dog's head. "I still love you, you big goof, but you need to learn not to jump on people." His plan was off to a rocky start.

Nothing to do but keep going. Once he was sure Bolt was calm enough, he stood. "I apologize for the way things started out. My dog seems determined to misbehave whenever we're together."

Emma knelt and petted Bolt, who tried to make it up to her by licking her face. She giggled. "You're so full of life, it's hard to contain all that excitement, isn't it? I know the feeling."

The setter's tail wagged so hard it whacked Sam in the leg. He bent to keep a tighter grip on Bolt's collar so she wouldn't leap on Emma again, but that put him near Emma's bowed head. The aroma of soap from her freshly washed hair urged him to bend closer. He straightened to avoid temptation. Keeping his promise to *Onkel* Eli might be harder than he thought.

"So you were out walking the dog?" Emma asked.

"What?" Sam forced himself to remember why he was standing on her porch. "Um, yes, we—Bolt and I—stopped by to see if you'd like to…" Emma's radiant smile almost made him lose his train of thought. "That is, I wondered if you'd like to try last week's walk again. You know, like if you had on shoes, and Bolt didn't go crazy and tangle us in the leash." Although with the way he was feeling right then, he certainly wouldn't mind if it happened that day.

Emma hesitated, and his heart sank.

"That sounds like fun, but…" She rubbed Bolt's ears one more time, then stood. "I have some pies in the oven. They'll soon be done, but I don't want to hold you up. I'm sure Bolt's eager to be on her way."

"We don't mind waiting, if you'd have time to walk after they're done baking."

"I'd enjoy that." Emma opened the door wider. "Would you like to come in while you wait?"

Sam maintained a tight rein on Bolt's collar. "I think we'd better stay out here. You know how energetic she is."

"I don't mind." Emma motioned for them to enter.

Sam shook his head. "*You* might not mind, but your sister might."

"You might be right. I'll hurry."

Emma waited until Sam settled into a rocker on the porch with Bolt beside him before she shut the door. Then she practically danced down the hall. Sam wanted to go for a walk together. She longed to burst into song, but she confined herself to rushing around the kitchen, doing a quick *redding* up while she waited to pull the pies out of the oven. Then she dashed upstairs to freshen up.

She almost collided with Lydia on the landing. Skidding to a stop, Emma reached out to steady her sister. Then breathing out a *sorry*, she brushed past her.

"Wait. What's your hurry?" Lydia used her big-sister-calming-wild-younger-sister tone.

Another tone that always irked Emma. She'd heard it so many times growing up. What a relief it would be to be around Sam. That was one place she could be herself. "Sam asked me to go for a walk." To keep her sister from getting the wrong idea, she added, "With Bolt. We're walking the dog."

Lydia followed her down the hall. "Do you think that's a good idea after last weekend? I'd hate for you to cause gossip."

"I already told Sam yes. He's waiting on the front porch." After he'd forgiven her for slamming the door in his face, she couldn't turn him down a second time. Emma walked into the bathroom, and her sister followed.

"Please think about this. What if the dog goes wild again?"

Emma already was thinking about it. Thinking about

how much she'd enjoy it. She couldn't admit that, or Lydia might forbid her to go. "Sam will keep his dog under control this time. Last time he was so busy listening to me, he didn't have time to pay attention to Bolt's antics."

"And you think he won't listen to you this time?"

"I'm sure he will." *He's so good at it.* "But we won't be talking about such important topics."

"Important topics? You barely know him."

"Oh, Lydia, stop worrying. The last time I was apologizing. I had to make sure he understood why I'd slammed the door in his face." Emma washed her hands and face. "Today we'll probably talk about the weather and things like that."

Lydia followed her to the bedroom and frowned as she switched from her kerchief to her *kapp*. "I'd still rather you not go." Lydia's face pinched up tighter than *Mammi*'s when her arthritis bothered her. "*Mamm* and *Dat* sent you to our house to get you away from the gossip at home. I wish you'd take care with your reputation *here*."

What did her sister mean by that? Yes, she'd been exuberant and lively as a child, but she hadn't been as bad as Lydia was implying. Other children were also a handful for their parents. Abner Zook, for example. He'd climbed up and jumped off a bench right in the middle of a sermon, knocking several people onto the floor. She'd mainly *rutsched*, whispered, and kicked the bench in front of them, sometimes earning a frown from the people sitting there— the same kind of frown her sister was directing her way now.

"I *have* to go." Emma realized she sounded defensive and tried to soften her words. "I already told him I would, and he's sitting on the porch waiting. It would be rude to tell him no now, unless..." Emma was unsure about putting her vague thoughts into words. "Well, if you know something about Sam or his reputation that makes him dangerous to be around."

Her sister looked startled. "Whatever gave you that idea?"

"You and Caleb don't seem to want me to be around him."

"That's because—" Lydia snapped her mouth shut.

Emma waited a moment for her sister to finish, but when she didn't, Emma shrugged. She didn't have time to wait around. Sam and Bolt were waiting, and the pies were ready to come out of the oven. Every minute she wasted here was a minute she could've been with Sam. "I'll be going then."

Lydia's pursed lips showed she disagreed with that decision, but she only shook her head. When Emma moved past her to head down the stairs, Lydia called after her, "Better to dash his hopes today than cause him heartache tomorrow."

What in the world did her sister mean? She seemed to be reading much more into the relationship with Sam than friendship. And Emma had no intention of causing him heartache—now or ever.

Eager to get back to Sam, Emma pulled the pies from the oven, breathing in the sugary aroma of the crispy crust bursting with juicy strawberries and rhubarb. She set them on the counter to cool and scurried to the porch. There she found Sam leaning back in the rocking chair, a smile playing across his lips, one hand stroking the dog's head.

When she shut the door behind her, Sam stood, and beside him Bolt rose to her feet and shook herself. Clamping his hand on the leash close to the dog's collar, Sam headed toward her. "That was fast. I'm used to my sisters' dawdling."

Emma hoped she hadn't appeared overeager. "The kitchen needed very little cleaning, so I only had to slide the pies out of the oven. It didn't take long."

Sam nodded. "And you washed up."

Emma laughed. "I had to. I had flour all over me."

"I know." Sam touched the tip of his nose. "You even had some here."

Emma's cheeks warmed. She must have been a sight.

Bolt yanked on the leash, dragging Sam down the porch steps. "I guess she figures she's been patient enough. I had no intention of taking you for an afternoon run, though."

Emma laughed. "A little exercise will do me good. I used to be the fastest runner in the *g'may* when I was younger, and everyone wanted me on their baseball team. That is until—"

"The accident?" Sam sent her a sympathetic glance.

"*Jah.* A lot of things changed after that."

"I've been meaning to talk to you about that." Sam looked away from her and concentrated on Bolt, who'd stopped to sniff around the oak tree at the edge of the walk.

"About what?"

Sam turned to her, his face serious. "I was thinking about how frightened Bolt was when I found her. She was wary of humans and cowered whenever I came close. I had to set out her food and leave before she'd eat even though she was so starved her ribs showed. I moved closer and closer each day until she eventually let me pet her."

"That took a lot of patience."

"It paid off, though. Look at her now. Oops!"

Bolt raced off, barking and tugging Sam off balance. He struggled to regain his footing while chasing the dog.

Emma caught up to them in the next block, where Bolt had treed a squirrel. Remembering the previous week's tangled leash, she kept her distance. The dog, though, didn't run in circles this time. Instead she stood under the tree and barked at the squirrel chattering on a branch overhead.

"So you were saying you helped Bolt get over her fear of humans." Emma giggled. "I'd say you've done a great job of that."

Sam's crooked smile lit a fuse in Emma's heart. She froze in place to prevent herself from moving closer. She needed to be careful about expressing her feelings; he'd been clear about only wanting to be friends.

"Well, maybe I went too much in the opposite direction with Bolt. I wanted her to be lively, and she's definitely that." He chuckled, but then sobered. "I wondered if that technique might help you."

Emma took a step backward. "What do you mean?"

"Taking small steps to overcome your fears. Like maybe just sitting in a buggy, one that's not moving or even hooked up to a horse. Then when you feel comfortable with that, you could try it with a horse attached, say, going a step or two."

The compassion on Sam's face and the earnestness in his eyes held Emma in place when all she wanted to do was run. Run as fast and far as she could. She bit her lip so she wouldn't scream out, "No, never!" Sam obviously had no idea of the depths of her fear. She trembled just standing here thinking about it.

Sam reached out and closed a warm hand over her shaking one. "Emma, I'm sorry. I didn't mean to frighten you like this. I only wanted to help. I thought if we could do it gradually..."

Emma couldn't stop the tremors. Her legs shook until they could barely hold her. Gray mist closed around her.

Shape-shifting monsters formed and dissolved in the blackness around her. Fear gripped her, pinning her down. She fought its hold, but she couldn't break free; shadows twined around her body, cutting off her breath. Her lungs ached, and she struggled for air. In the distance she heard murmuring, but she couldn't make out the words. Gradually they became more distinct.

"You're safe, Emma. It's all right. I have you," a deep voice repeated over and over.

Slowly it penetrated her consciousness that Sam had his arms wrapped around her, supporting her. She stopped thrashing and relaxed against his chest, but shivers still racked her body. Little by little the warmth of his arms and his whispered prayers for her safety soothed her, and the terror receded.

He waited until she stopped shivering, then, keeping his hands on her shoulders, he stepped back. "I didn't mean to frighten you like that."

Missing the comfort of his arms, Emma swayed toward him, but he held her steady an arm's length away. Her surroundings came into focus, and her heart swelled with gratitude. Sam had pulled her into a copse of trees, where no neighbors could witness her meltdown. He'd tied Bolt to a nearby tree.

Bolt had been lying on the ground, but when Emma looked in her direction, she leaped to her feet and lunged.

"Sit, girl," Sam commanded, but Bolt strained at her leash

until Emma worried she'd break free. Right then Emma was too fragile for Bolt's exuberance. It was as if everything had been scraped from inside her, leaving behind only a hollow shell, one that would blow away in a breeze. Sam's fingers gripping her shoulders were her only tie with reality.

Sam—what must he think of her? She must have been kicking and struggling against him, but he'd continued to hold her. With a great effort, she breathed in and pushed out the words "I'm...sorry..."

"No, I'm the one who's sorry. I didn't realize—"

Tears stung her eyes at the kindness and understanding on his face. After all he'd just been through, he hadn't turned his back on her or looked at her with pity or disgust. If he could handle what they'd just been through, surely she could trust him to help her work through her fears.

Her heart overflowed with so much gratitude, she couldn't express it in words without gushing and revealing her feelings. She swallowed back the words she wanted to say and opted for humor. "I guess...I'll be...harder to train...than..." She flapped a hand in Bolt's direction.

Sam's eyes widened. "You mean you still want to try?" He shook his head, an admiring smile on his face. "If I were you, I don't think I'd have the courage. You're amazing."

No, you're the one who's amazing, Sam. She'd never thought she'd find anyone besides her family who would stick around after witnessing one of her panic attacks.

Facing her fears was the last thing she wanted to do, and she might be risking Sam's friendship once he realized how persistent her panic attacks were, but if she didn't accept his offer and at least try, she'd be stuck in this prison of terror forever. To get her feelings under control, she kept her gaze fixed on the ground and sucked in several deep breaths while clenching and unclenching her fists. Finally she nodded.

Sam removed his hands from her shoulders and took her hands in his. "You're sure about this?"

She raised her head to meet his eyes, though his face appeared misty through the teardrops trembling on her eyelashes, and she nodded again. When he released her hands, she drew in another shuddery breath. "I didn't scare you off?"

He stood taller and threw back his shoulders. "I'm up for the challenge."

Emma managed a shaky laugh. "Aren't you afraid you might unleash a wild girl on the world?"

"As long as you promise not to leap on people and lick their faces, I think I can handle it." Sam led her from behind the bushes but dropped her hand as soon as they got in sight of the nearby houses.

"I can't promise that." Emma moved farther away as Sam unwound Bolt's leash. "Who knows what your training will turn me into." She bared her teeth and growled. "Bolt may be glad for the company."

Sam rolled his eyes. "Oh, great. I can see what I have to look forward to." His mouth stretched into a wolflike grin. "I hope you like dog biscuits and kibble."

"My favorites," Emma assured him. Although her breath still came in short, sharp gasps, she kept up with him as Bolt, glad to be released from captivity, trotted along at a brisk pace, chasing birds and barking at a cat.

As they neared her house, Sam asked, "When would you like to start?"

With only a slight hesitation, she responded, "Now?"

Sam studied her. "Are you sure?"

Although her voice shook, Emma answered, "Sooner started, sooner done."

Sam had said he was up for the challenge. Now he looked as if he weren't so sure.

Chapter Ten

EMMA STOOD IN the driveway of Eli's house while Sam took Bolt inside. He'd invited her in, but she preferred not to run into Eli. It would take all her courage to face her fears. No point in draining her bravery ahead of time. She'd acted strong in front of Sam, but she dreaded doing this.

Murmuring a brief prayer, she forced herself to take deep, even breaths rather than the sharp, shallow ones her lungs automatically reverted to when she thought about the ordeal ahead. Her feet itched to race home before Sam returned. What if she made a fool of herself? Hadn't she done that enough already?

She was still standing there undecided when Sam emerged, and his brilliant smile held her in place. Unclenching her fists, she tried to return his greeting, but her face had gone stiff.

"You're very brave to try this," Sam said. "Why don't we go inside the barn so nobody can see us?"

Emma trailed him, glancing over to the house where she longed to be instead. Not that she didn't want to be with Sam, but her heart was already knocking against her rib cage, and every nerve in her body was urging her to run.

When Sam opened the door and motioned for her to precede him, Emma hesitated. "I'm not sure this is a good idea."

A look of alarm crossed his face. "You mean the two of

us alone in here. I hadn't thought of that. Maybe your sister should chaperone us."

Emma hadn't been concerned about how it would appear if she and Sam disappeared into the barn together. "I wasn't worrying about what other people think." Though she should have been. Her fears had overshadowed common sense.

"Well, I am. I wouldn't want your family to get the wrong idea, and I certainly don't want to hurt your reputation. Bolt and I have already done enough damage to that."

Everyone was always worrying about her reputation. *Because you're so impulsive, you never think about it yourself. They're trying to prevent you from doing something foolish.* After the previous week's scene in the middle of the street, Lydia would have a conniption if she found out Emma had been alone in the barn with Sam. "Maybe we'd better forget this idea."

The disappointment in Sam's eyes spurred Emma to change her mind. As much as she wished to run from her fears, she wanted to see the joy shining in his eyes even more. "As long as we know the truth, I don't care what other people think. Besides, this probably won't take long." She'd be lucky if she managed to last a few seconds before collapsing.

"I don't want to stress your sister, but what if we asked your brother-in-law? He seems kind and understanding."

"He is." Caleb had been wonderful about the leash incident. "He knows a lot about recovery from comas, and he helped take care of me after the accident."

"Then he might be willing to let us try this." Sam studied her. "You've just been through a lot. Why don't I go to ask him?" He turned and jogged toward Caleb and Lydia's house. "I'll be right back," he called over his shoulder.

Emma hated to admit it, but she wasn't sure she could have made it the short distance to Lydia's back door. She slumped against the side of the barn while Sam crossed both backyards, knocked at the kitchen door, and had a short conversation with Caleb. Then the two of them headed her way. As Caleb got closer, Emma cringed inside. Much as she liked Caleb, having him chaperone meant two people watching her melt down. She'd been working hard to keep her terror under control, but now she crushed the fabric of her dress in her fists and struggled for breath.

"Emma?" Caleb's face radiated sympathy and understanding. "Sam told me about his plan. I think it's a great idea—if you're ready for it."

Emma couldn't meet his eyes, or he'd see the dread in hers. "I want to try." The wavering in her voice gave her away.

Caleb laid a hand on her shoulder. "It won't be easy, but it's very courageous of you. I've given Sam some pointers from the brain research I've done. It fits well with what he was thinking."

Emma managed a nod to let him know she heard. Caleb had studied a lot about recovery from traumatic brain injuries when his own mother was in a coma. After Emma's accident he'd been a big help to Lydia and *Mammi*.

"I've always wanted to experiment with something like this, but with Lydia and the babies and working full-time... Well, I never had the time," Caleb said. "I'm glad Sam is willing to try." He motioned to the door. "You two go ahead. I don't need to be there." He set a hand on Sam's shoulder. "No more than five minutes or so."

"Right," Sam said. "Then I'll walk her back to the house."

Caleb's permission lightened Emma's heart. Sam must be

okay, or Caleb would never allow them to be alone together. With a grateful smile at her brother-in-law, Emma stepped inside the dim barn and immediately wished she hadn't. Little sunshine filtered in through the cracks in the walls and through the small window high up near the eaves, striping the hard-packed dirt floor and bales of straw with light. To calm her racing heart, she closed her eyes and breathed in the familiar smells—the dusty air, the strong scent of cows and horses, and the ever-present stench of fresh manure. Sam touched her elbow, and her eyes flew open.

He leaned nearer. "Should I open the barn doors to let in more sunshine? You said you were scared of the dark."

Emma was torn between banishing the darkness and hiding her humiliation. This would be hard enough without Eli witnessing her panic. "I–I'll be all right."

Sam pointed to the vehicles parked in front of the stalls. "Would the wagon or courting buggy be better than the regular buggy because they're open?"

She managed to nod, although she was unsure it would decrease her terror. At least not enough to make any noticeable difference. She fixed her gaze on the ground and concentrated on Sam's presence beside her. She tried to mimic his steady, even breathing, and when he took the first step toward the wagon, she forced herself to follow.

Dragging her feet and averting her eyes, she inched toward the wagon. Each step seemed to take an eternity. Sam slowed to match his stride to hers. The closer they got, the harder her heart pumped.

Breathe, Emma, breathe. In and out. You remember how. Her grandmother's words echoed through caverns of her mind. Emma stumbled to a stop.

Long-forgotten sounds filled her head. The *whoosh* and *blips* and gurgle of machinery. The murmur of voices. The touch of a hand. Then silence. And the struggle to draw in a breath. The hand holding hers tightened in a gentle squeeze. A squeeze so real, so warm and comforting...

The hand holding hers drew her out of the past and back into the barn.

"You looked so far away." Sam's huge hand enveloped hers. "Are you all right?"

"I–I don't know." The green walls surrounding her dissolved into rough wooden boards. The *whooshes* and *blips* faded into the lowing of cows, the nickers of horses, and her own harsh breathing. She and Sam had stopped several feet from the wagon.

"We don't have to do this." Sam studied her face, his eyes full of sympathy. "Maybe this is close enough for today."

Emma shook her head. Hearing *Mammi*'s voice had instilled courage. "Let's keep going."

"Are you sure?"

Emma wasn't at all sure, but with Sam's hand around hers and *Mammi* urging her on, she squared her shoulders, took a deep breath, and stepped closer to the wagon. She tried to be brave in front of Sam, yet the nearer she got, the more her stomach roiled. Maybe if she didn't look at it...

Her eyes on the dirt and bits of straw under her feet, Emma shuffled forward one step at a time. Despite her not seeing it, the wagon's presence loomed larger and larger in her mind as she approached. From the corner of her eye, she glimpsed the wheel, and her gut seized. She would have doubled over if Sam hadn't spoken.

"What side were you on? Passenger or driver's?" he said in a quiet, soothing tone.

"I–I don't know."

Had she been driving? No one else had been hurt in the accident as far as she knew, so she must have been. To stop the nightmares and avoid the pain, she'd never raised any questions about that night. Even if she had, would anyone have answered? The whole topic had been taboo. It had created a rift between *Dat* and *Mammi*, and one between her and *Dat*. Rifts that had never healed.

She hung her head. "I never asked. *Mammi* might have told me, but Lydia refuses to speak about it. And *Dat*..." Her voice trembled. "All I know is that he avoided me afterward."

Sam squeezed her hand. "That must have been hard."

"It still is." Emma clamped her teeth down hard on her lower lip to stop its quivering. She hoped that after she returned from Lydia's, she and *Dat* could start fresh. Right now, though, she had other troubles to face.

Sam had distracted her momentarily, but standing beside the wagon brought all her fears rushing back. Calling on every ounce of courage she possessed and saying a silent prayer, Emma reached out and clutched the side. As soon as she did, her muscles stiffened, becoming as rigid as the wood under her hands. *I can't do this.* If Sam hadn't been standing behind her, she would have turned and fled.

He stepped closer and put his hands around her waist to boost her into the seat. "You can do this." He whispered those calming words over and over until she slumped onto the seat.

She hunched over and gripped the seat edges so fiercely the wood bit into her hands. All she wanted to do was curl into a ball and hide from the world, from the agony, from the memories clawing at her mind, her gut, her soul. What was lurking in those deep, dark recesses? Why couldn't she remember?

As if from a distance, Sam's voice penetrated the protective shell she was trying to pull around her. "Emma? Can you scoot over?"

Emma only clamped her hands more tightly on the seat and huddled farther down, hoping to stave off the shadows closing in. If she moved even an inch, it would destroy her last shred of self-control.

Sam blurred into a misty outline as he walked around the wagon to get in the other side. When he hopped in, the wagon rocked, pitching Emma forward.

Scenery whizzed by so fast in her peripheral vision, it made her dizzy. Dizzy and disoriented. She was on the right, the passenger side. But that didn't make sense. Who was driving? And why was that person speeding?

"Slow down!" she screamed, clutching Sam's arm. They were going to crash! She crumpled over and covered her head.

The roar of an engine filled her ears. A loud splintery crash, metal grinding, shattering glass...

Then silence.

Blackness swept over her; she was drowning, sucked under the waves, tossed upside down, her lungs exploding from lack of air. An invisible hand crushed her chest, squeezing all breath from her. A spasm of fear grew inside her until it filled every inch of space, expanding inside her skin until her body could no longer contain it.

Her chest and ribs ached. Her throat closed, choking her, blocking the rush of air. A scream built in her chest, pushing up, up, up, begging for release, but the opening had been pinched shut. Only a tiny whimper escaped.

Sam's arms closed around her. "Oh, Emma, I'm so sorry." His breath feathered across her forehead and fluttered tiny tendrils that had escaped from her *kapp*. If only she could relax into his embrace, revel in his closeness. Instead every muscle stayed on high alert, too tense to let go.

Sam's murmur, "Emma, Emma, Emma," drew her back to consciousness. The warmth of his arms, the laundry-fresh scent of his shirtsleeves, comforted her. She was safe. Her whole body shuddered with the pent-up tension. She forced herself to release long, slow exhales and breathe in the familiar odors of the barn, letting them wash over her until the terrors dissolved.

As Sam held Emma close, a sense of helplessness closed around him. He hadn't meant to upset her like this. He'd likened it to calming a mistreated stray. With time and patience, strays lost their fear and came to trust the person who fed them. But Emma was no stray, and he'd underestimated the depth of her trauma.

Lord, forgive me for assuming I could handle this. I don't know how to help her. Please show me what to do next.

For the time being, he did the only thing he could and kept his arms around her until she stopped shivering. After she sighed and rested heavily against him, limp and still, he said, "Emma, I apologize. I should never have done this." He had to lean closer to hear her whisper.

"I'll...be...all...right." Her voice quaked the way her body had. "It...takes...awhile."

He waited until she was somewhat steady before letting her go. Then he climbed out of the wagon and came around to help her down. "If you lean on me, do you think you can make it home?"

When she nodded, he took her arm, supporting her as much as he could. Still wobbly, she swayed against him as she walked, but a quick glance around told him that no neighbors were near, so he kept an arm around her all the way. He pulled open the back door for her, and she tottered through it.

He didn't like leaving her alone when she was still so shaky. "Are you going to be all right?"

"*Jah*, I'll be fine. I'll take a nap before dinner."

Sam watched through the window as she crossed the kitchen and headed down the hall. He hoped she'd be all right.

When he turned to head back to *Onkel* Eli's, he rubbed his arm where Emma's nails had dug into him. She'd sounded petrified of crashing. It seemed as if someone else had been driving. If only he knew more about the accident, maybe he could be more helpful.

He took several deep breaths. He was more drained than after working a long day in the field. He could only imagine how exhausted she must be. Guilt assailed him about what he'd put her through that day and about starting all this by asking her to go to the hymn sing.

If her dread of the dark was as intense as her terror of buggies, slamming the door on him seemed a mild response compared with the torrent of fears they'd unleashed that day. What if instead of healing those memories, he'd only made them worse?

Chapter Eleven

L
YDIA WOKE FROM her Saturday afternoon nap and headed down to the kitchen for a drink of water. Caleb stood at the stove, stirring a pot of soup.

"Hi, honey. Did you have a good rest?"

Covering her mouth to hide a yawn, Lydia nodded. "Where's Emma?"

"In her room. So how does grilled cheese sound with tomato soup?" Caleb pulled out a large skillet.

"Wait a minute. How come you're cooking?" Still a little disoriented from her nap, Lydia tried to figure out what was going on. "Why don't you wait for Emma to come down?"

"I peeked in her room on the way downstairs, and she was sound asleep. I think it's best not to wake her. I'll explain after we eat."

Emma napping in the afternoon? That made no sense. "Is she ill?"

"Not exactly. I promise to tell you when dinner's over. For now, I want to make sure you and the *bopplis* have a stress-free meal."

That didn't sound good. Evidently whatever Caleb planned to tell her would upset her. "Why don't you just tell me now? I'll only worry through dinner. You're sure Emma's not sick?" She admired Caleb's deft movements as he buttered the bread, placed it facedown in the skillet, laid the cheese on top, and topped it with another buttered slice of bread.

"I can assure you, Emma doesn't have anything contagious; she's only tired and drained. Just relax and wait till dinner is finished, and then we'll talk about it."

His words puzzled Lydia even more. She tried to put her worries out of her mind and enjoy the meal alone with Caleb. The sandwiches turned out crisp, and the melted cheese slid down—good comfort food. Lydia ate quickly so she could hear Caleb's news.

After he cleared the plates, refusing to let Lydia help, he sat beside her and covered her hand with his. "So about Emma…While you were napping, Sam offered to help her get over her fear of riding in buggies."

"What?" Lydia clamped her mouth shut to trap the shriek building in her chest. *Calm down, Lydia. Hear him out. Caleb would never agree to that, would he?*

"Anyway, after he explained his plan, it seemed sound. Actually it's very much what I'd hoped to do but didn't have the time."

Lydia swallowed back the fear rising in her throat. From the sound of it, Caleb liked Sam's idea. "You didn't agree, I hope."

Caleb's hand tightened over hers. "*Jah*, I did. I limited it to five minutes today. Depending on how Emma does, I might allow them ten minutes together next Saturday afternoon or the week after."

Nausea rose in Lydia's throat, and a kicking baby increased it. Surely she'd heard him wrong. He was letting Emma and Sam spend time together after they'd agreed to keep them apart? "Caleb, encouraging them to spend time together is dangerous."

"Don't worry. While they're together, Emma'll be in no shape to think about anything but her fear."

"Oh, Caleb…" She'd thought they were on the same side on this. "What if this makes her remember…?"

"Maybe it would be a good thing. Then we can put it all behind us."

Lydia shook her head. "How will she live with knowing the truth?"

"Sooner or later she'll have to face it."

Her chair scraping against the floor, Lydia stood abruptly. "If I had my way, she'd never, ever find out." Anger gave her voice a sharp edge. How could Caleb do this to her—now? With the babies coming? She regretted inviting Emma to stay. Maybe she should ask Sarah instead.

Caleb got to his feet and took Lydia in his arms. "Honey, you may not have a choice."

Lydia pushed her palms against his chest and turned away. "I might have, if you hadn't agreed to them spending time together." She dreaded to think what Caleb's permission might unleash—not only for Emma, but for all of them.

Late Saturday afternoon Emma lay on the bed, tossing and turning. She'd practiced with Sam three times now, with a week in between to recover. She tried to block those times from her mind. She was grateful Sam continued to work with her when she spent most of each session shaking, her eyes pinched shut to block out the fears that overwhelmed her. Sam probably had scars from her fingernails digging into his forearms. Yet he never lost his patience. And his "you're safe, you're safe" soothed her, although her throat was too dry and she was too choked up to thank him. She hadn't confessed to him about the aftermath of each session—how she collapsed into bed with panic attacks and migraines.

Last Saturday he'd hooked up the horse to the wagon, and earlier that day—

The nightmarish feelings rushed over her again. Her heart pounded harder than it had when she'd gotten off the wagon. She pressed her hands against her chest, trying to slow its racing. She gulped in air. Short, rapid breaths to stop smothering. Flashes of light exploded behind her closed eyes, and her head throbbed.

Would she ever get better?

Pressure built inside her head, and the trembling started again. She'd managed to control more of her emotions around Sam that day, but she was paying for it now with the worst headache of her life. She had no idea how long she lay there, numb and gasping.

Even after the tightness in her chest eased enough that she could draw in a breath, she lay shivering, too panicky to move. Her heartbeat slowed, and gradually the room came into focus. Her head still pounded, her eyes burned, and her muscles ached. After stumbling from the bed, she made her way to the landing. Her throat was parched; she needed a glass of water.

She had just started down the stairs when a wave of dizziness overtook her. She grabbed the handrail to steady herself.

Her sister's voice drifted up from the living room below.

"I'm worried about Emma and these panic attacks. If only we had someone to talk to."

As usual, Caleb soothed Lydia. "I've been reading about it. It's a normal reaction to facing fear, but if you're really worried, you could call your parents. I'm sure Eli would let you use the phone at the end of his lane."

"I don't want to alarm *Dat*. He might worry it's about the babies. *Mamm* said he was a mess after we lost the first one." Lydia choked back a sob. "For some reason, he blamed himself and was inconsolable."

"I understand how he feels," Caleb answered. "I had the same reaction. Helpless and guilty and inadequate. I trust it was God's will, but—" Caleb's voice grew hoarse, and he paused, then said, "We could call Emma's doctor, but I'm not sure it's necessary."

Emma stayed where she was, one hand grasping the railing for balance, until the dizziness subsided. Then she inched down to the next step cautiously, so as not to set it off again. Her heart ached for Caleb and Lydia. She thanked God they had two *bopplis* on the way who would bring them joy. And as for her own panic attacks, Emma was grateful that Caleb had calmed her sister. Lydia had always been a worrier. Emma took another careful step, trying to lessen the hammering in her head.

"If you think Emma's doing all right," Lydia said, "I won't fret about it. I am concerned about her spending so much time with Sam, though."

"Nothing to worry about," Caleb told her. "They're only friends."

"Doesn't seem that way to me." Lydia's voice had the

inflection she'd used in their younger years when scolding Emma for misbehavior.

Memories of *Mamm*, *Dat*, and Lydia frowning at her added to the pressure behind Emma's eyes. She'd always gotten into trouble back then, and now no matter how hard she tried, she still managed to cause trouble.

She should warn them she was there and stop eavesdropping, but she stayed where she was, each foot on a different stair, rubbing her forehead.

Caleb answered, "Relax, honey. Sam assured me they're only friends; he made it clear he has no interest in dating anyone here. I talked to him today after his session with Emma, and he started to say something about a girlfriend back home but never finished."

Sam? A girlfriend? The words penetrated the drumming in Emma's skull. She clutched the railing with both hands to avoid tumbling down the stairs and slumped against the wall, wishing away the pain in her head and her heart.

She recalled the tender way Sam had held her hands, placed his arms around her to comfort her. If he had a girlfriend, she'd misread his gentleness. She'd attached too much meaning to his kindly gestures. Likely he'd treat his younger sisters the same way. He expressed his caring through touch. Look at the way he treated Bolt. He caressed the Irish setter's ears, wrapped his arms around the dog, and buried his face in her fur. He'd even compared Emma's training to his dog's. Maybe she was nothing more than another stray to him.

The pressure inside her skull intensified, and she whimpered.

"Emma?" Lydia called.

Her throat too choked up to reply, Emma faked a cough

and stepped heavily on the next stair, a move that jarred her head.

"Emma, is that you?" The sharpness in Lydia's voice sliced through Emma's throbbing skull.

After croaking out a yes, Emma massaged her temples until the pain receded to a dull ache. Then she descended the rest of the steps to the living room.

"I thought you were napping." Lydia's accusatory tone was at odds with the guilt in her eyes.

Caleb stared at Emma, a worried frown creasing his brow. "Are you all right?"

"I have a bit of a headache." Pressing a hand to her forehead, Emma entered the living room, not sure she was up to participating in this conversation. She still felt shaky, and Lydia's irritation made her feel ashamed, even though she'd done nothing wrong.

"Again?" Lydia studied her closely. When Emma nodded, Lydia said, "I guess you heard our conversation."

"Only a bit of it." Enough to know her friendship with Sam upset them for some reason, something she'd heard before. And that Sam had a girlfriend. Emma lowered herself gingerly into the rocking chair opposite her sister and Caleb.

Caleb blew out a long breath. "I suppose it's time to talk about this."

Beside him, Lydia set a hand on his arm and shook her head vigorously. When Caleb turned to look at her, she shot him a covert look of alarm, and dread pooled in Emma's stomach. Something was wrong, very wrong.

Caleb wrapped an arm around Lydia and drew her closer. "Often the best way to clear things up is by being honest." He faced Emma. "You and Sam have been working together on your fears?"

Emma nodded, not sure where this conversation was headed. She hoped he wasn't going to forbid the two of them to meet. Having Sam help her with her fears was rather unusual, and people might assume they were more than friends. But if Caleb was right, they'd never be any more than that. Much as that hurt her, she tried to push the thought out of her mind so she could enjoy their time together.

"Do you think it's helping?" Caleb leaned forward a bit, eagerness in the lines of his body.

"I made it the whole way down the driveway today without having a panic attack." Emma had been proud of her progress, but what seemed like a big deal when she was in the wagon now seemed a tiny accomplishment.

Caleb didn't belittle her as she'd expected. Instead he smiled his encouragement. "That's pretty amazing. You're always exhausted afterwards, though?"

"Tired, and I have terrible headaches," Emma admitted. Not to mention the nausea and shaking.

"That makes sense. Your body, mind, and emotions are undergoing a lot of changes."

Emma twisted her hands in her lap. That was for sure and certain.

"Along with that," he continued, "have you noticed any differences in your memory?"

"Not really." Although the swirling fogginess had increased, intensifying the headaches and nausea. And she'd had a few frightening glimpses into the past—at least she assumed they were memories—but she'd had only vague impressions of sights or sounds. She opened her mouth to tell Caleb about the symptoms when Lydia interrupted.

Small frown lines creased her sister's brow. "Do you think we should take her to a doctor? They did say to let them know about headaches."

Caleb tapped a knuckle against his lip. "I'm not sure." He studied Emma for a moment before asking, "Do you have the headaches at other times or only after you've worked with Sam?"

"Only after Sam." Her lips quirked. "Just to be clear, Sam's not giving me headaches." She tried to keep her voice steady, but it wavered as she said, "It's scary to even sit in the buggy or wagon. And then when it moves..." Her hands trembled from the memory.

"So the headaches only occur after the buggy rides?" Caleb's tone was gentle.

"I wouldn't exactly call them rides." Emma had to be honest. They'd spent most of their time in an unmoving wagon. Still, she squeezed her eyes shut and clenched the fabric of her skirt the way she'd clutched the seat. Even now the terror of climbing in and sitting on the seat stayed with her.

"You're trembling."

Lydia's sympathetic words soothed Emma, and she forced her fingers to release her skirt. She smoothed the material down toward her ankles in an unsuccessful attempt to calm the nervous tremors in her legs and hands. After a brief swallow to release the tense muscles in her throat, she answered, "I try not to be scared, but it's terrifying."

Emma opened her eyes to see Lydia's brimming with tears. Was it because her sister was overly emotional now, or was she that deeply concerned?

Caleb, though, had relaxed his back against the couch. "I don't think we need to worry about the headaches. Rather than being random and unexplained, they seem to be directly connected with the buggy rides."

"But it wasn't a buggy. It was a ca—" Lydia clapped her hand over her mouth and gazed at Caleb with wide eyes.

He pulled her closer and took her hand. "I'm sure it won't matter. Getting used to any vehicle should help."

Emma wanted to ask what Lydia had meant, but the fireworks shooting off behind her right eye signaled the start of a migraine, an excruciating one. "I'm going back upstairs to lie down." She had questions she needed to ask. About her and Sam. About what Lydia and Caleb had been talking about. Now she couldn't remember any of them.

She rose, unsteady on her feet, gray shadows closing around her. No longer thirsty, she tottered toward the stairs and grasped the railing to keep herself upright. "I'll sleep until dinner."

"Don't worry about dinner. I'll whip something up." Caleb's response reverberated in the pain-filled recesses of her head.

Lydia's response floated up the stairwell. "That's one advantage of having a husband who used to be *Englisch*."

Caleb did know how to cook. He'd taken care of his younger brother after their parents died. Emma dragged herself up stair by stair until she reached the landing. She stumbled to the bedroom and curled up under the crocheted afghan. Caleb shouldn't have to fix meals every Saturday night. It was her job. That was Emma's last thought before she collapsed into bed and fell into a restless sleep where headlights glared in her eyes and emerald sweaters tangled around tree limbs.

Chapter Twelve

ARLY THE NEXT morning Emma fought her way out of
the nightmares. In the fog between sleep and waking,
the green sweater seemed to hold the key to her past.
Exhausted and bleary-eyed, she stumbled from bed to open
the drawer where she'd hidden it.

After lifting it out, she rubbed the wool against her face,
trying to stay in the hazy dream state. A light aroma of honey-
suckle and berries rose from the wool, teasing her with a
vague impression of a strange room. A room with a gray
metal door, mismatched furniture, a large mirror on the
wall, and glossy magazines on a coffee table. An *Englisch*
room, for sure and certain.

Emma shook her head to clear the last vestiges of the
dream. She'd anticipated a clue; instead she'd received more
riddles. She nibbled at her lower lip as disappointment
gnawed at her insides. How could this sweater and an unfa-
miliar room solve any past mysteries?

She was tempted to fling the sweater across the room,
but some instinct warned her to keep it hidden from Lydia.
Instead of returning it to the drawer, Emma tucked it under
her pillow. Then she made the bed and dressed.

Still groggy, she crept downstairs to gather eggs and start
breakfast. She wrapped her cape around her to ward off the
predawn chill. The fresh air blew away some of the cobwebs

tangling her mind and cleared away most of the pain from the previous night's headache.

Something shifted in the shadows by the chicken house. A fox? The large shape headed in her direction. Much too tall for a fox. A man.

Emma clutched the basket handle until it made indentations on her skin. Her mouth went dry. She knew she should flee, but her muscles refused to move.

"Emma?"

At the familiar voice, the tension in Emma's body melted away. "*Gude mariye*, Sam," she called as she hurried toward him, the empty egg basket banging against her hip. "What are you doing out here?"

"Did I frighten you?"

Now that she was close to Sam, Emma's pulse, which had been racing in fear, galloped with happiness and excitement. "Maybe a little."

"I'm sorry. I didn't mean to. I wanted to catch you early enough to ask you a question." Sam's smile, the look in his eyes, added brightness to the gray dawn. Behind him, a tiny sliver of sun slipped above the horizon, painting the sky around it pale pink and gold. Emma's mood brightened to match the sky.

"I should have thought of this yesterday," Sam said. "But I wondered if you'd like to go to church today."

"Oh." Emma couldn't keep the disappointment from her tone. Much as she'd enjoy going to church with him, she'd never handle the buggy ride. Yes, she'd made it down the driveway without a panic attack the day before, but Sam had no idea what that cost her afterward. Just the thought of trying that again made her ill.

Some of the joy drained from Sam's expression. "I thought we could walk there if—"

"Walk? Did you say walk?" Emma's voice squeaked on the last word.

"Yes, of course." It took a moment for Sam's face to register understanding. "Did you think I meant in the buggy?" At Emma's nod, the smile returned to his lips. "I need to be more careful with my invitations. Good thing you weren't in the chicken house when I asked, or I might have gotten another door slammed in my face."

Emma giggled. "I wouldn't have done that. At least I don't think I would. But did you really mean you want to walk to church? Us? You and me together?" Her cheeks heated. She hoped Sam didn't interpret her questions and the excitement in her voice to mean she was interested in him. Even if she was. She averted her eyes so he wouldn't read that message in them.

Now it was Sam's turn to laugh. "*Jah*, I meant for us to go together. It's at the Yoders' house today. That's about two miles from here, so I wanted to give you enough time to get ready. That is, if you want to go."

"Of course I would!" Emma wished she could clap a hand over her mouth.

If only she'd answered as demurely as Lydia would. Her sister would probably say, "*Danke* for the invitation. That would be nice." As usual, Emma had blurted out the first thing that came to mind, and she hadn't even thanked Sam. At least she could remedy that. Her overeager *danke* did little to erase the impression she'd already created. Emma groaned inside.

Sam's eyes twinkled. "I'll look forward to it. We should

leave soon after breakfast if—" He frowned. "We should probably ask Caleb and Lydia's permission first."

"I'm sure they'll be fine with it. They're always asking me to go to church."

"I'll see you soon then." Sam hurried across the lawn and was just opening the barn door as his *onkel* came out the back door.

Emma scooted into the chicken house before he saw her. She snatched the eggs and dumped them in the basket so quickly, she was lucky none of them broke. Then she practically danced across the lawn and into the kitchen.

Caleb was at the stove heating water for coffee. "You look chipper this morning."

Emma stopped herself before she blurted out the reason. She tried for a neutral smile before setting down the egg basket and heading to the refrigerator. She waited until she'd set the frying pan on the stove before she said as casually as she could, "Sam and I were planning to walk to church this morning."

Caleb's eyebrows shot up. "I'm glad you want to go to church." He smiled at Lydia, who was entering the kitchen. He rushed over to help her into a chair.

"What's this about Emma going to church today?" Lydia looked from Caleb to Emma.

Caleb took the pot of water off the stove and busied himself with making coffee. Emma guessed he was waiting for her to answer. She cracked several eggs into the hot pan, not sure how her sister might react.

"I'm walking to church with Sam this morning." It was difficult keeping the joy out of her voice.

"I'm not sure that's a good idea."

Lydia's mother-hen tone irritated Emma, so she retorted, "You don't think going to church is a good idea?"

Her sister sighed. "You know what I mean." She looked at Caleb. "I'm sure you agree it isn't wise."

Caleb stirred his coffee before replying. "I understand your worries, but I'd also like to see Emma go to church."

"My worries? Emma's cozying up to Sam doesn't worry you?"

Cozying up? Her sister made it sound as if she were chasing Sam. All right, so maybe she was a little. Emma flipped the eggs out onto the plates and realized in all her excitement over Sam she'd forgotten to start the toast.

She carried the plates to the table. "I'm sorry about the toast. Will bread and jam do?"

"Fine with me," Caleb said, earning a glare from Lydia. "I'm sorry, sweetie. I meant bread and jam are fine. I wasn't referring to the situation with Sam." He laid a hand over hers. "Although I'm not as worried about that as you are."

Emma set the bread and jam on the table and slid into her place. They all bowed their heads for the silent prayer. After she lifted her head, Emma determined not to let Lydia stop her from enjoying a walk with Sam.

Lydia and Caleb's discussion swirled around her. Emma tuned back in to the conversation to hear Lydia remark that someone should chaperone them.

"I'd offer to walk with them," Caleb said, "but I don't want you driving alone. I think they'll be fine on a public road."

"That's just it." Lydia looked close to tears. "What will people think?"

Emma set down the jam knife with a clang. "I don't care what people think."

"Exactly why you need a chaperone."

Caleb reached for the jam jar. "Let them walk to church without turning it into a big deal."

Lydia rubbed her forehead. "When we invited her here, I never imagined I'd have to worry about her courting."

"At least he's Amish."

Caleb's joking tone made Emma look up. What was that supposed to mean? Was he referring to the fact that her sister had fallen for him when he was *Englisch*?

"He's just a friend," Emma protested to both of them. "Besides, he has a girlfriend back home."

"Has he told you about her?" Lydia asked.

"No."

"Then how do you know?"

Emma waved her hand, not wanting to admit that she'd overheard Caleb say so. "Someone mentioned it, and Sam has made it clear he only wants to be friends. Besides, you've seen what a wreck I am after my sessions. Why would he want to court someone like me?"

The words were meant to soothe Lydia, but Emma had spent countless hours worrying over them. Why, indeed, would Sam want to court someone like her? She whisked the dishes off the table and left them soaking in the sink. Then she hurried upstairs before either of them could forbid her to go.

The breakfast conversation had punctured her excitement. Like a balloon pricked by a pin, most of her elation had leaked out, leaving her flat and drained. She tried to keep her mind off Sam's motives and his possible girlfriend and concentrate instead on the time they'd have together. As friends.

The thought of walking two miles with Sam brought the

smile back to her lips, the smile she'd suppressed during breakfast. Joy bubbled up inside at the thought of attending services. She usually spent church Sundays alone, reading her Bible. She tried to tell herself her happiness was only because she was looking forward to being part of the community, but her conscience jabbed her with the truth. She was equally thrilled to be spending more time with Sam. And for once, she'd be around Sam without having a panic attack.

Emma couldn't help humming a tune from the *Ausbund* as she dressed. As soon as she was ready, she rushed out to the porch to wait for Sam. The sun warmed her face and lifted her spirits even more. The perfume of early lilacs floated on the breeze, and the sparrows twittering in the bushes added to the song in her heart.

When Sam emerged from his front door, Emma hurried toward him, happiness adding a bounce to her step. She was delighted about finally going to church—at least that's what she tried to tell herself. If she were honest, though, some of her excitement had to do with Sam. And for once, she wouldn't be so terrified that she couldn't enjoy his company.

They'd left early enough that no cars or buggies passed them on the back roads, so they strolled along, enjoying doves cooing and wildflowers blooming. Bleeding hearts, bluebells, and lupines carpeted the ground at the edge of the woods. White dogwood blossoms coated the ground like snow. Interspersed among them, pink clouds of blossoms covered cherry trees. Emma flung her arms wide and inhaled the fragrant air. "What a lovely day!" Being with Sam, surrounded by all the beauty, made her want to run barefoot through the grass like a small girl or spin around until she was so dizzy, she collapsed in a heap.

Sam laughed. "It's great to see you filled with such enthusiasm. Your eyes are sparkling."

"Days like this make me grateful to God." Emma couldn't resist skipping beside him for a few steps. Then, worried that he'd find her too undignified, she stopped.

"Few people have your zest for life." Admiration, rather than disapproval, shone in Sam's eyes. "It's so refreshing being around you."

"Really? Even when we're in the barn?"

Sam sobered a bit. "That's different, but even there, your reactions are genuine. To me, being honest about your feelings is extremely important."

He likes being around me. Emma commanded her feet not to skip. She clasped her hands together to keep from throwing her arms around him. Of course, liking someone and enjoying their company were two different things. She needed to get a grip on herself. He'd assured her he wanted to be friends. Nothing more. Still she couldn't help hoping he might change his mind. For now, she was happy he stayed around after the panic attacks he'd witnessed in the barn.

She wanted to lighten the serious expression on his face. "I'm sorry to be a trial."

"You're not. I admire your courage, your willingness to tackle your fears. I can't imagine what it must be like to face a trauma like that."

Emma blinked back tears. His words touched a place deep inside her, a place she'd hidden for years. With Sam, she felt accepted and safe.

Ahead of them, blinking lights signaled a major

intersection. The sinking feeling in Emma's stomach slowed her steps.

Sam leaned toward her. "Are you all right?"

Emma swallowed hard but couldn't answer. All her energy and concentration centered on the crossroad ahead.

Sam followed her gaze. "I should have warned you, but this will be the only place with heavy traffic. It's Sunday, so traffic's lighter than usual," Sam said in the phony cheerful voice parents use to reassure small children.

When they neared the road, cars and trucks whizzed by, and Emma flinched. The sounds reminded her of the souped-up cars the teen boys often raced down their street on Saturday nights. The whine of their motors made her break out in a cold sweat.

Vehicles had stopped at the light by the time they reached the intersection. A single sports car turned into the lane on the opposite side of the street.

"We can cross the street now." Sam started to step off the curb into the street, but when she hesitated, he stopped and waited for her.

Beside her, a driver gunned his engine, and Emma choked back a scream. That noise. A motor revving. A dark tunnel sucked her inside, and roaring filled her ears, her head, her body. Ahead of her, a huge tree loomed, blocking her vision through the windshield. She was vaguely aware of Sam gripping her shoulder, repeating words over and over. She lowered her head, half in, half out of the nightmare.

Sam's murmur penetrated the mist surrounding her. "Emma, you're safe. You're safe."

She longed to slump against his chest, but Sam kept a

firm grip that held her away from him. The sound of car engines nearby receded, and silence fell. She raised her head.

Sam let go of her shoulders. "Are you all right?"

"I–I'm not sure. That car." She closed her eyes, but this time all that appeared was blessed blackness. "I had a flashback. At least I think it was a flashback."

"You remembered something?"

The memory in the barn flickered through her mind. Emma stared off into the distance, trying to recall the dreamlike image. "I heard a car engine roaring."

"A car crashed into the buggy?"

"I'm not sure." Emma knotted her fists and scrunched her eyes shut, but the screen in her head remained blank. "I don't remember anything but bits and pieces. And those pictures appear at random times. Forcing myself doesn't work."

"But you remember a car?"

A splitting headache began behind Emma's eyes, and she hesitated. "That can't be right."

Sam stood patiently waiting for her to gather her thoughts, but Emma couldn't make sense of what she'd seen.

"Just now it seemed like I was looking out a windshield at a silver hood."

"You were *in* a car?"

Emma shook her head. "That doesn't make sense. Why would I have been riding in a car?" Yet in the barn, she had the impression of speed. No one could drive a buggy that fast. And shattered glass.

"Does your family know what happened? Would they tell you if you asked?"

Emma heaved a sigh. "I suppose so. I've always avoided asking about it because I'm not sure I really want to remember."

Sam nodded. "Maybe you're better off not knowing."

"I imagine that's what my family thinks. I could ask my sister or Caleb about the car." If only she could remember what happened. Lydia wouldn't be happy if Emma started asking questions about the accident, but she had to find out why her visions included a car rather than a buggy.

Sam turned to her with a worried frown. "I don't like to think about you stirring up terrible memories."

"If I face what happened, though, it might help when we work together." Emma determined to ask Caleb and Lydia the next chance she got. Or maybe she could get Caleb alone. Lydia seemed to be taking her responsibilities as mother hen much too seriously.

With the intersection clear and the light now in their favor, they crossed the road without incident and continued their walk. The road they were on narrowed to two lanes instead of four, and the sidewalks soon ended, so they walked along the gravel shoulder. They went around a bend, where trees shaded both sides of the road.

An engine growled in the distance, and Emma gritted her teeth and willed her body not to react. Yet as the roaring increased, so did her shivering. By the time the red truck passed, she was shaking. "I'm sorry." Even her voice quavered.

Sam glanced around before reaching for her hand. "No one can see us, at least for the moment."

The warmth flowing from his fingers to hers soothed Emma. She longed for him to put his arms around her and hold her close until her racing pulse slowed. Although that might actually increase her heart rate more. Emma made herself breathe deeply and slowly. She concentrated on the strength and comfort of Sam's hand wrapped around hers.

"Perhaps we should keep walking so we're not late." Sam sounded as reluctant to move as she was.

Horses' hooves clip-clopped in the distance behind them, and Sam released her hand, leaving her bereft. After surviving the light at the intersection and hearing the car engines, the sounds of the clicking of buggy wheels and the trotting of horses were almost a welcome relief. They'd left so early that this was the first buggy to approach. A young mother holding a baby called out to ask if Sam and Emma needed a ride, but Sam thanked them before waving them on their way.

Emma released her breath in a long sigh. Although she'd tensed as the buggy neared, she had no flashbacks or reactions after it passed. She held out her hands. "I'm not shaking," she said in wonder. "I can't believe it! It's all because of your help." She was so overjoyed she almost threw her arms around Sam and hugged him, but she restrained herself just in time.

Sam's eyes shone. "That's amazing! But it had little to do with me. You're the one who did it."

The pride in his eyes made Emma's face heat. Lydia's voice echoed in her head, warning her about *hochmut*, so she lowered her eyes and squashed the smidgen of pride niggling its way through her mind. Besides, it never would have happened if it hadn't been for Sam.

Misty-eyed, she murmured, "I couldn't have done it without you." *Without you beside me, without your encouraging voice, without you, I never would have made it.*

"I'm glad I could help in some small way." Sam glanced around. "More buggies are headed our way. We should start walking again."

Emma kept pace with Sam's rapid stride, hoping no one had seen them standing there gazing into each other's eyes, or they'd have gotten the wrong impression. The road curved around another bend, hiding them from view for a moment, so Emma flashed Sam a broad smile. "I can't thank you enough. I never thought I'd be able to go near a buggy again."

"I don't suppose you'd be ready to ride in one?"

Emma shook her head. "Not yet. Even the thought still terrifies me. Although we did get the whole way down the driveway yesterday. That may not seem like a big deal to you, but for me, it's huge."

"I thought it was a major step forward."

Emma smiled so broadly her cheeks hurt. "It was." Maybe someday she'd be able to do it without a panic attack.

Chapter Thirteen

MMA AND SAM were just entering the Yoder house when Lydia and Caleb pulled in the driveway.

"Looks like they made it," Caleb said.

Lydia released a breath. "*Jah*, they did." She hadn't been worried about them getting to church; it was their opportunity for developing a deeper friendship that concerned her more. At least Emma and Sam would be apart during the service. The Yoders' home was small, so the women sat in a different room than the men.

After Caleb helped her out of the buggy and into the house, Lydia headed for the kitchen, where the women had gathered. Although women were chatting to one another and her sister, Emma looked lost and uncomfortable.

Lydia's heart went out to her sister. She'd been overwhelmed when she'd attended this *g'may* for the first time. Raised in the same *g'may* all their lives, the other members of their community became like family. Being among a crowd of strangers was never easy, but Emma had barely been out of the house since her accident, so it had to be overwhelming.

Emma spotted her, and the tension lines in her face relaxed. Emma's broad welcoming smile was accompanied by a *please-rescue-me* plea in her eyes, so Lydia hurried to her side and spent the time before the service introducing Emma and including her in conversations.

When the service began, Lydia sat beside Emma, her soul filled with joy that her sister was in church. Her mind flashed back to her own baptism day three years ago when Emma had attended church for the first time since her accident. What a joy that had been and how far her sister had come. Except for the gap in her memory, which Lydia hoped would never return, Emma had no lasting effects from the accident. Well, except for her fears.

Beside Lydia, Emma's lilting voice rang out as they began the second hymn they sang in every service, "*Das Loblied.*" Hearing her sister's enthusiasm for spiritual things touched Lydia's soul. She reached out and squeezed Emma's hand, surprising them both.

Her buoyancy lasted through the first sermon, the scripture reading, and the silent prayer. The bishop's sermon that followed, though, about *uffgevva*, soon had had her pondering her life and her relationship with Emma. As he reminded them that they needed to apply this principle of giving up or surrendering their wills to God's and submitting to the authority and the wisdom of the community, a tear trickled down Lydia's cheek. She'd been so busy forcing her will on Emma that she'd forgotten to trust God. She took her responsibility as older sister seriously and wanted only the best for Emma, but maybe it was time to let go of the burden she'd been carrying and let God work things out.

By the time Emma *redded* up the kitchen that evening and hung the dish towel to dry, Lydia and Caleb were cuddling on the living room sofa, *ooh*ing and *aah*ing over the stars sparkling in the sky.

"No moon tonight," Caleb noted.

Emma shivered, imagining the deep ebony sky closing around her, squishing the air out of her chest, choking her. Darkness inside the house made her slightly uncomfortable, but she'd grown up with that. *Dat* usually lit only one lamp in the living room, and everyone gathered there to work or play. Most nights they went to bed early so they could rise at dawn to do chores.

But the darkness outside overwhelmed her. Sometimes passing a window at night made her heart pound. This night was no exception. Emma squeezed her hands into fists and forced herself to take deep breaths to calm the thumping in her chest.

"Emma?" Caleb called. "Why don't you come join us? We're going to play Uno."

"Why don't we play at the kitchen table?" Emma preferred to be in a place where she could sit with her back to the windows. The living room couch and one chair faced windows.

Lydia sighed. "I'm too tired to move. I have my feet propped up."

Emma nibbled at her lower lip. Yes or no? Forcing her breathing into a natural in-and-out movement, she joined Lydia and Caleb. She averted her eyes from the huge picture window that revealed the moonless night outside and dragged the rocking chair to a spot where the windows loomed behind her.

"Oh, Emma." Lydia's words were more of an apology than a protest, but they made Emma feel she was a burden, a problem to be solved.

Although Lydia was a loving sister, she always knew the right things to say and do in any situation. Following the Bible and *Ordnung* came naturally to her. For Emma, doing the right thing was often a struggle. Her heart was generally in the right place, but somehow her actions never quite measured up. Like the way she'd acted when Sam asked her to the hymn sing or when she'd impulsively invited Eli to dinner or when...

"Are you ready?" Caleb interrupted the litany of mistakes and failures, which easily extended throughout her nineteen years.

Lydia tried to make her more comfortable by smiling, but the compassion shining in her sister's eyes only increased Emma's feelings of inadequacy. Emma sighed inwardly and picked up the cards Caleb had dealt.

The game barely held Emma's attention because her mind replayed the walk with Sam on an endless loop. She worked so hard to keep a gigantic grin off her face, she made foolish mistakes in the game. Finally she set down her unplayed hand. "I'm tired. I think I'll go up to bed."

"Already?" Caleb's face registered disappointment. "Why don't you finish out the hand?"

"So you can win?" Emma teased.

Caleb laughed. "Of course. I hate to end a game when I'm so close to being a champion."

Emma made a face at him but picked up her cards. After Caleb had won the hand, he turned to Lydia. "Ready for bed, love?"

The tenderness in his tone and the gentle way he helped Lydia up and supported her to the stairs sent frissons of loneliness and longing through Emma. If only someone cared about her that deeply. She pictured Sam in that role. Would he be interested?

Interested in what? She'd jumped from neighborly kindness to a serious relationship in the space of seconds. Yes, he'd been caring and compassionate, but their time together had been focused on her and her fears. And she could barely hold herself together after each session, so they never had time to talk about anything personal. For all she knew, he was helping her—another stray—the way he'd tamed Bolt. She hoped not, but she couldn't be sure.

Her heart heavy, Emma started for the stairs, but the distant sound of an ambulance froze her in place. As the shriek of the siren drew nearer, Emma hyperventilated, her breath coming in short, sharp gasps. *Breathe. In and out.* For some strange reason, she heard her grandmother's voice repeating those words.

"*Mammi?*" She wheezed out the word between rapid breaths. Her grandmother wasn't there, but her voice sounded in Emma's ear. *In and out. You can do it.* Emma's head spun, and she grabbed for the stair railing to catch herself as dizziness overtook her. Once again, wisps of the past floated by, but they were too nebulous to grasp.

Outside the howling grew louder and louder as if the ambulance were driving into their living room. Blue lights strobed through the window, and Emma clutched at the wooden post to keep herself upright. The world tilted, and she was lying on her back, gazing up at the stars. The light from the moon burned her eyes. Moon? There was no moon that night. Then a face blocked out the moon. Caleb? A mouth babbling *sorry*, salty tears dripping like raindrops onto her face. Had the ambulance been coming for her?

She concentrated on the smoothness of the wood beneath one hand, the plastic handle of the flashlight in the other. Her foot on the step. She was inside the house. She was safe.

The ambulance had pulled in next door. *Next door? Sam?* Was he all right? She had to be sure.

Emma rushed to the door and yanked it open. She froze in the doorway as the night sky closed in around her. Tremors shook her from head to toe. Squeezing her eyes shut against the flashing glare, she murmured a prayer for courage to cross the yard, but her muscles refused to move. Crossing that distance seemed more treacherous than walking through swamps filled with alligators, mouths wide open to expose needle-sharp teeth.

The siren ceased, but the bright pulsing light penetrated her closed eyelids. The ambulance doors clanged open, and Emma opened her eyes to see two EMTs rolling a stretcher toward Eli's front door. Who was hurt? Eli or Sam?

Light from the living room spilled out onto the porch as the front door flew open. Sam stood silhouetted in the doorway, one hand clutching Bolt's collar. Emma breathed a prayer of gratitude, quickly followed by a request for Eli's health.

When Sam opened the door wider for the stretcher, Bolt twisted free and zigzagged across the yard.

Panic and darkness forgotten, Emma plunged toward the furry blur streaking toward the street. Damp grass soaked through her stockinged feet. She gulped cool night air into her burning chest.

"Bolt!" she yelled as she closed in on the Irish setter. "Come here."

At the sound of her name, Bolt glanced in Emma's direction momentarily but then resumed running.

An engine roared as a car sped up the hill.

"NOOOO!" Adrenaline gushed through Emma. She raced the last few feet and threw herself at Bolt. With a flying tackle, she wrapped her arms around the dog and rolled to the side as headlights stabbed them. Brakes screeched, and the car swerved, missing the rotating mass of flesh and fur by inches. A blast of hot air whooshed past Emma's face as she rolled over again, the dog clasped tightly in her arms.

The car juddered to a stop a few feet away. Arms squeezing Bolt close to her, Emma lay, panting, air moving in and out of her mouth, but none flowing down to her air-starved lungs. Her heart banged against the inside of her rib cage, sending spasms of pain throughout her shuddering body. Tiny pinpoints of light swirled past her eyes.

When she could focus again, Caleb, an EMT, and a strange man bent over her. Sam, his face a mask of terror, knelt beside her. "Emma," he gasped.

Emma's teeth were chattering too hard to answer. *Sam.* There was something she needed to say to him, tell him, but her thoughts were spinning out of control.

Caleb grabbed Bolt's collar. "I'll take her into our house for now." He led the dog away.

"Can you stand?" The EMT reached out a hand to assist her, but Sam wrapped his arms around her and helped her to a sitting position.

Emma rested her head against his chest. She felt safe there in his arms.

The door to Eli's house banged open, and two EMTs wheeled out a stretcher. Sam sucked in a breath.

The EMT straightened. "If you're okay, miss, I need to go."

"I'll be fine." *Once I can catch my breath.* Although that seemed hard to do when she remained cradled in Sam's arms.

"I don't want to leave you," Sam whispered against her kerchief. "But *Onkel* Eli."

"Go," Emma wheezed out. "Your *onkel* needs you."

Sam helped her to her feet. "Are you sure you're..."

Caleb rushed out of the house. "I'll take care of Emma. I have some medical training. You go with the ambulance."

With one last glance at Emma, Sam dashed over and reached the ambulance as the EMTs slid the stretcher inside. The EMT who'd helped her slammed the doors behind them and jumped into the driver's seat. Sam got into the passenger side, and the ambulance screamed off into the night.

Chapter Fourteen

B OLT RACED AROUND the room, barking, skittering
from one end of the floor to the other. Still too shaken
and drained to help, Emma collapsed on the couch as
Caleb chased the dog around the living room, trying to tie a
rope to the Irish setter's collar.

"What's all that noise?" Lydia came halfway down the
steps and stopped.

Caleb leaped, nabbed the dog, and managed to clutch the
dog's collar. "Sit," he commanded after he knotted the rope.

Instead of obeying, Bolt twisted around and licked his
face. Startled, Caleb let go of the rope. With a joyous bark,
the Irish setter jumped on Caleb, knocking him backward.
Caleb struggled to his feet as Bolt dashed from the room.
The rope whipped through the air, and Caleb dove after it.
Triumphant, he held it up.

A wan smile was all that Emma could manage for their
antics. Lydia smiled and shook her head.

Staying on the steps, a safe distance from the lively dog,
Lydia asked, "What happened?"

"I don't know," Emma said. "They took Eli away in an
ambulance."

"Oh no. I hope he's all right." Lydia bowed her head and
murmured a prayer Emma couldn't hear. Emma added her

own heartfelt plea for Eli and one for Sam, who would be worried about his *onkel*.

Bolt dragged Caleb back into the living room, and the two of them headed for the front door.

"I'll take her out for a walk to calm her." Caleb managed to open the front door that Bolt was pawing furiously, and the Irish setter bounded out with Caleb sprinting behind. Caleb barely had time to slam the door behind him. "When I get back, I'll take care of you, Emma," he called before the door shut.

Half an hour later, a more subdued Bolt strolled into the house. Caleb followed, his expression more relieved than when he left.

After sniffing around the downstairs, Bolt returned and bumped Emma's legs, looking up at her with expectant eyes. She scratched the dog's head with trembling hands, while she continued the slow, deep breathing she'd been doing to calm her nerves.

Praying for the strength to conquer her fears, she made herself sit on the sofa facing the window even though it made her quiver. She didn't want to miss Sam when he returned. He'd want Bolt for company tonight.

Lydia had gone back to bed, and Caleb went up to check on her. A short while later, he returned with peroxide and a jar of salve. After he rinsed out dirt and gravel, he slathered salve on Emma's brush burns.

"Does anything else hurt besides your arms?" he asked.

Emma felt battered and bruised everywhere, but she shook her head. "I'll be fine." Once she got over the shock. She still hadn't processed it, and the deep breathing hadn't stopped her shivering. She'd been so intent on saving Bolt, she'd run out in the dark and landed a few feet away from a car.

A car. She'd almost been hit by a car. So had Bolt. Images played over in her mind. The engine roaring. Headlights glaring. Gravel crunching. Tires squealing. Glass shattering.

Wait. Glass hadn't shattered. That had been a memory. A memory she'd intended to question Caleb about. Now was the perfect opportunity.

Emma opened her mouth to ask, but snapped it shut again. She'd had enough trauma for one night. She couldn't face any more.

Caleb placed a hand on her shoulder. "Are you okay? You're still trembling."

If she admitted the truth—that she was still terrified— he'd insist on staying up with her, talking to her, when all she wanted was to be alone. Or in Sam's arms.

Caleb squatted down beside Bolt and ran a hand down the dog's back, but his eyes weren't on the setter; they were on Emma, assessing her. "That was a brave thing you did tonight. It would have been an act of courage for anyone, but for you..."

Inside, Emma squirmed. It hadn't been bravery. She'd acted purely on instinct. And look at her now. Teeth chattering, body shaking, stomach twisting. She couldn't handle the aftermath. Reminding herself she was safe on the couch did little to quell the fear still snaking through her, squeezing her chest until she could barely breathe. "I couldn't let Bolt get hurt."

"I know. It was a selfless act."

Not impulsive? Not foolhardy? That's what the scolding voices in her head had labeled it. And it hadn't been selfless.

She didn't want to be labeled heroic when she was so far from that. "You don't understand. I wasn't thinking at all."

Caleb scratched beside Bolt's ears. "Sorry. That's one problem with coming from an *Englisch* background where people praise each other. I need to remember *hochmut* is frowned on here."

His comment made Emma feel even worse. He thought she was being modest, avoiding the sin of pride, but she was only being honest. Better to change the subject. "I'm just glad Bolt is all right. I pray Eli is too."

"So do I." Caleb stood. "No telling how long Sam will be at the hospital. I guess we should get to bed. I can secure the rope to the newel, so we won't have to worry about Bolt racing around."

"She'll be fine here. I plan to stay up for a while. I can't sleep after..."

"I can understand that. Don't stay up too much later, though. Your body has been through a stressful experience and needs rest."

"I'll be sure to get some sleep." Once her heart stopped hammering and the chills running through her calmed. And once she'd seen Sam.

No matter how late he returned, she planned to sit up and wait for him. He'd want to reassure himself that Bolt wasn't hurt. And she longed to rest her head against his chest and hear him whisper the words, "You're safe."

For several hours Emma sat on the couch with the living room light on. She wanted Sam to know she was awake and waiting for him. Bolt lay on the floor beside her. Emma rested her hand on the dog's head. The warmth and soft-ness soothed her. She closed her eyes and imagined being in

Sam's arms. Gradually her pulse slowed, and her breathing returned to normal. Several times she dozed off and then woke with a start.

Once Bolt trotted to the kitchen door, whined, and pressed her nose against the glass.

Emma knelt beside the pup and ruffled her fur. "You want to go home, don't you?" She averted her eyes from the view outside, picturing the length of yard stretching between the back door and Eli's house.

She loved it when sunlight shone on the distant fields, the green grass a soft carpet underfoot, the chickens clucking behind the house, Sam opening the back door and looking straight at her, a welcoming smile tilting his lips. If she walked out there now, though, shadows would close in around her, smothering, suffocating. Thinking of it tightened her chest, tensed all her muscles.

But she'd gone out in that darkness. Fear for Bolt had overcome her terror of the night, but as she relived the screech of brakes, the squeal of tires, a tiny crack opened, and a memory slipped out. Those faces hovering over her, concern written in every line, brought to mind indistinct faces. And in the shadowy recesses of her mind, another ambulance siren wailed, coming closer, closer. Then blessed blackness descended.

Like swirling a stick in the creek to stir up the muddy depths, Emma poked and prodded at slivers buried under all the silt. The night's images mirrored long-buried memories, but murky depths obscured them. Emma concentrated on one tiny clear spot as the cloudiness cleared.

For a brief moment she glimpsed a face. A familiar face. Caleb. Why would he have been at the scene of her accident?

Chapter Fifteen

A TAXI PULLED INTO the gravel driveway next door, jolting Emma awake. She peeked out to see Sam paying the driver. He glanced over toward their house uncertainly. Lifting the blind, she waved to him. His face cleared, and he headed across the lawn. He tapped lightly at the door, and Bolt *woofed*.

One hand grasping Bolt's makeshift leash, Emma opened the door. Sam blinked and stared at her, seemingly dazed. He looked exhausted.

"Sam? Are you all right?" Emma stepped back and motioned for him to come in.

He nodded, but instead of moving, he stood on the step studying her. "And what about you?"

"I'm all right." Better than all right now that he was here.

Bolt whined and strained toward him, almost pulling Emma over. Sam reached out to steady her, and their eyes met. Was that a spark of interest glimmering in his eyes, or was she imagining it? Before Emma could decide, Bolt pawed Sam's leg, startling him. He shook his head as if to clear it and bent to hug the dog. "Are you all right, girl?"

Emma handed him the rope. "She seems to be fine."

"Thanks to you. I can't tell you what that meant to me." Sam swallowed hard. "If it weren't for you..."

"Glad I could help." Emma's voice quavered a bit, and she stepped back.

"I'm sorry. I didn't mean to keep you out here, especially at night." Sam shuffled his feet. "I should be going. It's late."

"I'd hoped...that is, I wanted to hear about your *onkel*."

Sam gestured toward the night sky. "But it's dark out here."

"You could come in," she said softly.

He looked reluctant, and Emma's spirits plunged.

"It's awfully late."

"But we're both awake," Emma pointed out, hoping to convince him.

"True, but I feel guilty keeping you up." When Emma insisted she didn't mind, he entered the living room. "I'm so sorry for all you've been through tonight."

"I'll be all right." Emma waved toward the couch. "How's your uncle?"

Sam settled on the sofa, so she headed to the chair opposite him. Just before she reached the rocking chair, she changed her mind and veered toward the couch to sit beside him. "This way we can talk quietly without waking Caleb and Lydia."

Sam clenched his hands together in his lap. Was she sitting too close? Making him nervous? Emma wished she'd thought over her decision instead of being so impulsive. Lydia would be upset if she knew they were down there together like that.

With Sam beside her, Emma was having trouble catching her breath. She'd asked him in to find out about Eli. Better to keep her mind on that instead of Sam's nearness. "Your *onkel*?" she asked.

"He had a mild heart attack, but he's in stable condition now."

"That must be a relief. I know how worrying it can be when someone you love is ill."

"It's a relief to know he'll be fine, and he'll be home soon. I'm exhausted, though."

"I imagine you would be after an ordeal like that."

"Not as tired as you, though, after what you went through rescuing Bolt."

Hearing her name, Bolt rose from the floor where she'd been curled up and jumped on Sam.

"Down, girl. You're much too huge to be a lap dog." Sam tried to push her off, but she wouldn't budge.

Emma giggled.

"You wouldn't think it was so funny if she was on your lap," Sam said with a grin, giving Bolt another shove that didn't dislodge her.

"Here." Emma stood and stepped a few feet away from him. She bent down and called softly to the dog.

Bolt leaped off Sam's lap, pounced at Emma, and licked her face. Emma lost her balance and tumbled to the floor. Bolt stretched out on the floor beside her, panting.

Sam rushed over to help Emma up, but once she was on her feet, he didn't let go of her hand. When the dog stayed put, Sam and Emma sat close together on the couch, and Sam turned to face her. "I haven't thanked you for saving Bolt. Knowing your fear of the dark and of cars, to think that you'd race out there to save her..."

When her hand trembled, he gripped it a little tighter. "That must have been terrifying for you."

"It was afterwards"—her voice wavered—"but at the time, I wasn't thinking. As usual."

"You must have been petrified. I wish I'd been able to help you afterwards."

"You had to take care of your *onkel*." Emma ducked her head and confessed, "I did wish you were here. You always calm me when I'm afraid."

"I'm so sorry I wasn't there for you."

His words and his hand around hers sent her nerves zinging so fast she could barely concentrate on the conversation. "It's all right. It's over now." She tilted her head and met his eyes. "I've had to confront so many fears in the past few weeks…"

"I know." Sam spoke in the soothing tone he used in the barn. "I still can't believe you ran out there tonight."

"Actually I can't either. I acted on instinct. The only thing running through my mind was how much you love that dog. I couldn't let her get hit."

"You risked your life for Bolt. I don't know how I can ever thank you."

Sam reached out as if to hug her, and Emma closed her eyes in anticipation.

Overhead the bed creaked, and soft footsteps shuffled along the hall. Emma jumped and slid to one end of the couch; Sam, to the other.

DeWalt light in hand, Caleb appeared on the stairs, his clothes wrinkled and in disarray. He shone the beam from one to the other, and his mouth tightened. No doubt it illuminated their flushed faces and guilty expressions. Not that they'd done anything to feel guilty about—talking and holding hands in a darkened room was hardly worrisome. But the way they'd slid apart made it look worse than it was.

Bolt perked up, and her tail thumped the floor as Caleb

descended the final steps into the living room. Caleb flashed a quick smile the dog's way before he pinned Sam and Emma with a flinty glare, his jaw tense.

Sam leaped to his feet. "I–I stopped by to pick up Bolt. But I was just leaving." His cheeks burned at the half-lie. Yes, he was leaving now, but if Caleb hadn't shown up, the idea of going home never would have entered his mind.

Caleb crossed the room in a few quick strides. "I'll see you out."

"Thanks." *I think.* Sam bent and picked up Bolt's leash. "Come on, girl."

"Oh." Caleb stopped abruptly, his body a barrier blocking Sam's view of Emma. "Forgive me. I forgot to ask. How is your *onkel?*"

"He had a mild heart attack." Sam cleared his throat to get rid of the thickness clogging his words. "They're keeping him overnight for observation, but he should be released tomorrow."

"That's *gut.*" Caleb moved past Sam to open the door. "Tell him we're praying for him."

"I will. We appreciate the prayers." Sam gestured toward the pup who was straining at the rope. "I also appreciate your willingness to care for my dog."

"No problem. We were happy to do so." Caleb edged himself back so he obstructed Sam's view of Emma again. He motioned for Sam to precede him.

Sam couldn't leave without thanking Emma one more time. He leaned over so he could see her and then wished he hadn't. Curled up on the corner of the sofa, she looked so sweet, so vulnerable, so appealing.

He adopted a neutral tone but couldn't prevent some of his emotions from seeping into his words. "*Danke* for saving Bolt's life tonight."

Emma raised her eyes, and her "You're welcome" came out soft and shaky, as if she were nervous, or perhaps she was experiencing the same rush of feelings he was.

"Sam?" Caleb clamped a hand on his shoulder. "We need to talk." Although he was only a few years older than Sam, Caleb seemed to be playing the role of overprotective father. The seriousness in his eyes compounded his ominous tone.

Sam's heart lurched, and heat flooded his cheeks. Prepared to be questioned about his intentions toward Emma, he was blindsided by Caleb's grim words after they stepped out on the porch and he'd closed the door behind them.

"There's something you should know about Emma."

Sam gripped the porch railing, but when Bolt tugged at the rope, Sam let her amble down the steps and into the grass. Caleb's tone had warned him it might be a long talk, so he tied the rope to a porch rail so she could sniff and play. Then he faced Caleb, whose mouth was set in a forbidding line.

"You've been helping Emma overcome her fears, so you know she was in an accident a few years ago. What you may not know is that Emma has no idea what happened the year before the accident."

"She told me about her memory loss."

"She did?" Caleb turned startled eyes toward Sam. "She never mentions it to anyone outside the family. Perhaps the shock of what happened tonight made her less wary."

Sam debated about telling him the truth. Emma had been quite open about it before that. Before Sam could correct him, Caleb gripped the porch railing and plunged on.

"Emma was sixteen, so it happened during *Rumschpringe*," he added darkly. "She was...How should I put this? Umm, wild."

Sam suspected that what her family considered wild was only Emma being Emma. Fun, free, exuberant, and spontaneous. "I don't want you to get the wrong idea about what's going on between us. I'm helping her with her fears, but that's as far as it goes."

Or as far as he'd let it go. Although he had to admit, that was much easier to say and think when he was standing out here and much harder to follow when he was around Emma. He tried to convince himself that that night's hug had been only gratitude, but his conscience prodded him to be honest.

Caleb's raised eyebrows indicated how skeptical he was of Sam's declaration. "I know you said you had no interest in dating anyone here."

Sam chewed at the inside of his cheek. He had to allay Caleb's suspicions, or he and Emma would have no chance to meet. He didn't want Caleb to forbid them to see each other, but he couldn't lie. As much as it pained him, he had to explain about Leah. "I started to tell you about a girl-friend, but I never finished. Leah is the reason I said I would never get involved with anyone."

Caleb rubbed his forehead. "That's right, you did. Perhaps another time. It's late."

Sam needed to explain about the betrayal, his fears of being jilted again, but Caleb turned toward the door.

As he reached for the knob, Caleb said, "Even if you're

committed to someone, it's easy to be tempted when you're apart."

It took a while for Sam's tired brain to process the comment. Caleb had misunderstood what he'd said about Leah. Sam needed to correct him. "But I—"

Caleb pivoted and pinned Sam with a serious gaze. "I trust you with Emma. But anyone who gets involved with her will face some serious consequences."

Sam gulped back his explanation about Leah. Caleb's words sounded like a threat. The Amish didn't believe in violence, but Caleb had grown up *Englisch*. Surely he didn't mean...The door closed behind him before Sam could ask what he meant.

Lydia was sitting up in bed when Caleb came upstairs. She'd been tossing and turning, unable to find a comfortable position.

His mouth set in a grim line, he asked, "Are you awake enough to talk for a while? Or are you ready to go back to sleep?"

Anything that could make her normally unflappable husband so tense needed to be discussed right away. "I can't sleep. What's the matter?"

"I thought I heard voices downstairs. When I went to check, Sam and Emma were in the living room together." Caleb paced back and forth by the foot of the bed.

Lydia gasped. *Sam and Emma?* "At this time of night? I thought Sam assured you they were only friends."

"He did, but with their guilty faces when I stepped into

the room, I had some concerns and decided to talk to Sam. I felt it was time to tell him about Emma. To be honest, I was hoping it would scare him off."

"Do you think it did?" Much as it pained Lydia to think of Emma never marrying, it wouldn't be fair to let someone fall in love with her without knowing about her past.

"He already knew about her memory loss. Emma had told him."

"But she's never told anyone. Ever." Why would Emma have confided this secret to someone she'd known for such a short time?

"That shocked me so much, I lost my train of thought, but I did let him know Emma had been wild." Caleb stopped pacing, rested his hands on the foot of the bed, and met Lydia's gaze. "I hope that was enough of a warning."

"Do you think he understood what you meant?"

Caleb shook his head. "It's hard to say, but I don't want to blacken Emma's reputation needlessly, and Sam started into some explanation about him and Emma only being friends because of a girl named Leah back home. I'm afraid I was a bit rude and cut him off."

"So he does have a girlfriend? That's a relief."

"I suppose. Although I did warn him about temptation when he's away from his intended."

Lydia sucked on her lower lip. "Is he still planning to work with Emma?"

Caleb rubbed his temples. "I believe so, but it looks as if you were right about it not being a good idea."

In church that morning Lydia had decided to let go and trust God to guide her sister's life, but that night's events made her long to take control and do things her way. But when Caleb reached for her hand and suggested they pray about Emma and Sam's relationship, Lydia bowed her head as he prayed and tried to let the burden roll off her heart.

Chapter Sixteen

EMMA TOSSED AND turned all night, wishing Sam's arms were wrapped around her. When she dozed off, terror wrapped its tentacles around her, squeezing the air from her chest. She woke in a cold sweat, her heartbeat thundering in her ears. As reality gradually replaced the nightmares, one image grew clearer and brighter: Caleb's face.

As the gray light of dawn filtered into the room, Emma rose, drained and weary. Her arms weighed down, each step dragging, she wrestled with her clothing, jabbing the straight pins in crookedly, pricking her fingers several times in the process. When she bent to tie her shoes, blood rushed to her head, pounding in a relentless rhythm, obscuring her vision. She fumbled with the laces, her movements clumsy, jerky.

After several tries she managed to tie bows a five-year-old might be proud of. Then she shoved herself up from the bed and slogged downstairs to gather the eggs before breakfast. When she pushed open the back door, the early morning chill set her teeth chattering. A soft mist enveloped her as she trudged through the dewy grass. The outside world mirrored her inward one, hazy and unclear.

The dull ache in her head expanded to a persistent drumming inside her temples. Indistinct pictures tumbled through her mind, puzzle pieces she couldn't fit together. Yet several faces stood out: Sam and Caleb, Sam and an

EMT, then Caleb next to a gray-shirted EMT, Caleb looking younger, his jaw clean-shaven, but with panic-filled eyes. Those panic-filled eyes often haunted her dreams, but the features surrounding them had always been obscured.

The night before, the cloudiness had dissipated, leaving behind a fuzzy image. An image of Caleb. But how could that be? Perhaps her mind had jumbled all the images together and had imposed a present image on the past. Or maybe Caleb's censure from the night before had impressed his face on her mind right before she fell asleep.

Unlike most mornings, when she timed her visit to the chicken house so she could wave to Sam, she'd overslept. He'd already left, and she'd be late with Caleb's breakfast. He'd certainly forgive her tardiness after the night before. Perhaps he'd even overslept himself. He'd been up late too. A murmur of voices had come from their bedroom for quite a while after Caleb went upstairs.

She wondered what Caleb had said to Sam when the two of them went out on the porch together. From the way Caleb had been acting, Emma worried he might have told Sam to stay away from her. He was certainly unhappy to see them together. He would have been even more upset if he'd come down a few minutes earlier.

Although she warned herself that Sam had been over-emotional after his *onkel*'s hospitalization and Bolt's dash in front of a car, the night before had stirred up a longing for time alone with Sam, for a deepening relationship. And even more, for a future. A future with Sam.

Preoccupied with sorting out her dreams, Emma wandered into the kitchen and put a dozen eggs in a pot of water. They could have hard-boiled eggs for breakfast and egg salad later in the week. She set out the dishes and prepared the cinnamon toast. Her muscles ached, and her brush burns stung, so every action took extra effort. As she laid silverware beside each plate, smoke curled from the oven. The toast. She rushed over and pulled it out. The edges were charred, but she could trim those off. She'd also forgotten to time the eggs, and the water had almost boiled away.

She sat slumped at the table, head in her hands, when Caleb entered the kitchen.

"Tired?" he asked.

Emma nodded. "And sore and mixed up." She hadn't meant to add that last one; it had slipped out because she was too weary to guard her tongue.

"The tiredness and soreness are understandable," Caleb said as he reached for a slice of crustless cinnamon toast. "But what's this about mixed up?"

"Who or what's mixed up?" Lydia sank into the chair beside Caleb.

His sunny smile created creases around his eyes. "I believe Emma is."

"About what?" Lydia glanced at Emma. "You look exhausted this morning. Maybe you should go back to bed."

"But the chores..."

"Can wait," Caleb finished. "Meanwhile we're waiting to hear what has you in a tizzy."

Emma regretted spilling her feelings. She'd mainly been talking about Sam. Did he like her as a friend? As more than a friend? Was he only being kind? Grateful? Those were all questions she needed to keep to herself. She wasn't ready to share her memories of the accident, and she was too tired to ask about the car engine. But with Lydia and Caleb's curious gazes fixed on her, she had to say something.

"Caleb?" Her question came out timid, uncertain. "W– were you there the night of my accident?"

Caleb cocked his head and studied her a moment before answering. Then he said in a slow, puzzled voice, "No, Emma."

Emma knotted her brow. She'd been so sure that brief glimpse had actually happened. But it seemed so vivid and real. "I thought…I remembered your face."

Lydia gasped, but Caleb stroked his beard and looked thoughtful. "My face?"

"When I was outside last night and you bent over me, a blurry picture came to mind of being on the ground with that ambulance screaming nearby." Emma shivered as the sound of the siren crawled up her spine and filled her ears.

Lydia's eyes widened, and she shot a look of alarm at Caleb.

He leaned forward. "Do you remember anything else?"

Emma shut her eyes, trying to recapture the image that had floated before her eyes. But it dissolved into nothingness. "I thought…I hoped maybe I'd remembered something. I guess not." She pushed her chair away from the table and stood, snatching up her plate so she'd have an excuse for turning away before she glimpsed the pity in their eyes. If it hadn't been real, it must be a figment of her imagination.

She gathered the pots and pans so she wouldn't have to face the other two. She bit her lip as she filled the sink, the heated water on her hands not enough to warm the chilliness overtaking her heart.

She'd been so sure she'd recalled something important.

And real. The memory had been so vivid. Caleb's lips had moved, but no sound came out. Emma closed her eyes and stared intently at the shapes his lips formed. She had to know what he was saying. Again and again she replayed the brief clip until she deciphered the message.

He'd repeated it like a litany: "I'm sorry, I'm sorry, I'm sorry."

Sadness welled up inside as she tried to reach out. But her arm remained glued to the ground until the scene faded and disappeared.

"Emma!" Lydia's sharp cry jolted her back to reality and a sink about to overflow.

"I'm sorry," Emma said automatically. *I'm sorry.* That phrase brought a fresh wave of pain. Whose lips had formed those words? And why?

The following evening at dinner Caleb turned to Lydia. "I ran into Sam at the hospital today when he came to take Eli home, and he invited us to dinner on Friday night."

Emma's pulse thrummed with excitement, but Lydia frowned.

"I don't think that's a good idea. Let's give Eli some time to heal."

"He's actually doing pretty well. They want him to walk every day and watch his diet, but he was lucky it wasn't more serious." Caleb dipped a spoon into his chicken corn soup. "Sam seems to think having company will cheer up Eli."

"And exhaust him," Lydia said.

Emma clasped her hands in her lap. *Please, Lydia, let us go.*

Caleb patted her hand. "I know how hard the last dinner was for you, so I can decline the invitation."

Emma squirmed inside. Sunday's sermon came to mind. As much as she wanted to see Sam, she shouldn't be putting her desires ahead of Lydia's needs.

After eating a few bites of her soup in silence, Lydia raised her head. "Going back to Eli's house and seeing that kitchen won't be easy, but if they've invited us, it wouldn't be neighborly to decline. I'll trust God to help me face it."

Admiration shone in Caleb's eyes, and Lydia beamed at him. Instead of feeling shut out this time, Emma tucked the memory of Sam's hand closing around hers into her heart. Maybe someday she and Sam would sit beside each other at a dinner table and exchange private looks like that.

Because Sam had to do his uncle's work in addition to his own, Emma had no chance to see him the rest of the week, so she looked forward to the dinner. On Friday she rushed through her chores so she'd have more time to get ready. She didn't want to appear overeager because Lydia might change her mind about going. She washed quickly and changed into a fresh dress, redid her hair, and pinned on her *kapp*. She hoped her sister and Caleb didn't notice the extra pains she'd taken with her appearance.

She needn't have worried. Lydia, her face pale and drawn, clung to Caleb's hand as they crossed the lawns to Eli's front porch. Emma whispered a prayer that God would give her sister the courage and strength to face this ordeal. She knew all too well how difficult it was to face one's fears.

Emma's heart leaped when Sam greeted them at the door and ushered them into the living room. "*Kumm esse.*"

He saved a special smile for Emma. "Thank you so much for saving Bolt the other night."

She lowered her gaze. "I hope she's doing well after her adventure."

"Very well. She's been her lively self, as *Onkel* Eli can attest." Sam stepped aside so everyone could enter the dining room, where Eli sat at one end of the table, dark circles under his eyes, his face gaunt. His lips lifted in a ghost of a smile when he saw Caleb, quivered a bit when he greeted Lydia, and turned down when he looked at Emma. She shrank inside; evidently he still held a grudge.

Caleb laughed. "I agree your dog's definitely lively. Speaking of Bolt, where is she?" He looked around as if expecting to find her hiding under the table.

Sam motioned toward the ceiling. "She's upstairs sleeping on my bed. I shut her in my room because she pesters us for food. I didn't want her to bother everyone."

Emma cocked her head to one side. "She's awfully quiet."

"That she is." *Onkel* Eli frowned. "And quiet with *that dog* is troublesome." He emphasized the two words sarcastically and nodded toward the upstairs room. "No doubt she's chomping on your shoes or tearing something to shreds."

"She does have a tendency to chew on things."

As soon as everyone was seated, they all bowed their heads for the silent prayer. Her heart brimming with happiness, Emma included extra words of thankfulness at the end of the Lord's Prayer, and then added a special prayer for Lydia. And one for Eli.

When she opened her eyes, Sam waved toward the

casserole dish in the center of the table. "Help yourselves." Steam rose from the golden brown cracker crumbs on top.

"This smells fantastic!" Caleb exclaimed as he heaped a large spoonful of chicken and rice casserole onto his plate.

"I thought you didn't know how to cook." Emma shot Sam a teasing glance. "It looks delicious."

Sam waggled his eyebrows. "Better wait until you taste it."

"That's for sure and certain," *Onkel* Eli said. "You should have been here for breakfast."

His tone indicated he was joking, but redness crept up Sam's neck. "Not one of my better attempts," he admitted. "Take it from me, charred eggs taste worse than they smell."

Emma giggled. "You should have seen the cinnamon toast I made the other day. I had to cut off the burned crusts."

Caleb chuckled. "And here I thought you were trying to make our breakfast fancier."

Emma stuck out her tongue at him. But when she looked around to see everyone watching and Lydia frowning, her cheeks heated.

"Of course she was." Sam turned in her direction and winked.

Lydia was reaching for her water glass, and Caleb was scooping up a forkful of chicken and mushrooms. As usual, Eli kept his head bent over his plate, although he didn't seem to be doing much eating. So unlike Emma's faux pas, Sam's wink passed unnoticed.

Except by Emma. Surely she hadn't imagined that. It took her a moment to process it, but Sam had winked at her. Her spirit soared, and she suppressed a smile. She'd been missing his company all week. After he'd held her hand the other night, she hoped it signaled a change in their relationship.

She'd even started imagining a future together. And now the wink.

After a glance around the table, Emma caught Sam's eye and slowly, deliberately winked back. He pinched his lips together to hold back a laugh and choked on a mouthful of food. Red-faced, he grabbed his glass of water, but his gagging caught everyone's attention. Eli thumped Sam's back, making him cough harder. Tears streamed down his cheeks as he tried to catch his breath. Water sloshed out of the glass and across the table. He held up a hand to stop his *onkel*'s pounding.

"I'll be fine," he croaked. "Let me drink some water." He took a sip from his glass and leaned back in his chair, eyes closed, chest heaving.

"You all right, son?" Eli's shaky question revealed his concern.

Sam sat up and looked at his *onkel* with affection. "*Jah, jah*. Something made me choke."

"Be careful now," Eli warned. "Eat slowly."

Sam waited until everyone was absorbed in eating before sending a mock frown Emma's way and shaking a finger at her.

He'd said he admired impetuousness, so Emma winked at him again and struggled to keep a straight face when both his eyebrows rose. This time, at least, he hadn't taken a bite of casserole. He pressed his hand against his mouth to stifle his grin, but his eyes danced with merriment.

They all ate in silence for a few moments until Eli turned his attention on Emma and cleared his throat. She tensed, waiting for one of the barbed comments he'd flung at her the last time they'd had dinner together, but he surprised her.

"Sam tells me you were quite the hero the other night. Seems I missed all the excitement."

Emma studied him a moment to see if he was being sarcastic, but he seemed genuinely interested. She dipped her head. "*Ach*, it was nothing."

"That's not what I hear."

Sam must have been filling his *onkel*'s head with nonsense. Why did everyone insist on making such a big deal out of a small incident?

"You heard right," Caleb said. "Emma was amazing. So brave, especially considering her fears."

"I agree." Sam's smile radiated such warmth, Emma basked in it across the table. "I've seen how frightened she is of buggy rides, and even more so of cars. For her to risk her life…"

Emma flapped a hand to brush away the compliments. She had done nothing special. How could she get them to understand? "Anyone else would have done the same."

"I'm not sure of that." His smile conveyed much more than gratitude. "I wanted to have you for dinner to thank you for that." He included Lydia and Caleb in his smile. "And for your wonderful hospitality. I only wish this meal were half as delicious."

"This is tastier than mine." Emma poked her fork into another chunk of chicken and brought it to her mouth. Chewing slowly, she savored the tender, juicy bite.

Sam's lips twisted comically. "If only I could say that about all my meals."

"Well, you haven't had to cook many dinners recently." Eli leaned back in his chair. "Like I expected, girls are always flitting around here like bees to honey."

Emma tried to keep her expression neutral, but inside she winced. Although she didn't blame other girls for being attracted to Sam, it hurt to think he might be interested in someone else. At least this time Eli hadn't twisted in the knife by glaring at her.

Eli smiled fondly at his nephew. "*Ach, vell,* Sam don't pay them any mind."

"There's no reason to." Sam stood and began clearing the dishes. "You know as well as I do they brought meals because you'd just come home from the hospital."

Emma had been about to push back her chair and offer her help when Eli spoke.

"There's a reason he avoids them all," he said to Caleb. "Back at home, Sam's girl, Leah—"

The fierce frown Sam directed at his *onkel* halted Eli's words, and he shrugged. "Guess I shouldn't be talking about my nephew's private business."

Emma remained glued to her chair like overly sticky bread dough. She ignored Lydia's subtle head shakes indicating she should assist Sam and turned her attention to spearing one last mushroom on her plate. She pretended to nibble at it while she worked to get her feelings under control.

"Don't eat yourself full." Eli set down his fork. "There's pie back yet."

Caleb's eyebrows rose. "Sam made pie too? That's quite a feat for a novice cook."

Sam returned with the pie and a small stack of plates. "*Ach,* no. I claim no credit for dessert."

"No need for him to go to the trouble," Eli said, "when we have so many desserts in the kitchen from girls eager to get to know him."

Emma froze with her empty fork halfway to her plate. He had a girlfriend. And girls lining up to bring him desserts. Had she been reading too much into his every look and gesture? She pushed away her plate.

"Are you done?" Sam asked.

Emma lowered her gaze before she nodded. She didn't want him to see the hurt in her eyes. When he extended his hand for the plate, she held it out to him, careful not to touch his fingertips.

While Sam cleared the table and cut the pie into wedges, Emma stared at her lap as she kneaded her dress fabric into a knot. A knot as big as the lump in her throat. A knot as twisted as the one in her relationship with Sam. A knot as tight as the one squeezing her chest.

Everyone complimented the flaky piecrust and tart cherry filling. Everyone but Emma, who ducked her head to hide the tears welling in her eyes. She blinked to clear them and forced her hands to pick up the fork Sam had set on her plate. In slow motion she tilted her fork sideways and pressed down to cut off a bite.

The red cherries reminded her of hearts. Broken hearts. Bleeding hearts. She struggled to lift the bite to her mouth. Her stomach churned as she imagined Sam with another girl. Someone other than her.

This shouldn't have hit her so hard. She'd heard about Sam's girlfriend. Caleb had warned her. So had Sam when he insisted that he only wanted to be friends. *Friends*, she repeated to herself. *Friends*. How could a word that stood for warmth and caring seem so cold and empty?

Chapter Seventeen

EMMA HAD JUST finished the Saturday morning baking when someone knocked on the door. She brushed the flour from her hands and apron, tucked a few loose curls under her kerchief, and hurried to answer it.

"Sam?" After the night before, he was the last person she expected to see on the doorstep. She had to remind herself his cheerful smile was for a friend. *Friend, Emma. A friend.* But no matter how often she repeated the word, she interpreted the look in his eyes as something more. She concentrated on the boards running across the porch floor, studying each knot and whorl.

"I know you're probably still busy with chores, but I wanted to catch you early enough to see if you'd like to play baseball this afternoon. I forgot to mention it last night."

Emma's head jerked up. "Baseball?" She loved baseball. She almost blurted out that she'd been the star pitcher in her *g'may*, but she caught herself in time. Not only would it be *hochmut*; it likely wasn't true anymore. That had been before the accident. She hadn't played since.

Sam's mouth slipped down into lines of disappointment. "I guess that doesn't appeal to you?"

It appealed to her, and so did he. She'd be better off staying away. "*Jah*, it does, but…" She needed an excuse. Her chores were almost complete, Lydia napped in the afternoon, and Caleb would be home from work by midafternoon.

"But?" Sam prompted.

"I really shouldn't go." No need to tell him why.

"You'll be finished with your chores, right?"

Emma didn't trust herself to speak. She might blurt out the truth. So she only nodded.

"And Lydia naps, doesn't she?"

If he kept probing, he'd discover the real reason. She took a step backward and made as if to close the door. "*Danke* for the invitation, but I think I'll pass this time."

"Wait, Emma." Sam grasped the edge of the door to prevent her from closing it. "Fishers' Farm is less than a mile away. We could walk or ride scooters. We don't have to stay long if you need to get back. And if you don't like playing baseball, we can just watch." His words rushed out so fast, Emma barely caught them.

But then she made the mistake of glancing up. How could she say no to the pleading in his eyes? "I–I'll check with Lydia. Do you want to come in and wait while I ask?"

As soon as Sam stepped inside, Emma flew up the stairs. "Lydia? Lydia?" She banged into the nursery, where Lydia was mending more of the baby dresses.

"Emma, you frightened me. Is everything all right?"

"Sam's here, and he wants to know if I can go to a baseball game this afternoon, and I told him I'd ask you." Emma ran out of breath.

"Slow down. Now tell me again." Lydia rested her sewing in her lap and gave Emma her full attention.

Emma repeated herself and added, "The game is at the

Fishers'. Sam said it's less than a mile away, so we could walk or ride scooters."

"As you know, I've had some concerns about your relationship with Sam." Lydia tapped a finger against her lip. "Caleb thinks I worry unnecessarily. I must admit Sam seems like a very nice person, but he does have a girlfriend."

"I know!" Emma wanted to scream. "We're only friends." She clamped her teeth on her lower lip to keep it from quivering. *Only friends.*

"He was nice enough to walk you to church, and he seems responsible."

"Honestly, Lydia, it's only a baseball game. He's waiting downstairs. All he needs is a simple yes or no. You act like I'm a five-year-old, and you're my mother."

Tears formed in Lydia's eyes. "*Mamm* asked me to take care of you, to make sure you..."

"To make sure I behave? To make sure I don't get into trouble?"

Lydia avoided Emma's eyes. "Something like that." She drew in a shuddery, trying-not-to-cry breath. "I know I've been hard on you, but I'm trying to be responsible."

Emma felt guilty for making Lydia cry, but her sister needed to realize that she could take care of herself. "I know I've been"—What was the word Sam used to describe her? Not impulsive—"exuberant. Maybe even irresponsible at times, but I'm old enough to make my own decisions."

"But the accident, your memory."

"So I don't remember one year. That doesn't make me an invalid. I don't need to be coddled."

Lydia pinched her lips together and shook her head. "There's so much you don't know."

"So tell me."

"I–I can't. But you need to understand that Caleb and I are only trying to protect you."

Protect her from what? This was the closest Emma had ever come to asking for information from Lydia, but Sam was still waiting downstairs. "I appreciate that, but you can't swaddle me in blankets and keep me safe like your *bopplis*. All I'm asking to do is go to a baseball game for a few hours."

"Oh, Emma, forgive me. I have been trying to treat you more like my child than my sister. I didn't mean to. It's just that this is such a heavy responsibility."

"I'm that much of a burden to you?"

"No, no. That's not what I meant at all. It's only that Caleb and I took care of you for so long, it's hard to remember that you can take care of yourself." Her furrowed forehead created deep vertical lines beside each eyebrow. "And with my fears about the babies, well, it's hard not to worry about you too."

"Oh, Lydia," Emma threw her arms around her sister and hugged her. "You've done so much for me, I can never repay you. If you don't want me to go to the game, I won't."

Lydia stepped back, her eyes wet with tears. "Of course you should go. After all, you were the star pitcher in our *g'may*."

"I almost told Sam that, but then I remembered all your lectures about *hochmut*, and I managed to keep my mouth shut."

Her sister's shaky laughter followed Emma as she bounded down the stairs. She slowed before she reached the living room and walked the rest of the way with dignity.

"I can go to the game," she announced before she met Sam's eyes.

It was good she hadn't looked up because the words would have gotten stuck in her throat. Sam was sitting on the couch in the same spot where he'd been the other night, and it took all of Emma's willpower not to go over and curl up next to him.

⌒∞⌒

A few hours later Emma was gliding along, admiring the yellow blossoms of the rhododendron bushes lining the driveway of the house they were passing. The combination of spring air, freshly mowed grass, flowers blooming, and Sam's company had her smiling from ear to ear.

"Emma?" Sam moved up beside her. He'd insisted on riding behind her in the narrow lanes to protect her if a car came. "I need to talk to you about something."

The seriousness of his voice worried Emma. She wasn't sure she wanted to hear what he had to say. Sam's next words wiped the smile from her face and the light from her heart.

"Do you remember my *onkel* mentioning Leah last night?"

How could she have forgotten? Emma nodded without looking at Sam. All she wanted to do was plug up her ears so she wouldn't have to listen. Or better yet, turn around and go home. Instead she watched the front wheel rotate until she was dizzy and waited for the words that would rip her world apart.

"From what my *onkel* said last night, I was afraid you might have gotten the wrong impression about Leah." Sam's voice was low and shaky. "Like he said, she was my girlfriend."

I know. Why do you have to tell me this and spoil my day?

Sam was silent for a while, and then he said, "The thing is...she *was* my girlfriend, but she's not anymore."

Emma braked so fast she almost fell. By putting one foot on the ground, she managed to keep her balance.

"Are you all right?" Sam screeched to a halt a few feet ahead and circled back.

"I'm fine." *More than fine. Glorious.* Wunderbar. *Ecstatic.* Sam didn't have a girlfriend. Emma couldn't stop grinning.

"Is the scooter working properly? You stopped so suddenly."

"That was my fault. I tromped on the back fender."

A puzzled frown crinkled Sam's brow, but Emma wasn't about to enlighten him. This was her secret. Just because he had no girlfriend didn't mean he was interested in her. But at least there was a chance. If she hadn't been on the scooter, she might have danced along. So much happiness filled her she could have floated into the sky.

Then Sam continued, "But the real reason I haven't wanted to date anyone is because—"

A car rumbled up behind them.

"Emma, get over! Onto the grass!" Sam shouted and gave her a push toward the side of the road.

She almost toppled but managed to keep her balance on the bumpy ground. Sam rode up next to her, staying between her and the road as the car zoomed past.

After the car whizzed by, her scooter teetered and almost tipped. She planted her feet on the ground and stood there shaking.

Sam repeated the litany he'd used in the barn. "You're safe, Emma. You're safe." Gradually her hands relaxed their grip, and her breathing slowed.

When Sam suggested they walk their scooters back out to the road, Emma trailed behind him as if in a daze.

"Think you can make it to the Fishers'?"

"I'll try." Emma weaved onto the road and kicked to start her scooter. After she'd gone a few yards, her trembling lessened.

Sam pulled up beside her, and she managed a weak smile. The rest of the trip Sam entertained her by describing the antics of his four younger brothers and three older sisters. The stories made her laugh and helped to reduce her anxiety. She suspected Sam was doing it on purpose to keep her mind off the road, and she was grateful. Twice Sam started to bring up Leah, but Emma changed the subject. It pained her too much to think of Sam having a girlfriend. Maybe once she conquered her own fears, she'd be ready to hear about Sam's past. In the meantime she enjoyed hearing about his family and hoped his sharing stories about his childhood meant she was more to him than just another stray he was rescuing.

Two more cars passed as they rode along, and each time Emma's recovery afterward took less time, but she breathed a sigh of relief when they turned into the Fishers' driveway. She dismounted and walked her scooter partway up the driveway, but then she slowed.

Sam teased, "Where's all that exuberance? If you were Bolt, you'd be all over these people."

Emma gave him a wan smile. "I think I left it back on the road."

"Frights like that do sap a lot of energy."

Sam's understanding look lifted Emma's spirits, and she

couldn't help teasing, "Besides, if I were Bolt, I'd be barking and licking their faces. Is that what you want me to do?"

Sam laughed. "That would be interesting. I guess this is what I get for training you with dog biscuits."

Emma started to retort, but one of the girls waved them over. She introduced herself and her five sisters, including two sets of twins who looked almost identical. All their names blended together in her head until Emma was positive she'd never keep them straight. Soon she'd met so many people her head was spinning. Everyone welcomed them with friendly smiles, and within a few minutes Emma was laughing and talking with the others, something she hadn't done since the accident.

Once a few more people arrived, they divided up into teams. Three Fisher sisters played on each team. Emma wished she could remember who was who. She was thrilled when she and Sam were assigned to the same team.

Though she had no idea if she could still do it, Emma offered to pitch. Once she got on the mound, her muscles moved easily into old familiar patterns. She wound up and threw a fastball, followed by a curve ball, and then a slow ball that seemed to hover over the plate before it dropped unexpectedly.

Strike one! Strike two! Strike three!

The other team stared dumbfounded as Emma struck out three batters in a row. Her team rushed over, whooping and hollering, to clap her on the back.

A boy named Mark tossed his hat in the air and caught it. "That was terrific." He gazed at Emma with awe. "You can play on my team anytime." As the game continued, he took every opportunity to stay close to Emma.

And he wasn't the only one.

By the end of the game, she'd brought in several runs every inning. When the game was over, a crowd surrounded Emma, congratulating her and begging her and Sam to come back. They also invited them to several other events. Emma was so grateful to be back to normal in this one area of her life, she had to hold back tears of joy. She never thought she'd be able to have a crowd of friends again.

"*Danke*, Lord," she murmured under her breath, "for this wonderful *gut* blessing. And for Sam's help in overcoming my fears." She glanced up, and her gaze met Sam's; she tried to pour all her gratitude into her smile and was rewarded with a dazzling smile in return.

Mark hurried over. "Great game. You're amazing out there." The light in his eyes suggested he appreciated more than her playing skills.

When Emma smiled her thanks, he added, "I notice you haven't been to any hymn sings yet. You should come next time."

Sam interrupted before she could respond. "Don't you need to get home, Emma?"

The edge in his voice made Emma wonder if he might be jealous. If only that were true.

"Sam's right. I need to take care of my sister and get dinner on the table," Emma said to Mark. "It was great to meet you."

As they walked their scooters down the driveway, Sam said, "And I thought I was good at baseball." He whistled between his teeth. "That was amazing. I'm glad you were on my team."

Emma ducked her head. "I used to be better before..."

"Before your accident?"

A brief flicker of pain flared in her heart, but then she nodded.

Temporarily hidden from view of the others by a bush, Sam reached for her hand and squeezed it gently. "I'm sorry."

Emma's spirits overflowed with happiness, and she returned the squeeze, but then wondered if she'd been too forward. Reluctantly, she released Sam's hand to mount her scooter when they reached the end of the gravel drive.

The farther they rode from Fishers' Farm, the more Emma relaxed. Being around Sam had a soothing effect on her, and hearing his funny stories about his cooking disasters at his *onkel* Eli's soon had Emma recounting some of her own childhood escapades. Each time they pulled over for cars, she shivered less.

Hot and disheveled, they set their scooters beside Emma's porch, and she turned to Sam. "Would you like to come in for a glass of root beer?"

Unlike the last time she'd made that offer, he didn't hesitate. To Emma, his answer sounded almost eager. She hoped she wasn't reading it wrong.

As Emma led him down the hall and into the kitchen, she couldn't keep her mind from replaying the other night or her heart from longing to have him hold her.

Chapter Eighteen

E MMA WAS KNEELING in the garden, waiting, when Sam pulled the farm wagon into the driveway on Monday evening. They'd had so much fun together on Saturday after the game, talking, drinking root beer, and later making lemonade ice cream. She'd missed him yesterday when he and Eli went visiting. Tonight just the sight of him bumped up her pulse. He headed for the barn, but when she called out, he pulled the horse to a stop.

She hurried toward him. "Sam, if you're not too tired, I thought maybe...well, these May evenings stay lighter longer."

"You want to practice?" His words came out flat.

Emma nibbled on her lower lip. She shouldn't have bothered him, especially not after he'd had a long day of work. "Never mind." Her shoulders slumped, and she turned to go.

"Emma, wait. I didn't mean to sound like I didn't want to do it. I was just surprised, that's all. I'd be happy to work with you. The horse is already hitched up."

She grinned and pivoted. "Are you sure? I know you had a long day." She started to approach the wagon, then stopped short. "I forgot about your *onkel*. You need to make dinner."

"Since *Onkel* Eli's been home from the hospital, he's been taking a nap every evening before dinner. We'll be back before he wakes."

Sam held out his hand to help her up, and when his fingers closed around hers, blood rushed through her veins. Though she usually hunched over, Emma made herself sit straight, and she clenched her hands in her lap rather than gripping the seat edges.

Sam's eyebrows rose. "You're looking much braver."

"I'm feeling more courageous. I think riding the scooter and chasing Bolt helped."

But when Sam flicked the reins and the horse took its first step, Emma couldn't hold back a small gasp. She pressed her lips into a tight line and sat motionless beside him as he turned the wagon and headed down the driveway.

Before he turned onto the street, he glanced at her. "Stop or go?" She hissed out a breath from between her teeth that Sam took as a *stop*.

He pulled the wagon to a halt.

The last time she'd staggered from the wagon and into the house. This time she climbed down with a quiet *danke*.

The next night the horse trotted into the driveway, and once again Emma was waiting.

"Sam, guess what? I didn't have a panic attack last night. I felt a little queasy and had a slight headache, but that was all. Isn't that amazing?"

Her enthusiasm made him smile. "It is."

Emma's excitement bubbled over into her words. "I noticed when we rode the scooters, as each car passed, I became less shaky. So I thought...if you don't mind, that is, maybe if we practiced several nights in a row, it might help."

When he hesitated, she added, "You don't have to do it. I know I'm asking a lot of you."

"It's not that; it's just that...I don't want you to have a setback."

"I think I'll be all right." She took his hand with greater confidence than she felt, but once she sat on the wagon seat, some of the old dread surfaced. "I hope," she whispered.

"You will. Look how brave you've been so far."

So each evening for the next three days, they went a little farther, and afterward Emma waited in the barn for Sam to unhitch the horse. To thank him for taking her out after his long days of work, Emma made casseroles and dessert for him and Eli. On Friday they went out after dinner so they'd have more time together.

"I hope I haven't kept you from your *onkel* too much," Emma murmured as they drove. This was the first time she'd felt calm enough to start a conversation during a ride, and she relished the small victory.

"So far we've only been out when he's napping. And tonight he was exhausted and went to bed early."

"But does he mind you helping me like this? I'm not so sure he approves of me."

Sam turned to her with a twinkle in his eye. "He certainly approves of the delicious meals. He was amazed at how much my cooking had improved this week. I had to confess I hadn't been making the casseroles and tell him what we'd been doing."

Emma was curious what Eli's reaction had been, but Sam had deflected her previous question in his usual diplomatic manner. If Eli supported their plan to cure her fears, Sam would have said so. She wouldn't put him on the spot by asking.

Approaching a busy intersection drove all thoughts of Eli from her mind. This was the farthest they'd ever traveled in the wagon, and Emma's whirling stomach and jittery nerves were warning her to call a halt, jump out, and run in the opposite direction.

"S-Sam?"

He slowed the wagon and studied her. "Time to stop?"

Emma's lips started to form the word *please*, but her heart urged her to conquer this fear. Cringing, she whispered for him to keep going. The traffic coming back from Harrisburg had thinned, but the sun was sinking. Rainbow colors streaked the sky and clouds.

"Are you sure?" Sam asked. "We won't get back until dark."

"I want to try, Sam." She prayed for courage and strength, and felt God's peace despite her trembling. Taking a deep breath, Emma pointed to the sunset. "What gorgeous colors." She hadn't been outdoors like this since the accident. Every evening when the sun sank lower in the sky, she always averted her eyes, knowing the dark soon would follow. Tears welled in her eyes.

Sam glanced over. "Are you all right? Should we turn around?"

Emma shook her head. "I've never stayed outside during a sunset before. At least not since the accident." Her voice was shaky, but not with fear. "I can't believe I've missed all this beauty."

A tear trickled down her cheek, and Sam longed to brush it away with his fingertip. Instead he swallowed hard, clutched the reins, and stared at the road ahead. When he could speak, he said, "We best be heading back."

"I wish we could stay out here forever."

Sam would have been happy to comply, but Emma had never been out on the wagon after dark. He didn't want her out too late. They drove home in silence except for Emma's hushed exclamations over the majesty of God's creation. The first stars were twinkling overhead as they drove into the barn.

Sam closed the barn door, but before he could unhitch the horse, Emma opened the small door on the side of the barn and gasped.

"The moon, Sam. Look."

She spread her arms wide as if to embrace the sky, and Sam ached to hold her. He ventured as close as he dared and stood behind her to stare at the star-studded darkness. Without warning, she whirled, her face alight with joy, and hugged him. Sam's muscles tensed, and he reached out to push her away.

Instead his arms wrapped around her, cradling her close. "Oh, Emma," he breathed.

Moonlight illuminated her face as she lifted her head to look at him, gratitude sparkling in her eyes. "Thank you, Sam, for one of the most beautiful experiences of my life."

Sam sucked in a breath and fought temptation for a moment before tilting her chin higher with one finger and pressing his lips to hers.

And thank you, Emma, for the most beautiful one of mine.

Chapter Nineteen

T HE NEXT MORNING Emma raced down the stairs and into the living room. "Caleb! Lydia's water broke!"

Caleb sat talking to another man, one who bore a remarkable resemblance to him. Both men stared at her, panic in their eyes. The man on the rocker, his face drained of color, tipped forward and gripped the wooden arms as if he'd seen a ghost.

Eyes wide, Caleb jumped to his feet, tension in every line of his body. "No. It's too early. She can't lose these babies too." Fists clenched at his sides, teeth clamped on his lower lip for a second, he turned to the other man. "Kyle, could you stay here while I call the midwife? Our neighbors have a phone in their lane."

So this was the elusive Kyle, Caleb's younger brother. Emma stared at him curiously.

Kyle darted a look at her. "You can't ask me to stay when…" A flustered look in his eyes, Kyle reached in his pocket. "Here, use my cell. It'll be faster." He handed Caleb his phone, adding sarcastically, "You do remember how they work, don't you?"

Caleb looked dazed, as if he didn't remember anything.

Snatching the phone from Caleb's hand, Kyle snapped, "Tell me the number, and I'll dial." He pushed a button and swore. "It's dead. And I don't suppose you have electricity to charge it?"

"No, we don't," Emma said tartly.

Caleb's brother glanced up at her with pain-filled eyes. Had she hurt his feelings? She had no time to worry about that now with Lydia in labor.

She softened her tone. "Caleb, you need to call the midwife now."

"Right, right." He headed for the door. "Kyle, you'll keep an eye on Lydia?"

Despite Caleb's frantic plea, Kyle shook his head.

"Please?" Caleb begged. "Just until the midwife arrives. You've had EMT training."

Kyle glanced wildly from Emma to the door. "You can't ask me to do that." His voice hoarse, he said, "I have to go. To get out of here."

Caleb strode across the room, gripped him by the shoulder, and lowered his voice to a whisper. Emma caught only a few snatches of their conversation—"doesn't remember" and "please don't tell."

What was going on? Emma cleared her throat and interrupted Caleb's pleadings. "Have you forgotten Lydia?"

Caleb dashed for the door. "I'm leaving." He threw one last glance at Kyle. "Please?"

Caleb, his voice shaking with fear, begged, "Lydia won't be able to bear it if she loses another baby."

A stricken look came over Kyle's face. Then his jaw hardened. His words came out stiff and mechanical. "I'll stay until the midwife arrives and not a minute more."

"I owe you one." Relief washed over Caleb's face. "Sorry,

old habit." He rushed out the door, heading for the phone box at the end of Eli's driveway.

Emma turned to find Caleb's brother studying her with a strange look in his eyes. Almost as if... As if *what*? As if he didn't trust her? As if he were afraid of being hurt? But he didn't even know her. And she'd barely even spoken to him. The pain in his eyes seemed to go far beyond a reaction to a sarcastic remark, but maybe she should apologize.

Before Emma could identify the look, the man squeezed his eyes shut. When he opened them again, they were blank, shuttered. Had she imagined it? When she was younger, Lydia had often scolded her for a too-vivid imagination.

"You're Kyle?"

He started.

Had Caleb made the right choice in leaving such a nervous person in charge of Lydia's life and safety? Emma knew nothing about delivering babies, but she might be the one who ended up with all the responsibility. One thing was for certain: they needed to get back to Lydia.

Emma motioned for the man to follow her upstairs. "Caleb didn't have time to introduce us," she said over her shoulder. "I'm Emma."

As he rushed up the stairs behind her, the man said, "I know—I mean, nice to meet you."

After they reached the top of the stairs, Emma turned to face him. "Lydia's room is down the hall here." She was struck again by his resemblance to Caleb. "You look so much like Caleb."

His brow creased, he studied her with a wary, hunted expression, as if she were a hawk swooping down for an attack. Yet he was too tall and broad-shouldered to resemble a helpless rabbit. "That's because he's my older brother."

"I figured that." But they had no time for questions or explanations. "Hurry, Lydia needs help."

With his awkward gait and the sweat beading on his brow, this man exuded panic or fear. Perhaps it wasn't she who scared him. Maybe he had no experience delivering babies. Emma's heart went out to him, but she needed to get him calmed down before they reached Lydia. Her sister was already terrified.

"Have you ever delivered a baby before?" Emma asked in her most soothing voice.

Kyle tensed up. "No," he said sharply. "But I learned about it in my EMT training."

"Oh, that explains why you're so nervous." Emma wished she could stuff the words back into her mouth. Would she ever learn not to be so impulsive?

"What? No! It's not that; it's—" Kyle clamped his mouth shut. Then in a clipped, professional tone, he asked, "Where's the patient?"

Now it was Emma's turn to stare. This man had gone from a quivering mass of fear to a stiff wooden puppet. What was wrong with him?

She led him into the master bedroom, where she'd left Lydia pacing the floor. But she was unprepared for her sister's reaction.

Lydia's face paled, and she gasped out, "Kyle?" Then her gaze darted from the man to Emma and back again. Lydia looked as if she were about to faint.

Kyle dashed forward and grasped her forearms. "It's all

right," he said, lowering her into a nearby chair. "Caleb explained."

Lydia looked as if she were grasping for straws. "He did?" Her gaze, full of concern, rested on Emma. Then she turned a questioning glance to Kyle.

He nodded. "Everything is fine. And the babies will be too." Kyle's words were gentle, reassuring, but his voice shook when he said the word *babies*.

Frustration rose in Emma. It was as if two conversations were occurring here—one on the surface and another underneath, one whose meaning she wasn't privy to. Who was this Kyle? And why had his presence caused so much distress?

Lydia's brows drew together. "But why?"

"Why am I here?" Kyle's voice held a note of harshness.

Lydia waved a hand in protest. "You are always welcome here, but—"

"Now wasn't an appropriate time." He glanced at Emma. "I see that."

Somehow she seemed to be a problem, but Emma didn't know how or why.

"I only have some papers Caleb needs to sign. I thought coming in person would be quicker. Then I'll be on my way. Don't worry."

"I'm not worried." The nervous timbre of Lydia's voice didn't match her words.

Kyle bent lower and spoke so low that Emma could barely catch the words. "I promised Caleb I'd stay until he brings the midwife. Then I'll leave."

Suddenly Lydia clasped her hands around her belly and moaned.

"A contraction?" Kyle asked sympathetically. He helped her to her feet. "Try walking it off." He took Lydia's arm. "Lean on me, and try to relax."

Emma stood in the doorway, fearful for her sister but at the same time feeling useless, an unwanted burden.

"But it's...much too...soon." Lydia panted between words. "I...can't lose...these babies too." Her face contorted, a combination of grief and pain.

Kyle's face mirrored her anguish. When he spoke, his voice was husky. "Twins often come early. Nothing to worry about."

But standing across from him, Emma clearly saw his mouth form the words "I hope."

Caleb called up the stairs. "Mollie wasn't expecting you to go into labor so soon. Her husband took the buggy to run some errands. She doesn't know how long he'll be, so I need to drive over to get her. We'll be back soon. Lydia, I love you." With the slam of the door, he was gone.

Lydia stumbled to a stop and groaned, her body trembling.

"How close are the contractions?" The alarm in Kyle's tone worried Emma.

Lydia flapped her hand, indicating she couldn't talk, so Kyle turned to Emma. His facial expression flickered from concern to guardedness.

"I don't know. Pretty close, I think."

He pinched his lips together for a few seconds, then rasped out, "Time them. They seem to be coming very quickly." He took off his watch and handed it to Emma. When their fingers brushed, he jumped back as if burned.

A swift, sharp pain shot through Emma's midsection, and the cool metal in her hand seared her skin. She almost dropped the watch as swirling blackness closed around her. *No. Not now.* She needed to take care of her sister. The babies. She shook her head violently to dislodge the mist of memories slithering through her mind. *Concentrate on Lydia.*

Sweat beaded Lydia's brow, and she shuffled along beside Kyle, one hand cupped under her belly. Then she bent over and gasped.

A look of alarm crossed Kyle's face. "Don't bother timing the contractions. You'd better get the bed ready. Now."

Emma handed Kyle's watch back and rushed to the closet. Lydia had all the bedding and supplies stored in a plastic bin. Swiftly Emma stripped the bedding and put on the plastic sheet. Then she laid out the old, clean towels.

"Would you be more comfortable on the bed, Lyddie?" The pain in Emma's stomach had turned to cramps—sympathy cramps mingled with fear. "Hurry, Caleb, hurry," she whispered under her breath.

Kyle assisted Lydia onto the bed. "We'd better get ready for delivery."

Emma could barely push the words out through her constricted throat. "But the midwife's not here yet."

"These babies aren't going to wait for the midwife." Kyle's cold, clipped tone sent even more dread spiraling through Emma's stomach. "You and I will have to deliver them."

Chapter Twenty

I N THE KITCHEN Kyle directed Emma how to wash up, and then he scrubbed at his arms until his skin turned red while she put water on to boil. As if he'd wiped away his emotions at the same time, his face became blank, his tone professional as he described each step.

"You'll need to take care of the first baby while I deliver the second," he said as they hurried back upstairs to help Lydia. "With babies arriving this early, the most important thing is to keep them warm. Wrap the baby tightly in several blankets, and only wash his or her face. We'll leave the vernix, er, cheesy white covering on the rest of the baby's skin to protect it from germs."

The minute he walked back through the doorway of the bedroom, Kyle took control, switching from his matter-of-fact voice with Emma to a gentle cajoling with Lydia. While Emma rushed downstairs to sterilize the scissors and other supplies Kyle had requested, he encouraged Lydia through each contraction.

When Emma reentered the room, Kyle was urging Lydia to push. Shivers coursed through Emma. Kyle's earlier trembling seemed to have transferred to her. Hands shaking, she gathered the blankets and washcloth while whispering, "Please, God, let both *bopplis* be healthy. Keep Lydia safe, and give Kyle the wisdom to know what to do."

She stood beside Kyle with several soft receiving blankets in her hands and a warm, damp cloth nearby for cleaning the *boppli*'s face.

"You can do it, Lydia," Kyle said. "One more push."

Eyes squinched and fists clenched, Lydia followed his directions.

"You did it." Kyle's voice shook. "It's a girl."

Through misty eyes, Emma watched her niece slip into the world. Kyle, his eyes brimming with tears, cut the cord and handed the wailing *boppli* to Emma.

"She's tiny but seems to be breathing fine on her own," he assured Lydia. "Try to rest a bit before the next contraction."

"Thank You, Lord," Emma murmured as she swaddled her niece in layers of blankets. When she cradled the *boppli* close, tears trickled down her cheeks. She wiped the baby's face and settled into the rocking chair. The wails settled to mewls as Emma rocked her back and forth. How she wished she had a *boppli* of her own.

Suddenly a fog closed around her, and she was clawing her way through the darkness surrounding her. Wisps of memories drifted through her mind, leaving her weak and trembling. Fear reached out to choke her, a monster that grew until it towered over her, about to devour her. Emma clutched the baby closer. "No, no, don't take the baby," she cried.

"Emma!" Kyle's sharp command startled her back into the room.

She shrank back in the chair, tears coursing down her cheeks. She'd almost penetrated that thick black curtain separating her from the past. "I'm sorry," she said through sobs.

Kyle knelt beside her and put an arm around her. "Are you okay?"

Emma bit down on her lip until the nightmare faded. "I'm fine." The weight and warmth of the *boppli* in her arms brought her back to reality. "It was just…"

"You remembered something?" Kyle's tone combined hope with dread.

Emma shook her head. She shifted the little one in her arms so she could wipe away her tears. "It was nothing." She wasn't about to explain to a stranger about her memory loss, even if he was Caleb's brother. "I–I think I'm just overwhelmed."

Lydia moaned, and Kyle gave Emma one last desperate glance and a quick hug before hastening back to the bed.

Downstairs a door banged.

A calm, authoritative voice floated upstairs. "Relax. First babies take their time."

Thank the Lord, Mollie's here. Emma was about to call out when the infant in her arms squalled.

"What was that?" Caleb charged up the steps and into the room, the midwife on his heels.

Kyle spun around. "Are you the midwife?" He backed away so she could reach Lydia. After a swift glance at Emma cradling the *boppli*, Kyle's face paled, and he rushed from the room.

"Kyle, wait!" Caleb's gaze skittered from the *boppli* in Emma's arms to Lydia and back again. He stood transfixed as if not sure which direction to head in first.

Lydia's groan made the decision. He dropped a quick kiss on his baby daughter's head, ran a finger gently over her cheek, and then rushed to Lydia's side. She grabbed his hand as if it were a lifeline and gazed up into his eyes.

He smoothed tendrils of damp hair back from her forehead. "Are you all right?"

Turning pain-filled eyes toward him, she barely nodded. Then she doubled over with a sharp gasp.

Emma swallowed hard. The love shining in their eyes started an ache deep inside. The night before, she thought she'd seen a look like that in Sam's eyes, but he quickly shuttered it. Yet he'd kissed her after they'd looked at the stars. A kiss so tender and filled with promise...After shifting the *boppli* into one arm, she touched a fingertip to her lips, reliving the precious moment with Sam. Then she pressed lightly as if to imprint the kiss there forever.

Lydia's groans shook her from her reverie. This second *boppli* seemed to be taking longer than the first one. Emma was grateful for the midwife. Helping to deliver a baby had been awe-inspiring, but also nerve-racking.

It must have been even worse for Kyle. He'd had the main responsibility—a responsibility he hadn't wanted to accept in the first place. He'd seemed so in control as he barked orders during the delivery, but he must not have been as sure of himself as he seemed. He'd looked sick when he left the room. Emma hoped he was all right. Still cradling the baby, she hurried downstairs and found him sitting in the living room, his head in his hands, his whole body shaking.

"Kyle?" she whispered, keeping her voice low and gentle so as not to startle the *boppli*. "Everything went well. You did a good job."

He looked up when she said his name, but he winced at each word as if she were punching him in the gut, as if looking at her pained him, as if seeing the infant in her arms were an unimaginable horror rather than a special blessing.

"You don't understand." His voice was a harsh rasp, and he buried his face in his hands again. "What have I done?"

Emma longed to find a way to comfort him but couldn't figure out what was wrong. Her niece opened her mouth and rooted around. Emma slid her knuckle into the *boppli*'s mouth to stop her from crying. "Sorry, love, but your *mamm*'s too busy to feed you yet." The *boppli* sucked hard at her finger, and Emma bent over and kissed the soft down on her niece's head.

When she looked up, Kyle was staring at her, his eyes shimmering with tears.

A sharp knock on the door startled both of them.

Kyle jumped to his feet. "I–I'll get that. The baby shouldn't be exposed to drafts or strangers."

"Thanks," Emma said softly.

Kyle dashed a fist across each eye and straightened his shoulders, but the pain he'd tried to scrub out of his eyes had slipped to the thin, compressed line of his lips.

The deep voice greeting Kyle sent warmth spreading through Emma. She peeked out to see Sam standing on the doorstep, his eyes wide in surprise to see an *Englischer* at the front door. After a once-over of Kyle, Sam gazed over Kyle's shoulder, and his mouth went slack. At the look in his eyes, Emma's heart pattered, and her mouth went dry. It was the same look Caleb had given Lydia.

Sam stood facing a stranger in the doorway. A slightly taller version of Caleb. No one had mentioned that Caleb had a brother, so this replica in the doorway shocked him. But what froze him in place was Emma.

She glowed like an angel as she cooed over the *boppli* in her arms. His first thought was of Mary, the mother of Jesus, a heavenly light surrounding her. He shook his head. He shouldn't be comparing Emma to Mary, but a halo of sunshine streamed through the windows behind her, illuminating her and the infant in her arms with a soft glow. A glow that radiated through him, warming him, melting the ice around his heart. A glow that made him want to sweep her into his arms and kiss her. A glow that made him wish the *boppli* in her arms was his.

The man in the doorway cleared his throat, and slowly, reluctantly, Sam pulled his attention away from Emma. "I'm Sam," he managed to get out. On seeing Emma, all other thoughts had fled. He couldn't remember why he had come. He only stood there dumbly, lost in a haze.

Kyle cleared his throat, and Sam broke eye contact with Emma.

"I'm Kyle, Caleb's brother." The man thrust out his hand.

Sam reached out to shake but couldn't keep his gaze from straying to Emma and the infant in her arms.

"Come in," Emma said, her voice breathless. "You're early."

They usually took their Saturday wagon ride in the afternoon, but Sam had hoped she might be free now. "I, um, was just passing the house walking Bolt, so I came to see if you wanted to walk the dog," he stammered. "With me," he added lamely.

"I can't. Not right now. But why don't you come in." She gestured with her chin toward the living room. "Lydia just had her baby. The first one, that is."

"Already?" Sam asked. That explained why she had a *boppli* in her arms.

"*Jah*, she went into labor early." Emma nodded toward Kyle. "Luckily Caleb's brother is an EMT. He helped deliver the first *boppli*. A girl."

Sam's gut clenched as she bent and kissed the baby. She'd make a wonderful *gut* mother. He tore his gaze away from Emma and made himself look at Kyle. "It's good that you were here then."

Kyle winced. "I guess."

Caleb's voice boomed overhead. "It's a boy."

"Congratulations," Sam called. But neither of the other two said a word.

Kyle was staring at Emma, his face twisted in a strange expression Sam couldn't decipher. Some men reacted strangely toward babies—cold or nervous—but this almost resembled anguish. Before Sam could figure it out, Caleb called again.

"Bring my sweet daughter up here, please, Emma. Her *mamm* wants to see her."

Emma started for the stairs. "I'm coming," she whispered so she didn't wake the sleeping *boppli*.

"Oh." She stopped. "Someone should call *Mamm* and *Dat* to let them know."

Kyle whipped out his cell phone. "My phone's dead, and there's no place to plug it in." He shook it as if hoping it would get a signal.

Sam stood. "If you give me the number, I can call."

"You have a phone?" Kyle's tone was derisive. "Thought the Amish weren't supposed to have phones."

"Many don't, although some have cell phones now. My *onkel* has a phone box at the end of the driveway. He had it installed after my *aenti* died." He swallowed hard. "The ambulance didn't arrive in time."

Kyle looked as if he intended to make a cutting remark, but he only lowered his eyes. "Sorry, man."

Sam answered with a gruff, "Thanks."

After shifting the baby to one arm, Emma jotted a number on a scrap of paper and held it out to Sam. "This is an *Englisch* neighbor of my parents. Can you ask if they'd please let the Eshes know about the twins?"

When Emma's fingers touched his, a jolt went through Sam. She quickly withdrew her hand and tucked it around the *boppli*. Had she felt it too? He grasped his galluses to prevent himself from reaching out to her again.

"Sam," she said over her shoulder, "if you want to come back after you call, I'll introduce you to my niece and nephew once they're fed and cleaned up. Maybe they'll even have names."

"I'd like that." Sam headed for the door, but added, "After I call your family, I need to walk the dog and do some chores, but I'll be back later for sure."

Emma paused before mounting the stairs and turned to Kyle. "Do you want to come up now?"

Kyle shook his head. As Emma climbed the stairs, he watched her until she was out of sight, then placed his hand over his face and groaned.

Sam now had a clue to the agony he'd seen on the man's face. Kyle had stared after Emma with longing. The same longing Sam was struggling to keep under control. If Emma hadn't acted so casual and indifferent toward this *Englischer*, Sam might have been jealous.

Instead he empathized with Kyle. This man's anguish went deeper than unrequited love, though. The sadness on his face was combined with—Sam couldn't quite put a finger on it—guilt, maybe? Or shame?

⚭

Upstairs Emma helped the midwife clean up, put fresh sheets on the bed, and get Lydia settled. She filled the tub with water to soak the sheet and towels. When she returned to the room, her heart filled to the brim at the sight of Lydia and Caleb, snuggled together on the bed, each holding one of the babies. Her eyes stung as she thought about someday holding a baby of her own.

A baby of her own. The words echoed through her head as she slumped into the nearest chair, and a gray cloud enveloped her, pressed down on her. Like a heavy, dank prison, it blinded her, dampened her spirits, leaving her twisting, turning, uncertain. One small thread dangled just out of reach. If only she could pull it, the curtain would open, revealing all that was hidden behind its murky folds. She reached for it...

One of the babies cried, sending a searing arrow through her heart. Emma waved her hands in the air to dissipate the mist around her. She had to help the crying *boppli*. The room came back into focus. Caleb took one infant from Lydia's arms and handed her the crier to feed. From this distance she couldn't tell whether the bawling baby was

Elizabeth or Aaron, the names Caleb and Lydia had chosen for their twins.

Emma pressed her hands to her cheeks, and her fingers came away soaked with tears. She stood abruptly, setting the rocking chair in motion, and fled from the room before the darkness could descend again.

Lydia called after her in alarm. "Emma? Is everything all right?"

Her voice clogged with tears, Emma said, "I–I'm just overly emotional after seeing the babies born." She rushed down the stairs and into the living room to find Kyle, his head in his hands. If only Sam were here. She needed his calming presence and support. She pictured him and the smile he'd given her earlier. A smile that warmed her from head to toe.

Chapter Twenty-One

W HEN SOMEONE KNOCKED at the door an hour later, Emma raced from the kitchen to answer it and almost bumped into Kyle. Perhaps it was Sam returning. Kyle gave a quick nod and slumped back into the chair where he'd been sitting.

Emma opened the door, and her younger sister, Sarah, rushed toward her and enveloped her in a hug. "Emmie! It's so good to see you. I've missed you!"

Emma was startled at the changes in Sarah in just a few short months. Her blonde hair twisted neatly back under her cap, her delicate features, and her pristine dress had stayed the same, but she looked older, more mature than her seventeen years. Hugging her ferociously, Emma asked, "How did you get here so fast? I thought it would take you hours."

Tears swam in Sarah's eyes, but she smiled. "*Mammi* insisted on coming along, so *Dat* hired a van driver. A trip in the buggy would have been too much for her arthritis. This way we could all come together."

Reluctant to let go of her sister, Emma glanced over Sarah's shoulder to see *Dat* helping *Mamm* out of the back seat of the van. Her eyes misted as her younger brother Abe helped *Mammi* out of the front seat. *Mammi!* It seemed like forever since she'd seen her grandmother. *Mammi* still looked the same. With her sparse gray hair tucked under her *kapp* and her body curved forward, she tottered across the grass, leaning heavily on Abe's arm.

Emma gave Sarah one last squeeze, then twisted out of her sister's embrace to race over. Arms wide, she flew toward her grandmother.

"Patience," *Mammi* counseled. "Don't knock me over before I have my feet steady on the ground."

"I didn't intend to knock you over, *Mammi*."

"Hmm, could have fooled me with the way you barreled toward me." Her grandmother's peppery retort belied the happiness shining in her eyes.

Emma put her hands on her hips and pretended to lift her nose in the air. "Well, if you don't want me to hug you, I'll just go back in the house." She whirled around and started walking.

Before she made it two steps, *Mammi* barked, "Emma Esh, you get back over here right now. I need two strong arms to lean on. Abe here won't be enough."

Emma turned and raised her eyebrows. "First I come running out to help you, and you scold me. Now you want me to help?"

Emma had meant her words to be light and teasing, but her mother sucked in a breath and said, "Emma, whatever has gotten into you? Since when do you speak so disrespectfully to your elders?"

Oops, maybe Sam had influenced her more than she thought. "I'm sorry, *Mamm* and *Mammi*. I was just fooling."

Mamm frowned. "Confine your jokes to something we all find humorous."

"Yes, *Mamm*." Emma tried to be meek, but her words had

enough of an edge to them that *Mamm* might think she was being disrespectful.

Dat scowled.

What had she done to deserve a look that fierce? Although if she were honest, one of the reasons she'd been eager to come and help Lydia had been *Dat*'s coldness toward her. She'd hoped being away might have softened his heart toward her, yet it seemed the opposite had happened. Once she'd been *Dat*'s favorite. If only she could figure out what she'd done to make him so hostile. Today, though, he seemed to be frowning at everyone.

Before the accident she'd enjoyed spending her days in *Dat*'s business doing the billing and accounting, but now she struggled with numbers. Staring at columns of prices made her eyes sting, and when she wrote down sales, she sometimes transposed numbers or forgot simple equations. She could no longer work for *Dat*, but that didn't seem to be the source of her father's annoyance, or even more painful, his avoidance. It was almost as if he couldn't bear to look at her.

Mammi had advised her to ignore her father's slights. According to her, *Dat* suffered from guilt, but *Mammi* refused to explain why. And forgiving him did little to ease Emma's heartache.

She turned and headed back to assist *Mammi*.

When she reached out to take her grandmother's arm, *Mammi* shook her head. "I thought being around Lydia would teach you some decorum. Doesn't seem to have helped." Yet Emma was positive she'd seen a twinkle in *Mammi*'s eyes.

Emma, *Mammi*, and Abe followed *Mamm* and *Dat* to the

front door. Her other brother, Zeke, had raced toward the house, but Sarah caught him on the porch steps and tried to calm him.

"We need to see if they're ready for visitors," Sarah said, holding him back from racing upstairs.

He thrust out his lower lip. "But I want to see them NOW!" He shouted the last word and struggled to free himself.

"Zeke," *Mammi*'s voice cracked like a whip, snapping him to attention. "All in good time. You listen to your sister."

"As soon as I get *Mammi* settled, I'll take you up to see the babies," Emma told him. "But you'll need to calm down and be gentle. Lydia needs peace and quiet right now."

"Like this?" Zeke did an exaggerated tiptoe up the porch steps.

Emma bit back a laugh that almost dissolved into tears. She'd missed her younger brothers' antics. Zeke reminded her a lot of herself at that age. Always charging ahead and getting into trouble.

Sarah patted his shoulder. "That's the way, Zeke. Nice and quiet."

Abe and Emma helped *Mammi* mount the steps. She tottered toward one of the wooden rockers and sank into it. "I'll just catch my breath a minute before we go in."

Emma turned to her parents. "No need to stand on the porch. Make yourselves comfortable in the living room. Once *Mammi*'s ready, I'll help her in."

"I don't need any help," *Mammi* snapped. "Go on in with your parents. I'm certainly capable of walking to the front door."

Emma tapped a finger against her chin. "Hmm, seems to

me I recall someone who couldn't walk without two people supporting her. Don't you, Abe?"

Abe's eyes widened, and then he stared at the ground and mumbled, "I guess so."

Mammi swatted at Emma's arm. "Go on with you, girl. You've gotten much too sassy. Maybe you'd better come back home, where we can teach you proper manners."

"I've missed you, *Mammi*." Emma kissed her startled grandmother on the cheek. But as much as she longed to be home with her family, part of her wanted to stay at Lydia's. Now that the babies were here, Lydia and Caleb likely wouldn't need her for much longer. Maybe a few months or so until Lydia got the twins into a routine. Then what would she do? Emma's stomach twisted. Going home meant she'd never see Sam again.

Mammi pushed herself to her feet. "Well, let's go see those babies." She ignored the arm Emma held out to help her, but Abe stayed close to *Mammi*'s side, one hand out to help her if she needed it. She stumbled in the doorway, and Abe assisted her over the threshold.

By the time Emma stepped inside, her parents had entered the foyer. *Dat* faltered in the doorway of the living room and stared at the figure slumped in the chair.

Mamm said in a puzzled voice, "Caleb?" When Kyle lifted his head, she drew in a sharp breath, and *Dat*'s brows drew together.

Kyle jumped to his feet. "I didn't expect you all to get here so soon. I–I'd better go."

Emma let go of *Mammi*'s arm and rushed toward Kyle. "Wait. Don't go yet. Caleb hasn't signed the papers you need, and you haven't seen baby Aaron."

"Maybe I should come back another time," Kyle said hoarsely. "I don't think—" He glanced around wildly and made as if to dash out the door, but Sarah and Zeke entering the doorway blocked his exit.

Mammi took a few steps toward him. "Calm down, young man. No need to get yourself into a panic." She held out a hand. "You must be Caleb's brother. Kyle, is it? I don't believe we've met."

Kyle stared at her extended hand as if it were a snake about to bite. Then swallowing hard, he shook her hand and mumbled something Emma didn't quite catch. It almost sounded like, "Sorry," but that didn't make sense.

Emma's head was spinning. How did *Mammi* know he was Caleb's brother? And why was Kyle so uncomfortable? Was he shy around strangers? Or did having so many Amish people surrounding him make the *Englischer* nervous? And oddly, her parents seemed as uneasy around Kyle as he was around them. *Dat*'s face had settled into a cold frown, and *Mamm* looked anywhere but at Kyle.

Emma shook her head. No time to sort through this now. Instead, she announced, "If everyone wants to sit down in the living room, I'll run upstairs and see if Lydia and the babies are ready for visitors. And Kyle, I'll remind Caleb you're waiting for him."

"Can I come too?" Abe followed Emma to the stairs.

"If he goes, then I'm coming too." Zeke rushed after Abe.

Grateful for the distraction, Emma set a hand on each of their shoulders. "Remember what I said about being quiet?"

Abe smooshed his lips together to show her he wouldn't make a sound. Zeke copied him and repeated the exaggerated tiptoeing he'd done earlier.

Satisfied that they would behave, Emma led the boys up the steps. It seemed like only yesterday they'd been babies. Now they were nine and ten years old.

Before they got to the door, Emma held up a hand. "Wait here a minute. I want to be sure Lydia is ready for visitors."

Zeke's expression was mutinous. "We're not visitors. We're her brothers."

Emma hid her smile. "I know. But let me check first." She opened the door a crack and peeked in. Lydia sat in bed, a *boppli* cradled in her arms. Caleb was diapering a wriggling Aaron.

"Lyddie?" Emma stuck her head through the door. "*Mamm* and *Dat* are here with everyone."

"Already?"

"*Dat* hired a van."

Caleb looked up. "I just need to change my beautiful daughter." He beamed at Lydia, who gazed at him adoringly. "Her lovely *mamm* just fed her."

"I can change her," Emma said.

"You've done enough for one day helping deliver Elizabeth." Caleb's grateful smile warmed Emma's heart. "Besides I need to get used to this. With two babies to care for, all three of us will have plenty to do."

"But your brother..."

Caleb looked stricken. "Oh no. In all the rush, I forgot. Tell him I'll—" He froze, and an almost fearful look crossed his face. "Never mind. I'll tell him myself."

Before Emma could decipher Caleb's strange expression, Abe and Zeke pushed past her to peek into the room.

"Tiptoe and whisper," Emma warned.

In their haste to get into the room, the boys collided. They glared at each other, but when Emma's hands descended on their shoulders, they shrugged and moved toward the *bopplis*. When Abe headed toward Lydia and Elizabeth, Emma steered Zeke toward Caleb, who was now swaddling Aaron in a blanket. Both boys stood, mouths agape, gazing at the infants.

Finally Zeke whispered, "It's so tiny." He turned to Emma. "Is this one a boy or a girl?"

"A boy. That's Aaron," she said.

"And this is Elizabeth," Lydia told Abe.

"Her hands are so small." Awe in his eyes, Abe touched the baby's finger. Elizabeth curled her hand around Abe's finger. "She likes me."

"No fair." Zeke pouted. "My *boppli* isn't doing anything."

"Come here, Zekey." Lydia unwrapped the lower part of the blanket. "Look at her tiny toes."

Zeke's quiet stomping motions ended when he glimpsed the toes. He reached out a hand, but drew it back. "Is it okay to touch them?"

"Of course." Lydia smiled at him. "I'm so glad all of you could come. I guess we should invite everyone up to see the *bopplis*." She wrapped the blanket back around Elizabeth's toes and handed her to Emma. "Can you give her to her *dat* to change?"

Again a feeling of gloom overwhelmed Emma as she cuddled the tiny, warm bundle close. Grief rolled up in waves from a well deep within, a long-forgotten place. Maybe it was only a longing for a child of her own, someone to hold in her arms, someone to care for, to love.

Emma, lost in a swirl of sadness, barely heard Lydia's

attempts at settling another minor argument between her two brothers.

She snapped out of her fog when Lydia asked her to bring the rest of the family upstairs. After Caleb set Aaron in the cradle, Emma handed him Elizabeth, and he carefully supported the *boppli*'s head and then leaned down to kiss her.

The tug on Emma's heart increased, and she turned away to hide her distress; she didn't want to spoil Lydia's and Caleb's bliss. Would she ever have a child of her own to fill this emptiness?

Chapter Twenty-Two

E MMA DESCENDED THE stairs with Zeke and Abe in the lead to be the first to announce the babies were ready for visitors, and everyone headed for the stairs. Everyone but Kyle, who sat slumped in the chair in the corner of the living room. Like her, he seemed to be locked in a world of pain. Perhaps the lines on his face were only exhaustion after delivering the baby. It must have been even more frightening for him than it had been for her. If anything had gone wrong...

"Caleb will be down shortly," she said softly.

Kyle's head jerked up, and he stared at her, grief in his eyes. He swallowed hard, and his lips moved as if he were about to speak, but then his face hardened, and he glanced away.

Her natural instinct was to reach out to him, to ask what was wrong. She curbed the impulse and said instead, "You're welcome to join us."

His eyes averted, Kyle shook his head and mumbled something.

Uncertain, Emma stood in the doorway. She didn't want to leave him there when he was so upset, but he seemed uncomfortable in her presence. "I'll tell Caleb to hurry," she said and rushed after her family.

When she reached the bedroom, Caleb was sitting beside

Lydia, and they were each holding a *boppli*. *Mamm*, her face shining, stood near the foot of the bed, gazing from one infant to the other, and *Mammi*, who usually pretended to be stern, had tears in her eyes. *Dat* stumped into the room, not even glancing up.

Lydia beamed to see her family. "Who wants to be first to hold the *bopplis*? The boys had their turn seeing them earlier."

"Aw," Zeke crossed his arms and stuck out his lower lip. "We didn't get to hold them."

"But you will wait until all your elders have had their turns, won't you?" Sarah smiled at Zeke until he subsided with a sulky *jah*. She ruffled his hair. "You can take my turn so you don't have to wait so long."

Abe stepped closer. "What about me?"

Sarah's smile grew even wider. "With two babies, you can each take my turn. Isn't that great?"

Abe mumbled, "I guess so," and stepped back so the grown-ups could hold the baby.

"I want to be first." *Mammi* pointed to the blanket-wrapped bundle in Lydia's arms. "Which one is this?"

"Elizabeth." Lydia returned *Mammi*'s beatific smile as she handed over her newborn daughter.

Mammi cradled Elizabeth while Emma took the other baby from Caleb and headed toward *Mamm*, who had her arms open wide.

"Meet Aaron," Emma said as she placed the *boppli* into her mother's eager hands.

A look of contentment descended on *Mamm*'s face as she wrapped her arms around her grandson and cooed at him.

Beside her, *Dat* inched away. He appeared ready to flee from the room.

"Impatient for your turn, Reuben?" *Mammi* asked.

"No, no. Plenty of others waiting for a chance." He waved a hand. "I don't need a turn. I'm too clumsy."

Mammi brushed aside his concerns. "Don't be silly. You held all of yours when they were newborns."

Sadness flickered across his face to be quickly replaced by irritation. "A long time ago."

"Nonsense," *Mammi* insisted. "It's not a skill you ever forget." She turned to Emma. "Take this *boppli* over to your *dat* for a few minutes, but mind you, I want another turn. And a chance to hold Aaron too. I need to get to know my great-grandchildren."

Emma took Elizabeth from her grandmother's arms. She couldn't resist hugging the baby close. Inhaling the newborn scent sent sharp pains through her stomach. The longing for a child of her own mingled with a rush of sorrow, a sense of mourning so overwhelming it was beyond tears.

But when she held the baby out to her father, he shrank back and waved a hand in front of him as if warding off evil. "No, no, give her to someone else."

"Stop being so ridiculous, Reuben." *Mammi* scolded. "Put that baby in his arms, Emma. The minute he touches her, it'll all come back to him. Babies are fragile, but they're not breakable."

Dat's lips were pinched so tightly, they formed a thin white line. He shook his head as Emma lowered the *boppli* toward his waiting arms. He avoided her eyes and didn't look at Elizabeth, but his arms moved automatically to cradle her.

Instead of cuddling her close, though, he held her out at an awkward angle as if trying to keep from touching her.

He looked so uncomfortable, Emma stood there uncertainly, not sure if she should take Elizabeth back. *Mammi's* barked order sent her scurrying away.

"Move, Emma, so I can see my son. Give him a chance to get used to being a grandfather."

Emma's heart ached for tiny Elizabeth. *Dat* seemed to be rejecting the *boppli*. Emma knew how that felt.

Mammi didn't seem to notice. She beamed at *Dat*. "See now, that isn't so bad, is it? What a blessing to have two healthy *bopplis*." Her face softened as it rested on Lydia. "It's wonderful to have great-grandchildren. Thank the Lord for His grace."

"I am, *Mammi*." Lydia's eyes were wet with tears. "I'm so grateful."

Sarah moved a little closer to *Dat* and stood with her arms outstretched as if to catch Elizabeth if she fell.

Lydia looked over at *Dat*, and her brows drew together in a worried frown. She too held out her arms, as if to encourage him to return the *boppli*, but she stopped when *Mammi* frowned at her.

"How does it feel to hold your first grandbaby, Reuben?" *Mammi* asked.

Dat's face screwed up in anguish. "Oh, *Gott*, forgive me," he cried. "Someone take the *boppli*."

Sarah reached for the blanket-wrapped bundle he thrust toward her. The minute her arms closed around Elizabeth, he burst out, "She isn't my first grandchild."

Emma cringed. What was wrong with *Dat*? Why was he bringing up Lydia's miscarriage now? Why would he recall past sadness and spoil the joy of the two new *bopplis*? This was so unlike her *dat*, at least the *dat* she remembered from childhood. The one who'd always taught them to be careful of other people's feelings, to be thoughtful and considerate.

Sorrow flickered in Lydia's eyes as *Mamm* stepped closer to the bed and leaned down so Lydia could stroke Aaron's downy hair. As her sister's eyes filled with tears, Emma wanted to hug Lydia or shout at her *dat* to stop, but like everyone else in the room, she stood silent, transfixed, staring at him as he wrung his hands.

"I don't deserve..." His voice broke. "I don't deserve...to be blessed...with grandbabies." He rushed from the room with a sob.

Tears streaked down Lydia's face. "Go after him, Emmie. Find out what's wrong."

Emma hesitated. She was the last person *Dat* wanted to see when he was upset, but when *Mammi* added her sharp command to Lydia's, Emma ran downstairs after him.

As she neared the living room, Kyle was still sitting in the same chair he'd been in earlier, but now he sat on the edge, staring in the direction of *Dat*'s cries, as if unsure whether to go after him or flee the house. He held a pen in one hand, and papers were spread across the table.

When Emma reached the bottom of the stairs, he scrambled up from his chair. "Is everything okay? Are you all right?" Even though he was a stranger, he sounded genuinely concerned and caring.

"I'm fine." *I think.* "It's my *dat*," she said helplessly. "He held the baby and then..." She motioned toward the kitchen, where *Dat*'s sobs could be faintly heard.

Her reluctance to enter must have shown on her face

because Kyle straightened and threw back his shoulders. "Do you want me to go with you?" he offered.

"No." Then worried she sounded rude, Emma added, "It's a family matter. I don't want to trouble you."

He quickly masked the hurt look in his eyes, a look that puzzled Emma. She had little time to think about it because she had to find out what was the matter with *Dat*.

"You shouldn't go in there alone." Kyle followed Emma to the kitchen. "He sounds hysterical. I've had some medical training; it might help."

It felt odd to have this stranger taking care of her. But she supposed as Caleb's brother, he must feel some responsibility. Or maybe his EMT training made him a natural helper. Either way, Emma was grateful for his presence behind her when she entered the kitchen.

Dat was stumbling around the kitchen, his face contorted, his eyes red and swollen, crying out and praying, "*Gott im Himmel*, forgive me."

When he saw them in the doorway, he stopped, and all color drained from his face. "Both of you here together at the same time the babies are born?" Then he hung his head and mumbled, "*Gott* must have brought you here to show me it's time to confess."

Emma shot a look at Kyle. She hoped he'd take the hint and leave.

His mouth a tight line, Kyle shuffled in the doorway. "I shouldn't be here. As Emma said earlier, this is a family matter. I'll leave so you can talk to your daughter in private."

Dat held out a hand. "What I have to say concerns you too."

"I don't see how."

"Please stay." *Dat*'s quiet plea halted Kyle's escape.

With evident reluctance Kyle remained just outside the doorway.

Dat closed his eyes and lowered his head. "I owe everyone an apology for my behavior the past few years, but you most of all," he said in a raspy voice. "I've been fighting an inner battle, and I have a confession to make."

Behind Emma, Kyle moved restlessly, clicking his pen open and closed, an annoying sound, one that distracted her from what her *dat* was saying, but Emma stood motionless, her gaze fixed on *Dat*.

In a voice thick with tears, he continued, "I've been carrying this burden since…since the…accident."

Kyle sucked in a breath and edged backward. *Dat* pinned him in place with a pleading look.

Emma leaned forward. Maybe he'd explain why he'd been so irritated with her. Ever since she'd had that memory of being in the passenger seat, Emma had wondered who had been driving. Had *Dat* been taking her somewhere? She sucked in a deep breath to steel herself for his revelation, but nothing could have prepared her for his bombshell.

He placed a hand across his forehead, shielding his eyes from view, and hung his head. Then in a tone so quiet Emma strained to hear, he confessed, "After the accident I signed for Emma to have an abortion."

Chapter Twenty-Three

T HE PEN FELL from Kyle's hand and rolled across the floor. The clatter rang in Emma's ears, blocking out the words she'd just heard. Nothing made sense.

Dat gulped back a sob. "They said Emma was at risk and that without the baby, they had a better chance of saving her life. But that's not why I signed those papers."

His shoulders slumped lower until his chin almost touched his chest. "I wish I could say I did it to protect my daughter's life, but I didn't. I did it to protect her reputation. And mine. I signed those papers because I was ashamed. Ashamed for anyone to know the truth. Ashamed for people to know I'd failed as a father."

"Y–you?" Kyle burst out, sidestepping around Emma. "You let me believe I killed our baby? All this time—" His fists curled at his sides, and he started toward *Dat*.

"I'm so, so sorry, son." *Dat* wrung his hands. "I had no idea you knew. They said she wasn't very far along." He swiped at his damp eyes with the back of his fist, and he choked out, "I thought no one knew. No one would ever know. But I've been living with the guilt ever since."

Kyle took another step in *Dat*'s direction. "I could barely forgive myself for what I'd done to Emma. She lost months of her life because of me. But making her lose the baby... I've never forgiven myself for that."

Sounds swirled around Emma, buzzing in and out of her ears like swarms of bees, some alighting, some stinging, but always a constant drone that refused to separate into words.

Dat rasped, his voice unsteady, "That wasn't your fault, son. I made that decision. A decision I'll regret every day of my life."

Kyle cut him off with a wave of his hand. "It doesn't matter what anyone else thinks. I blame me." He thumped his chest with a fist. "I caused that accident. I was furious Emma was leaving me, especially when I knew..." He sank onto the nearest chair, head bowed, shoulders shaking. *Dat* tottered a few steps, lowered himself onto a bench, and buried his head in his hands. "I hope that someday you'll find it in your heart to forgive a foolish, prideful old man, one who doesn't deserve it." He glanced up, his eyes filled with tears, and looked Emma in the eye for the first time since the accident. "Blaming you made it easier to avoid facing my own guilt. I wish I could go back and undo all my cruelty." He drew in a shuddering breath. "Please forgive me."

Emma stood immobile. She couldn't move, couldn't process anything. White noise still whined in her head. Fuzzy memories kept slip-sliding in and out of view. A metal band tightened around her head. Pounding began inside her skull.

No, she whimpered. Bits and pieces jumbled together. The green sweater.

She raced from the room, darted up the stairs, and yanked open the dresser drawer. She pawed through the clothes, tossing things to the floor. The green sweater had disappeared.

Sinking onto the bed, she cradled her head in her hands, her thoughts as jumbled as the pile of garments littering the floor. *Dat*'s story had been a whirring in her ears, the words indistinguishable. They had no meaning. She needed something tangible, not abstract. An object, not words.

The pillow. She'd put the sweater under there the other day to keep it close when she dreamed. Emma slid her hand under the pillow. Her fingers closed around the emerald sweater, and she clasped it to her chest. She rubbed the wool between her fingers. She needed this sweater.

This sweater held the key. The key to unlocking the memories.

A hazy image formed in her mind. The same one she'd glimpsed before. A gray metal door, mismatched furniture, fashion magazines scattered across a coffee table. Emma moved around the room touching each item. Metal door, cold and icy against her cheek. Nubby brown plaid couch arm, rough under her palm. She smoothed a hand over the frayed, worn patches on a green velour armchair. She fingered the shiny, slick surfaces of magazines, each with a skinny, scantily clad model on the cover. An *Englisch* room. With a huge gold-framed mirror on the wall.

Mist obscured the reflection in the mirror. A figure dressed in jeans and an emerald sweater stayed blurred around the edges. Emma leaned forward and strained to see the clouded face. A scarf came into focus, then shoulder-length blonde hair.

No! The face staring back at her was one she'd seen in puddles and panes of glass. Why had she been preening in front of a mirror dressed in *Englisch* clothes?

The minute she asked that question, the room swirled. Images rolled around her, over her, coming so fast they blurred, making her seasick. She was rocking in a boat without an anchor, adrift on stormy seas. She clutched her stomach with one hand to slow the waves of nausea rushing over her, threatening to choke her.

Her other hand held a white stick. A white plastic stick. With two pink lines.

No, it couldn't be true.

"Emma?" Kyle stood in the doorway.

His deep voice vibrated through the corridors of her mind, sending groundswells crashing over her. When his lips moved, a raging current closed over her. Rushing water blocked all sound, turning his words to gurgling.

He stepped closer, and his face ballooned toward her, huge and scary, his features distorted. A bulbous nose. Immense eyes staring at her, twirling like pinwheels. Then they receded, shrinking until they settled into human features. A face she recognized. A face she remembered. From her nightmares.

Images whirled around her like a carousel, blurring as they passed. Too many to remember. Too painful to forget.

Hugging the sweater to her chest, Emma pushed by him and raced down the hall, past Lydia's bedroom, crowded with family, babies, and love. While she had only heartache, shame, and loss.

She had to get away. Away from the staring eyes. The haunting memories. The shame of the past.

She sprinted down the steps, her only thought to escape. The garden called to her. Digging her hands in the warm, moist soil. Mindlessly pulling weeds. She'd find healing among the plants. The garden was where she could breathe freely. There she'd find Sam. She needed his accepting eyes, his understanding expression, his comforting arms as she poured out her story. *Nooo.* She skidded to a stop before she reached the kitchen. She could never tell Sam. Never.

And *Dat* was in the kitchen, and she couldn't face him. Not if what he said was true. His confession seemed like a lie. Wind, sound, and fury, signifying nothing. But why would he lie?

The kitchen door slammed. *Dat* must have gone outside. Whenever things got too emotional at home, he retreated to the barn, where the comforting smell of horseflesh soothed his spirit and God could soothe his soul.

But who would soothe hers? Not Sam. And not God. She hadn't forgiven *Dat* when he asked, so God couldn't forgive her. Her whimpered *no* hadn't been an answer to his question. Or had it? Her thoughts were too topsy-turvy, whirling too fast to even catch the tail end of one before another crowded in, and then another, and another...Which were real, and which were imaginary?

Maybe it was all a dream. A nightmare. But unlike the monsters that sometimes loomed over her, threatening her in the dark, the apparition that followed her into the kitchen had a human face. And a voice that stirred up the murky waters of the past.

In a fog she crossed the kitchen and turned the knob of the back door. She had to flee...

"Emma, wait. Please? We need to talk."

That voice from her dream again.

Emma let go of the doorknob. If it was a dream, she wanted to wake up. Kyle stood in the doorway across from her. She twisted the green wool between both hands. This sweater was real. And so was Kyle.

Pain distorting his features, Kyle stared at the green sweater. "You saved that?"

Emma followed his gaze. She shook her head. She hadn't saved it; Lydia had.

"You were wearing that when you told me about the baby." Kyle gestured to the sweater she was now hugging to her chest. "Do you remember?"

Like a marionette with someone else pulling the strings, Emma's head moved from side to side. The only thing she recalled was the sweater and the white plastic stick.

"You called me that afternoon. Twice. But I didn't answer." Kyle's voice carried oceans of regret. "If I had, maybe all this would have been different." He gripped the doorjamb until his knuckles turned white.

Emma studied the furrows etched between his brows. The lines around his tightened lips appeared to have been carved into stone.

"I was in a meeting with the manager. He offered me a promotion. When I called back to tell you, the phone rang and rang. I guess you were talking to your sister."

"Sister?" That didn't make sense. No one in her family had a phone.

"You don't remember?" Kyle's voice was gentle. "Lydia visited you that day."

A faint memory surfaced of Lydia's worried face, of her own anger at her sister. But the puzzle pieces didn't fit.

"Your sister wanted you to come home." Kyle's voice quavered.

The scene became clearer. She and Lydia had argued, and she'd sent Lydia away. Then she'd cried. Emma slid the pieces around in her mind, twisting and turning them. They still didn't fit. That visit was before this...this stick.

"Y–you told me about the baby first." Kyle's voice was thick with tears. "And I—" Moisture glistened in his eyes. "Emma, do you remember?"

Emma squeezed her eyes shut, trying to push beyond the blackness, beyond the barrier that had fallen like a prison door, locking the truth behind it.

When she opened them, anguish filled Kyle's eyes. "You don't, do you?"

Emma's heart had expanded so much it hurt to breathe. Hard as she tried, that night was a blank.

Kyle crossed the room. "I got down like this." He bent on one knee in front of her and reached for her hand. "I knelt like I am right now. And I asked you to marry me."

Marry him? This stranger? Emma's heart stuttered to a stop. Why couldn't she remember? What had she answered? Were they married? No, please, she couldn't bear another revelation. But she'd only been sixteen. She struggled to find her voice. "W–what did I say?"

Kyle dropped her hand and rocked back on his heels. His voice harsh, he said, "You'd been planning to leave the Amish to marry me, but I guess the thought of having a baby..." He shrugged. "You insisted you were going to raise the baby Amish. It was like you'd changed completely in the few hours I was at work. I don't know if it was something your sister said, or knowing your grandmother was ill..."

Mammi, ill? The word *hospital* shot through the blackness like a flare, but spluttered out. But Emma chanted the word tonelessly, "Hospital, hospit—"

"That's right. You remember?" The hope in Kyle's voice

died when she shook her head. "Your sister had stopped by to ask you to care for your grandmother—*Mammi*, isn't it?—when she came home from the hospital."

Mammi, hospital. Emma put the two words together. Then she added *Lydia*, and a flash of anger surged through her.

"That part I understood. I didn't want you to leave, but if it was only for a few weeks, well, then I would have accepted it, even though I wanted desperately to be with you and the..." He gazed off into the distance, his eyes unfocused. "And I know what it was like when my mother—"

So many missing pieces floated past her eyes, Emma tensed. *His mother?* Was that someone else she'd forgotten?

"You don't remember that either," he said flatly.

One tiny fragment slid into place. If he was Caleb's brother, then she did remember. "Yes, I do. Caleb took care of me after the accident because of his mother—your mother." Caleb had studied brain injuries because their mother had been in a coma before she died, so he'd known how to help Emma recover.

At the word *accident*, Kyle sucked in a deep, pained breath. "I should have been there for you. Instead, I avoided you because I couldn't bear to face what I'd done." His breath hitched. "My whole world fell apart that night."

"What happened? I mean with us." Emma was frightened to know, but Lydia would never tell her the truth. Maybe something Kyle said would unlock hidden memories.

Kyle's face contorted. "You said you'd marry me if I became Amish. Me? Amish? No way. You begged and pleaded. When I refused, you insisted on going home, confessing, and joining the church so you could raise our baby Amish."

The earlier nausea returned with tsunami force. Emma pressed her hands over her mouth. What more had she done that she couldn't recall?

"Then you went into the bedroom and came back out dressed in those"—Kyle waved a hand toward her Plain clothes—"and asked me to drive you home. I was so hurt, so furious, I drove recklessly. The car fishtailed. I–I lost control. We smashed into a tree. It's all a blur after that."

The tree looming in the windshield. The vision she'd seen the night she rescued Bolt. *Scenery whooshing by the window.* She'd been a car. In the passenger seat.

"I never meant to hurt you."

The pleading in Kyle's voice released a flood of images. Emma balled up the sweater, crushing it against her with one arm. She staggered to the table and clutched a chair with her other hand to steady herself as pictures surged by. Kyle on his knees, begging, "Please, Emma, please." Kyle, jaw clenched, hands tight on the steering wheel. "Don't do this, Emma." Kyle, tears running down his cheeks, bending over her. "I'm sorry. I'm sorry."

The vision she'd seen while doing dishes.

Emma's lungs refused to draw in air. Black specks floated by her eyes. She had to breathe, or she'd pass out.

Mammi's stern voice filled her head. "In and out. In and out. You can do it, Emmie." She'd done this before. Emma sucked in one shaky breath. Then another. And another. Until the past faded into the present.

Kyle was there now in the kitchen with her, his face as scared and frightened as it had been that night.

"Emma, are you all right? Maybe I shouldn't have told you all this. You blocked it out for a reason."

But now that she knew, she needed to face the truth, all of it, no matter how painful. Emma sank into a chair. She gestured to the chair opposite her, but Kyle only shook his head and stood a few feet away.

"Tell me everything," she said heavily.

Kyle hesitated. "Are you sure?"

At Emma's nod, he began. She rested her chin in her hands and forced herself to focus on Kyle's face, though every word made her want to hang her head in shame as he told of their Friday night trips to Yoders' Barn to dance and of apartment hunting together.

"We were in love, Emma. Do you remember that?"

Emma lowered her eyes.

"You don't, do you?" The roughness of his voice revealed the depth of his pain.

Vague impressions drifted through her mind but disappeared into gray mist. Squeezing her eyes shut, she tried to focus. Music and laughter. Hope and plans. Pain and heartache. Fighting. Arguing. Leaving.

Shattering glass. An ambulance siren screaming, coming closer, closer. Faces in the dark, staring down at her. An EMT and Caleb. *No, Kyle.*

Then Sam's face crowded out the others. Sam kneeling beside her. Helping her up. She longed to feel Sam's arms around her, to hear him whisper, "You're safe." Her heart cried out to him, but once she told him the truth, she'd lose him forever.

A tear trickled down her cheek.

"I didn't mean to make you cry." Kyle reached out and caressed her hand.

Emma didn't trust herself to speak. If only it were Sam's hand holding hers.

"I've done nothing but hurt you." The anguish in Kyle's eyes tore at Emma's heart, and some of her old feelings for him came rushing back, a tumultuous jumble of attraction, passion, rebellion, excitement, anger. And caring. She *had* loved him. But that was three-years-ago Emma. Who was she now?

Kyle stepped closer. "I'm so sorry."

She stared at him, still processing not only Kyle but also who *she* had been. She had been rebellious. She had dressed in *Englisch* clothes, gone dancing, lived with an *Englisch* man. Worst of all, their carelessness had killed a baby. If she'd followed the church's teachings, none of this would have happened. She'd disgraced her family and driven *Dat* into violating his conscience. No wonder he couldn't bear to look at her.

Filled with shame, she lowered her head. "You're not to blame. If I'd done what I should have, none of this would have happened." She waved her hand weakly. "Lydia. She tried to warn me. I should have listened..."

Kyle leaned forward, gripping the table edge with both hands. "How can you possibly think any of this is *your* fault? You weren't the one who had a fit of rage. You weren't the one who took your eyes off the road. You weren't the one who let temper blind you to patches of black ice. You weren't the one who slid the car across the road and into the tree."

Emma placed a hand on his sleeve to stop the torrent of words. "We never would have been on the road that night if it weren't for me."

Kyle shook off her hand and strode to the window, his

back to her. His voice when it came was low and harsh. "The only one who deserves blame here is me. And I've paid for it every day and night for the past three years. Do you have any idea what it's like to spend your life visualizing the woman you love bleeding on the snow, knowing it was your temper that almost killed her?"

"You didn't..."

He turned on her almost savagely. "I loved you with every fiber of my being, yet I almost destroyed you. And I was such a coward, I didn't even visit you in the hospital. I couldn't face seeing you, couldn't face knowing what I'd done."

"Don't tear yourself apart like this. Please." Emma slipped over to him, laid a hand on his sleeve. "I recovered." But had she really? And why was she comforting him when she was so torn up inside? Shouldn't he be comforting her? *No.* She didn't want him comforting her. She wanted Sam's comfort. Something she'd never have ever again.

He turned toward her and grasped her shoulders, his fingers digging into her soft flesh. "You lost a year of your life because of me. A year. And don't tell me you're fine. You had no idea who I was when you saw me this morning." Bitterness tinged his tone. "Maybe it would have been better if it had stayed that way."

She stared at him, memories of her love for him warring with the guilt and shame of what she'd done. "I needed to know."

Kyle let go of her shoulders. "But not like this."

"No one else would have told me." All those whispered conversations between Lydia and Caleb, the glances when they thought she wasn't looking. They'd deliberately kept the truth from her, but they weren't totally to blame. She'd never asked them what happened; she'd never tried to find out about the past. Instinctively she must have known it would be too awful to face. Had they been trying to protect her? Or had they been worried she would return to her rebellious ways? Or were they afraid Kyle would hurt her again? After all, Kyle hadn't proved himself capable of really taking care of her. And maybe they were afraid of how she would handle Kyle's abandonment. They probably couldn't bear to see her go through any more pain.

What did it matter how she'd learned the truth? Suppose she hadn't discovered it until after she and Sam married? Surely Lydia and Caleb would have told her before that happened. Or would they have? Now she understood why they were so concerned about her relationship with Sam.

"It doesn't matter," she murmured finally. Not anymore. When he heard the truth about her past, Sam would walk away, out of her life for good.

"It does matter." Kyle waved his hand to the scar running down his arm. "I got stitches, a broken arm, and a concussion. That's all. That's freaking all." He gulped in a breath. "You almost died."

"But I didn't." Moved by his pain, she wanted to reach out to him but held herself back.

"No thanks to me. You lay in the snow, the life bleeding out of you." He covered his eyes as if to block out the vision. "And I did nothing. Nothing but call 911. Nothing but watch as they took you away." He rubbed his forehead. "All my EMT training, and I couldn't remember one thing."

"You were probably in shock. You'd been hurt too."

He lifted his head, searching her face, and a rush of

compassion overcame her. She'd lost so much...but then, so had he.

Seeing the softening in her expression, he moved closer, but she took a step back, tried to bring the conversation back to normal. "You did great this morning delivering Lydia's baby."

Kyle pinched his lips together, and tears formed in his eyes. He swallowed hard before he said, "That was one of the hardest things I've ever done, aside from losing you. Working beside you and remembering the night of the accident."

Emma squirmed; it sounded as if he still cared deeply for her. Three years had passed. She was a different person now. It seemed he was still living in the past, still blaming himself for everything that had happened—still loving the people who had died in that accident: her former self and their baby.

Eyes damp, Kyle stared down at her. "I lost our baby twice that night. First when you left...and then later in the emergency room." His chest heaved, and sobs racked his body.

"Oh, Kyle." They'd both suffered. Her own cheeks damp with tears, Emma reached over and laid a hand on his arm. She wanted to comfort him, to ease his hurt, his pain. "I'm sorry you had to bear that alone." So when his sobs increased, she did the only thing she could—reached out and wrapped her arms around him.

Kyle hugged her closer. "Emma?" Her name on his lips sounded like the cry of a drowning man.

Emma could barely get out a "Yes?" She lifted her head to look at him, and through the window behind him, her eyes met Sam's.

The tears clogging Emma's chest turned to ice. She stood

frozen, her mouth open, her gaze locked with Sam's shocked eyes as Kyle held her close.

∽

Sam's brain and body screeched to a stop. He stood rigid, unmoving, unable to tear his gaze from the couple framed in the window. From a distance he'd assumed it was Caleb and Lydia in an embrace. Then the woman lifted her head.

Not Lydia. Emma.

Emma, his Emma, in another man's arms. No, not his Emma. Not anymore. She belonged to someone else. And the worst part, the part that drove the arrow tip even deeper was that Emma had been the one to hug the *Englischer*.

His whole world ground to a halt. Each second ticking by lasted hours as the chill in his heart crept through his whole body, seeping through muscle, bone, tissue, and blood until it penetrated his skin, freezing him in place. Harsh gasps issued from his still-open mouth, and his eyes stayed focused on the scene before him. His only coherent thought—to close his eyelids to blot out the betrayal. But his nerves wouldn't obey. The cold seeping through him had iced his eyelids open, his gaze fastened on the scene before him. Inside, he was dying a slow, painful death.

Behind the glass, Emma met his gaze, her face ashen. Her mouth pursed into an O. She shook her head and tried to convey a frantic message with her eyes. A message Sam's frozen brain could not interpret. One he had no need to interpret. He'd already received a similar message. The same message Leah had given him. A message of betrayal.

Emma pushed herself out of the other man's arms, waved at him to wait, moved jerkily toward the back door.

A burst of adrenaline shot through Sam, propelling him to move his rigid muscles and spin on his heels. Wooden-legged, he staggered toward the door of his *onkel*'s house.

"Sam, Saaaamm…"

Emma's cries followed him. The distress in her voice almost made him stop and turn. But he couldn't, wouldn't face that agony again. The stammered excuses, the half-truths. Leah's betrayal had wounded; Emma's had ripped his insides out.

"Wait, Sam!" Emma shouted as she dashed across the lawn after him. She had to explain. She couldn't let him think being in Kyle's arms meant anything. When the door slammed behind him, she sank onto the grass. "Nooo."

She longed to pound on the door, to demand to talk to him, but what could she say? She needed to tell him he was mistaken, that what he'd seen wasn't what it seemed. To do that, though, she'd have to tell him about Kyle and why she'd been comforting him. About their relationship. Her cheeks burned with shame. What would he think of her? He deserved a woman who'd stayed faithful to her beliefs, who was pure. Sam already had a low opinion of her now. He wouldn't have anything to do with her after this. He could go on to another relationship with one of the many single girls in the *g'may*. The ones Eli claimed were lining up on their doorstep.

"Emma?" Kyle touched her arm. "Are you okay?"

No, she wasn't, and she might never be again. But she couldn't share that sorrow with Kyle. Her body ached as if a sudden punch had stunned her, almost knocked her out. Her shoulders slumped, and Kyle released his grip.

He came around and squatted in front of her. "Is that your boyfriend?"

"Just a friend." She emphasized the *just*, but Sam had been more than a friend. He'd been a lifeline, a breath of fresh air, and her hope of recovery. Now she'd been plunged deeper into the tangles of the past. Unraveling some of the mysteries today had destroyed her future. Who knew how many others remained untold? She didn't want to ask Kyle any more about their relationship. No point in hurting him, stirring up old feelings she'd never reciprocate.

"He seems pretty upset. I think he wants to be more than just friends." Kyle stared into her eyes. "I know how he feels. It's been three years, but not a day goes by that I don't think of you and regret everything that happened. I don't know if I'll ever get over you."

"Don't, Kyle, please." Emma couldn't bear to see the pain etched into his face. Her own heart overflowed with a similar grief. The grief of unrequited love.

"You're in love with him, aren't you?" he said flatly.

Emma lowered her head so he couldn't read the truth in her eyes. "It matters little what I feel. I'd never be worthy of a man like him."

"He'd reject you because of your past? If so, he's not worthy of you."

"You don't understand. Our faith—"

Kyle held up a hand. "Stop. I don't want to hear about

your faith. I've gotten enough pressure from my brother about coming back to the Amish."

"You should. It's your family heritage, and Caleb is happy he joined the church."

"I don't want a lecture about religion. I'm not going to give up my future. I'm going to medical school when I'm done with college. I never, ever want to stand by helplessly again while someone I love lies bleeding on the ground."

He stood and held out a hand to help Emma up. "Besides, we got off track in this conversation. Your neighbor, who's *just a friend*, saw us hugging, didn't he? I can go over there and set him straight."

"No, no." Emma swallowed down the lump of fear blocking her throat. "Whatever was between Sam and me is over." She had too much to hide.

Kyle started toward the house next door, but Emma grabbed his sleeve.

"Please don't," she begged. "It'll only make things worse."

"It's the least I can do after all I've done to ruin your life." The bitterness in Kyle's tone made Emma's heart ache. "I've only been here a day, and I've already managed to mess up your life all over again."

"Don't blame yourself for this. Or for anything that's happened to me." Emma held out an imploring hand. "I made my choices, and now I have to live with them." And Sam had to live with them too.

Chapter Twenty-Four

~

A s the door slammed behind him, Bolt ran up and nosed Sam, nudging him to pet her. He dropped to the floor and wrapped his arms around the Irish setter, burying his face in her soft red fur. The warm doggie scent enveloped him, comforting him. But not even the pup's kisses could penetrate the ice block inside.

Sam marveled at the change in Bolt. From the skittish stray she'd been a few months before, she'd grown into a happy, affectionate dog who loved to play and cuddle. He'd seen a similar change in Emma. She too had been wary and nervous but had blossomed into a loving, spontaneous friend. More than a friend. A sharp pang shot through him, and his gut twisted at the thought of her in someone else's arms. He'd imagined holding her like that someday. Even asking her to be his wife.

What a fool he'd been. He'd come here to forget Leah and ended up falling for another faithless female. One who'd appeared to care about him, possibly even love him. One he loved with every fiber of his being. One who had played him false.

Sam groaned at the memory of her shocked face staring at him through the window. He could still hear her voice calling him, begging for a chance to explain. Like a coward, he'd fled from the confrontation. What more was there to say?

In his mind Leah stood before him, her hands clenching the folds of her skirt, her head bowed so he couldn't see her eyes, her words soft as she delivered the fatal blow. "I'm sorry, Sam, I–I love someone else. I shouldn't have..."

Blood roared in Sam's ears, blocking out the rest of her confession. The only thing he knew in that moment was that she no longer loved him. Why and how didn't matter. Now Emma had done the same.

In a few short hours he'd gone from discovering he was in love, imagining marrying Emma and having children with her, to being alone with the tattered remnants of his dreams.

An hour later Emma stood at the window of her bedroom, following Kyle's hunched form moving slowly along the front walkway to the driveway as if he were crippled by a weight too heavy to bear. He tossed the envelope stuffed with papers into the backseat and climbed into the now familiar-looking silver car. The front end had been smashed in the accident, but Kyle had it repaired. She'd sat in that car. She struggled to remember. Had Kyle been a wild driver? She had a vague impression of being in that car as it whipped around curves. Now he inched his way along the driveway to the road. Were his eyes as blurred with tears as hers?

She stood by the window, staring off into the distance long after Kyle's car disappeared from view, as the gray sky, heavy with rain, darkened into evening. She thought she should go and start dinner, but it was as if she had hardened into place and might never move again.

"Emma?"

The soft voice startled her, and she whirled around. "Lydia! What are you doing out of bed?"

Her sister's face was drawn and tired, and she leaned against the doorjamb. "Kyle talked to Caleb when they signed the papers. I wanted to check on you to be sure you were all right."

For a moment Emma's resentment flared. Lydia, ever the older sister, taking care of her, making her feel small and inadequate. But as quickly as it blazed up, it died down at the sight of Lydia, exhausted, her hair matted and disheveled, her body listing to one side. In spite of her exhaustion and pain, she'd gotten out of bed to check on Emma's well-being.

A lump rose in Emma's throat. Why had she never seen Lydia's mothering as caring instead of interference? If she'd obeyed it when they were younger, she might have a clean conscience and a relationship with Sam. Almost too choked up to speak, Emma crossed the room and took Lydia's arm. "You need to get back in bed. Now."

She wasn't used to ordering Lydia around, and her sister wasn't used to taking orders. Lydia bristled. If they'd been young schoolgirls again, Lydia might have put her hands on her hips and declared, "You can't make me." That was the expression on her face, but her muscles were too weak to protest when Emma steered her out the door and down the hall.

In the bedroom both babies were sound asleep in their cradles, and the blockage in Emma's throat grew larger and spread into a hollowness, an emptiness inside. An ache in her stomach radiated through her chest, constricting her breathing and squeezing her heart into a tight knot.

She barely managed a croaky, "Get in bed." Surprisingly her sister complied without a protest. In fact, she looked grateful. As soon as Lydia was settled and covered, Emma headed for the door. She had to get out of there. That day's news was too much for her; she was about to collapse, and being around the babies after *Dat*'s announcement only added to the pain, especially now that she knew babies weren't in her future.

"Emma, wait." Lydia's words reminded her of the futile chase after Sam earlier, and Emma wanted to scoot away and disappear, take some time to grieve. But when Lydia patted the bed beside her and said, "Please sit," in such a pleading tone, Emma couldn't leave.

As soon as Emma sat down, Lydia studied her and then asked, "Are you all right?"

Emma started to nod automatically but then shook her head. No, she wasn't all right, and she never would be. Her whole world had shattered. Like with a dropped glass, shards had flown everywhere. And no matter how she tried to glue the pieces together, the cracks would show. She'd never be whole again.

"Oh, Emma."

Those annoying words again, but this time Emma heard the concern behind them. How had she missed that before? This time they echoed in her mind and wrapped her in warmth. Lydia cared what happened to her.

"I'm so sorry Kyle showed up. I wish you'd never learned about the past."

She turned to face her sister. "Why didn't you tell me?"

Lydia set a hand on Emma's shoulder. Emma cringed but didn't back away. "You didn't seem to want to remember, and I thought it would be better if you didn't. Caleb disagreed, but I asked him to keep silent." Lydia's eyes filled with tears, and her lips quivered. "I never thought it would happen like this."

"You knew all about the accident, about Kyle, and never said a word." Emma struggled to process this—this betrayal. "And you invited me here to help with the babies, knowing I'd lost—"

"Oh, Emma, no. I had no idea about that. Not until Kyle told Caleb." Guilt flickered across Lydia's face. "I did wonder…But I didn't know. None of us did. Except *Dat*." She waved a hand, imploring and helpless. "I never would have asked you here if I had."

Holding the babies had opened a wound—a deep wound. Emma wrapped her arms around herself to stave off the pain. Inside, she erected a wall around her bruised and battered heart. A brick wall, strong and sturdy enough to block out anyone and everything. No one would ever gain access again. "It doesn't matter now." She made her voice as toneless as her feelings.

"But it does." Lydia extended both hands. "I love you and care about you. I never meant to hurt you, but I have. I'm sorry."

Lydia's teary plea opened a chink in Emma's wall, one she quickly cemented over. Throughout childhood Emma had learned God would forgive her if she forgave others. But how could God ever forgive her for her past mistakes?

Emma couldn't mouth empty words. Her soul burdened, she started to scoot off the bed.

Behind her, Lydia said in a broken voice, "I know it isn't much help, but I do understand what you're going through."

Emma twisted around, fists clenched. "How could you possibly understand? You have Caleb, a happy marriage, *bopplis*. I have nothing."

Lydia's eyes filled with tears. "I lost a baby too. And even these two babies can't take the place of that precious life."

Emma closed her eyes. Now, with her own grief over the baby so close to the surface, she understood the depths of her sister's pain over her miscarriage. But Lydia had a happy ending, something Emma would never have.

Lydia bit her lip. "I'd hoped to save you from the hurt I knew that Kyle would bring. Caleb tried too. We weren't successful back then. And we failed again today."

Another memory snapped into place. Standing in their bedroom at home, accusing Lydia of teaming up with Caleb to break up her and Kyle. And her pent-up fury when Lydia trailed her to a car. The silver car Kyle was driving that day. The sick feeling in her stomach intensified.

"That wasn't the only reason I didn't want you to remember." Lydia hung her head. "I didn't want you to remember our arguments and how much you despised me. My actions drove you away from home and from the faith." She looked up, her eyes glistening with tears. "I feared losing you again." Her voice barely a whisper, she added, "I'm sorry. Please forgive me."

The defeated slump of her sister's shoulders, the sadness in her voice, and her heartfelt apology tugged at Emma's heart. Being angry with Lydia and building a wall couldn't erase the shame.

"You're not to blame. I am." Emma's voice quavered. "If only I'd listened to you. Maybe Sam and I..." She gulped back tears at the sympathy on Lydia's face.

How different her life might be if she'd chosen to obey rather than to rebel. Her heart ached for what might have been. She could never put things right with Sam, but she could make a start with her sister. Taking a deep breath, she asked the question on her heart. "Can you ever forgive me?"

"Oh, Emma." This time Lydia's "Oh, Emma" vibrated with love and acceptance, the same love and acceptance brimming in her eyes.

Emma leaned toward her, arms outstretched to embrace her sister.

"Careful," Lydia said and held out a hand to stem Emma's liveliness. "I don't want to be knocked backward. I'm still not that steady." But she laughed as she said it, and Emma knew she'd been forgiven before Lydia said the words.

Lydia's gentle hug warmed Emma's heart because her sister had never been physically affectionate except with Caleb. Emma relaxed in her sister's arms and let the closeness soothe her frazzled nerves and spirit. But this bond with Lydia marked only one small step on the long and lonely road to forgiveness. Forgiveness Emma wasn't sure she deserved.

She slipped from Lydia's arms and trudged back to the bedroom, kicked off her shoes, and curled up under the quilt folded at the foot of the bed.

All her energy had drained from her. She'd lost everything— her reputation, her chance to marry, and her baby. Emma wrapped her arms around herself and rocked back and forth. Worst of all, she'd lost Sam, her future, and God's forgiveness.

Chapter Twenty-Five

~

LIGHT FOOTSTEPS TRIPPED up the stairs. No doubt Sarah's. Emma knew the moment Sarah entered the room; she sensed her presence and the peace her sister brought to every situation.

"Emma, are you all right?" Sarah's voice, barely a whisper, was hoarse with tears.

Soft-hearted Sarah cried for everyone else's pain. Emma hated to hurt her more, but honesty wouldn't let her lie. She kept her back to her sister and pressed both hands over her heart as if it could stem the ache inside. "No, Sarah. I'm not all right." She squeezed her eyes shut. "And I'm not sure I ever will be."

Sarah moved closer and rested a hand on Emma's shoulder. "It may not seem like it now, but God will give you peace."

Emma gritted her teeth. Sarah meant well, but all was always right in her sister's world. She had an unshakeable faith, an inner certainty that Emma lacked. What would it be like to have such surety, such assurance?

She longed to snap at Sarah, to inflict some of her own doubt and pain on her sister, but that wouldn't be fair. Sarah had done nothing to deserve it. And the truth of it was Emma had chosen her path. And now she must live with it.

Emma rolled over to face her sister. "Sarah? Promise me you'll not follow my example."

"Don't be silly. You are a wonderful *gut* example."

How Sarah could see good in her Emma had no idea.

Emma protested, "I'm talking about—"

Sarah waved a hand to shush her. "I know what you mean, but you needn't worry about me."

The deep sadness underlying her sister's words made Emma look up at her. Small, dark half-moons shadowed Sarah's eyes. And pain flickered in the depths of her eyes, but she quickly shuttered it and put on a halfhearted smile.

"I'm destined to be an old maid." Sarah's words were light, teasing, but they held wistfulness. "I'll remain a school teacher. I love my job helping Rebecca, and the children are a joy."

"No boyfriend?" With Sarah's soft speech, sweet demeanor, and gentle heart, Emma expected that boys would flock around her.

Sarah shrugged and turned her head away, but not before Emma caught the trembling of her mouth. "None that interest me."

"You can't find one appealing boy in the whole *g'may*?"

Sarah's sharp little, "Oh," as if she'd been deeply wounded, tore at Emma's heart. She must be pining for someone.

Emma sat up and slipped her arm around Sarah's shoulders. "You set your sights on a boy who loves someone else?"

Sarah ducked her head, and her cheeks crimsoned. Her, *yes* was barely audible.

"Oh, Sarah, I'm so sorry."

"You needn't be. I have the teaching. I can be content with that."

"Well, I guess we'll be old maids together then."

"You're so beautiful and generous. You won't be an old maid," Sarah declared stoutly, then clapped a hand over her mouth. This time her "Oh" sounded apologetic. "I didn't realize...I'm so sorry. Please forgive me."

"There's nothing to forgive."

Sarah looked about to protest, but after a quick look at Emma's face, she said, "I thought you might not feel up to cooking dinner tonight, so I came up to see if I could do it instead."

"*Danke*." The thought of cooking food or eating made Emma's stomach roil. Even worse would be sitting across the table from the family, knowing what she did now. How could she ever face them again? "All I want to do is sleep."

"That might be wise. I'll ask the others to be quiet so they don't disturb you." Sarah's smile was apologetic. "I'm sorry I can't stop the babies from crying. But I'll help Lydia in your place."

As Sarah slipped out of the room, Emma stretched out on the bed. Why couldn't she have been like Sarah—content to do good, obey her parents, and love everyone? That's the kind of girl Sam should marry. One who'd come to him pure and wholehearted. One who was as kind and good as he was. One who was worthy of his love. Worthy to be his wife.

She wrapped the afghan around her like a cocoon, but she lay restless, her mind in a tumult. Downstairs the noise and confusion hushed. Except for occasional squalling from the babies, the house was quiet. The tension and stress of the day had been replaced by bone-deep exhaustion. But sleep wouldn't come. Memories rushed back—drowning

Emma the way the rain was drowning the world outside the window.

The door snicked open. Sarah crept into the room and tiptoed toward the bed. Emma watched from beneath slitted lids. If she lay still enough, perhaps her sister would leave.

Sarah gently shook Emma's shoulder. "Forgive me for waking you, but *Dat* asked to talk to you."

Emma tucked the afghan more tightly around her, wishing she could pull it over her head. "I can't talk to him now." Not after what she'd just been through. Her heart was still too raw; the pain, too fresh.

"Oh, Emmie, you must." Sarah's eyes filled with tears. "I've never seen *Dat* like this. He's heartbroken and ashamed. He needs your forgiveness."

Her forgiveness? Sarah had gotten things mixed up. Emma needed his. How could she face him after what she'd done? If it hadn't been for her behavior, he'd never have been put in that situation.

When Emma didn't respond, Sarah patted her back. "Please? I know this is hard for you, but think of *Dat*."

Emma had been thinking of *Dat*, of his anger and rejection. She knew now why he'd avoided her, why it pained him to look at her. He was the only one who'd known the truth.

With a moan, Emma dragged herself to a sitting position. She tuned out Sarah's chatter as she rose and headed to the door. Her mind was on one thing—making peace with *Dat*.

Sarah escorted her downstairs and into the living room. *Dat* hunched in the rocking chair, his head in his hands. The rest of the family had gathered in the kitchen, where the low murmur of conversation and clanging of pots and pans indicated dinner preparations were under way.

Sarah turned and headed toward the noise, saying over her shoulder, "I'll leave you two alone and go help *Mamm* with the cooking."

Dat's brief nod was the only acknowledgment he'd heard her. Emma stood, hands clasped in front of her, throat dry. She'd moistened her lips and opened her mouth to apologize when *Dat* spoke.

"Please sit down, Emma." He motioned to the chair beside him without looking up. "I have some things that need saying."

Emma sank into the seat he'd indicated, her heart heavy. She deserved a lecture, but she couldn't bear any more that night. But when he lifted his head to look at her, the pain in his eyes mirrored her own. She had never seen her *Dat* so broken, so guilt-ridden.

"I've failed you as a father and need to ask your forgiveness." Before she could respond, he hurried on. He listed his faults and mistakes, begging her to forgive him for being so prideful, for setting a bad example...

The Bible speaks of heaping burning coals on your head. *Dat's* every word added one more coal of shame to her fire. When Emma tried to interrupt, he waved a hand to silence her.

"I treated everyone so unkindly—especially you. But it was my guilt, my shame for what I'd done."

"*Dat*, please." Emma cut him off in mid-sentence. "You and *Mamm* were good parents. You're not to blame for my behavior. I chose to rebel."

He shook his head violently. "You don't know the whole story. How I opposed them bringing you home and..."

"*Dat*," Emma protested. She squeezed her eyes shut; she didn't want to hear this. *Dat* shouldn't be confessing to *her. She* was the one with the heavy burdens weighing down her soul.

All her life Emma had said the Lord's Prayer at every meal, and the need to forgive everyone had been instilled in her from early childhood: God forgave you as you forgave others. If anyone asked for forgiveness, the Amish community gave it freely and quickly. Growing up, Emma had taken advantage of that because she'd never fully understood how she was imposing on others by repeating the same offenses and then blithely asking for and expecting forgiveness. She hadn't been sorry or repentant; she'd only mouthed the words to stay out of trouble.

But her childhood misbehavior paled in comparison with her teen years. Now when she really needed it, how could she ask for forgiveness for something this huge? And even worse, she needed God's forgiveness for a whole lifetime of offenses.

Dat droned on, listing a litany of sins, but Emma couldn't focus on his words, the wrongs he claimed he'd done. Like her, he needed his burden of guilt lifted. Only God could do that, but she could be an earthly example.

She reached out and placed a hand over her father's rough, callused hand, stopping his flow of words. The dampness in his eyes, the anguish on his face tore at her heart. "*Dat*, you don't need to say any more. I don't blame you." She almost added, *I blame me*, but that guilt was something she would wrestle with alone.

"Emma, how can you ever forgive me for what I've done, for how I treated you?"

She waited until *Dat* fixed his full attention on her, and

she held his gaze. Then words welled up from the depth of her soul. "I forgive you. For everything."

For a moment *Dat* only stared at her as if he couldn't process what she'd said. Then he reached out, his hand unsteady, and awkwardly patted her shoulder. Emma blinked back tears. Her undemonstrative father touching her?

The gentleness of his hand brought back a hazy memory. Through the ether surrounding her, she sensed her family gathered around her hospital bed, showering her with a chorus of "I forgive you's." Only *Dat* was missing. But now, as if from a great distance, his lips formed the sentence she'd longed to hear to release her from her coma.

"I forgive you, Emma," *Dat* said.

Emma didn't hear the actual words; instead they echoed through that deep, empty space inside and reverberated back through her past to erase the damage, the bitterness, the heartache.

But they couldn't erase the guilt and shame. Only God could do that.

Chapter Twenty-Six

To Emma's relief, her family left the following evening. Dat needed to get back to work, and Sarah had to teach school on Monday morning. Emma stayed home from church to help with the babies, so she'd only had to endure the afternoon with her family. She couldn't look anyone in the eye. Although she'd only found out about her past the day before, everyone else, at least the adults, had known about it all along, and their pitying looks added to her shame.

Sarah and *Mammi* tried to keep the conversation light and pleasant, but it often sputtered out. Emma was grateful when the *bopplis* woke. Her *dat*, his conscience relieved, took more readily to holding the babies, and of course, the twins were the center of attention.

"Thank the Lord for that," Emma breathed, grateful the day before had finally ended and a new day had begun. After Caleb left for work, taking care of Lydia and the babies kept Emma too busy to think about herself or Sam until the late afternoon, when Sam's wagon pulled into the driveway next door.

Emma peeked out from behind the shades as Eli climbed down and headed into the house, before Sam drove into the barn. She waited until Sam came out of the barn and disappeared through the back door. The sight opened a new wound in her heart, but she couldn't resist watching him.

"Emma?" Lydia called. "Did you heat the bottle yet?" Unable to keep up with the appetites of both babies, her sister had resorted to bottle-feeding one and nursing the other.

Grateful that Lydia was upstairs in bed, Emma tore her gaze from Sam's house and glanced at the stove, where the pot of water was sputtering. If Lydia hadn't called, the water would have boiled away. Guiltily, she turned off the heat and tested the formula. Ouch! She scalded her wrist. She ran the bottle under cool water until it was the right temperature.

Then she hurried upstairs, where Lydia was nursing Elizabeth. Aaron was grizzling, waiting to be fed. She picked him up to comfort him, but she couldn't resist another glance out the window to see if Sam had come out to walk Bolt. He was nowhere in sight.

Her gaze strayed to the garden. After the heavy rain, weeds had sprouted everywhere, but she couldn't bear to go outside to pull them. Someday soon she'd need to, but for now even looking at the garden was too painful. Being in the garden would remind her of Sam. And of all she'd lost.

She averted her eyes as she tipped the bottle into Aaron's mouth, but her mind drifted to thoughts of Sam. She crossed the room and settled into the rocking chair, letting images of their time together float past until the pain of "never to be" made her stomach clench.

Emma cuddled Aaron closer, grateful for the warmth and comfort from his tiny body. She'd never have a *boppli* of her own, so Lydia's babies would have to fill her empty arms.

Grief stopped up her throat, constricted her chest. All she had left now were her dreams.

Restless, she got up to stare out the window once again, in time to see Sam drive the buggy, not the wagon, out of the barn. Emma's chest hurt at the thought that he might be calling on one of the many girls in the *g'may*. Any one of them would make him a better wife.

As the buggy rattled down the driveway next door, Lydia asked, "Was that Sam and Eli?"

"Just Sam," Emma clarified but didn't add what she'd been thinking.

"Speaking of Sam, it was nice of him to call *Mamm* and *Dat*. I'd like to thank him. Maybe with a pie?"

When Emma winced, Lydia gave her an apologetic glance. "Sorry. I wasn't thinking. But we should at least say *danke*."

"I can make a pie." Picturing Sam eating it, Emma swallowed hard. Would he even want it after she'd hurt him?

A short while later she set about rolling out the crust and preparing the filling. When the pie was ready, Sam still hadn't returned. Emma tortured herself with pictures of him enjoying some other girl's company. But what if he'd only gone to run errands? The thought made her hesitant to go over to Eli's. But if she went quickly, maybe she could leave the pie before he returned.

Swallowing hard to block out the memories, she mounted the stairs of Eli's porch, a hot-from-the-oven blueberry pie in the wicker carrier on her arm. The heat penetrated the basket and scorched her side. She should have waited for the pie to cool, but she wanted to get it delivered and scoot home before Sam returned.

When Eli opened the front door, she muttered a hasty, "Good afternoon" and thrust the carrier toward him.

"Ouch!" He yanked his hand back so suddenly, she almost dropped the wicker carrier. "That's hot. Maybe you'd best bring it in and set it on the counter."

The last thing Emma wanted to do was enter the house and be reminded of the last time she'd been here, but Eli opened the door, and she stepped over the threshold. "This is to thank Sam for calling our family about the babies," she explained.

He waved her toward the kitchen, and she followed his direction, her eyes brimming with tears. As they walked through the dining room, Emma imagined Sam poking his head out from the kitchen doorway, and his deep *"Kumm esse"* boomed in her ears. She stumbled as she passed the table where they'd all eaten together. The place where Sam had winked at her.

"Careful," Eli said. "We don't want any accidents." His face crumpled as he said the last word, and Emma sympathized. His past had as strong a hold on him as hers did on her. And they'd both lost someone they loved.

She set the basket where he indicated and turned to find him staring at her. "I hope you ain't doing this to get in my nephew's good graces. If so, it would've been better if you'd stayed away after what you done to him." Bitterness incised lines around his mouth, but his eyes held deep pools of pain.

Sucking in a sharp breath, Emma ducked her head so he couldn't see the sadness in her eyes. "I didn't mean to hurt him."

Eli shook his head. "I don't understand you *youngie*. In my day once you started courting someone, you stayed faithful. None of this going behind people's backs, dating other people."

"I wasn't—" Emma swallowed the rest of her protest. If she admitted that she had no relationship with Kyle, she'd have to explain who he was. She could never expose her past. Better to be condemned for being faithless than to let everyone know about her sins. "I'm not the right girl for Sam."

"That's for sure and certain. He needs someone like my Martha—God bless her soul." He wiped a tear from his eye. "Someone upright and true. Once she gave her heart, she never wavered."

I never wavered either. I still love Sam with all my heart. This conversation was tearing Emma apart inside. She wanted to be Sam's helpmeet, to share all the love she had for him. But he deserved someone with a pure past, someone as upright as he was. Someone other than her.

Though she could hardly push the words past the lump in her throat, she managed to croak out, "She sounds like a wonderful woman."

"She was. And a wonderful *gut* wife." He pulled out a handkerchief and dabbed at his eyes. Turning his back, he blew his nose loudly before saying in a tear-choked voice, "I want the same for my nephew."

I do too. More than anything in the world, Emma wanted Sam to be happy, to be loved. If only she could be the one to love him.

"He's as kindhearted as they come." Eli escorted her to the door as if he couldn't wait to get rid of her. "He came here to get over a broken heart. He don't deserve to get cheated on twice."

Twice? Had Leah cheated on him? *Oh, Sam, I'm so sorry. If only I'd known.* Emma swallowed back the bile in her throat. No matter how shameful it would be to confess her past, she couldn't let Sam go on believing she'd betrayed him.

Emma hurried back to the house to avoid running into Sam if he got home early. As she passed the garden, her gut twisted. She pictured Bolt tearing through the garden, the plants strewn everywhere, and Sam chasing his dog. In her imagination he knelt beside her, and together they turned the soil, the earth warm and moist under their hands.

Weeds poked up from the ground, choking the plants the way her sorrow was choking off her breath and squeezing her heart. The garden needed to be tended, but she couldn't bring herself to weed, not that night, not while the pain of losing Sam was still so fresh. The best remedy for heartache was work. Hard work and plenty of it; the twins provided that, but she couldn't let all the hard work she and Sam had done in the garden go to ruin.

Chapter Twenty-Seven

E ARLY THE NEXT morning Emma forced herself to head to the garden, but someone was already there, kneeling in the rows, weeding. "Sam?" Her voice wavered.

"Emma?" He stared at her as if he were seeing a ghost. Before he shuttered them, his eyes expressed all the anguish she'd seen in that awful moment when he'd spotted her with Kyle. Then his lips turned up in a semblance of a smile, nothing like his usual broad grin. She'd hurt him deeply, but what she was about to do would hurt even more. Still, after all he'd done for her, she owed him the truth.

She stared at the pile of weeds near her feet that Sam had already pulled. If only she could pull the weeds of her past and toss them into a pile to burn. But the things she'd done could never be eliminated. Shame kept her head bent; she didn't want to see Sam's eyes. If she did, she'd never be able to tell him what she'd gone there to say. Even thinking about it made her ill.

Bile rose in her throat, almost closing off the words. "I have a confession to make."

Sam held up a hand. "Emma, you don't owe me a confession. As long as your heart's right with God, that's enough."

"But I want to..." She wanted to what? Wrap her arms around him and kiss him. See the warmth and caring in his eyes. Hear his gentle and understanding words. Words that soothed her heart and made her feel that no matter who she was, no matter how she acted, he'd still accept her and love her just the way she was. Emma blinked back tears. That was fantasy. This was reality. She'd be lucky if Sam could bear to look at her after she told him the truth.

She'd spent hours thinking about what she'd say to him. Now that she was there, looking him in the face, all the speeches she'd rehearsed disappeared. Then Eli's words replayed in her mind. *Two betrayals.* That's what she'd needed to tell him. She hadn't betrayed him. But the only way to do that was to tell him the whole story.

She mashed her knuckle against her mouth and stood there mute, all the words she needed to say pressing against her lips. No, she couldn't do this, not now. Not yet.

She turned and would have fled, but Sam's quiet "Wait" made her spin around. This wasn't about her; it was about him.

A steady light of acceptance shone in Sam's eyes although he'd pressed his lips together in a thin, tight line. "What is it, Emma? You know you can tell me anything." When she didn't respond, Sam said, "Why don't we weed the garden together? Sometimes it's easier to talk when you aren't face-to-face."

How did he always seem to know just what she needed?

"But you don't have to help me. I can weed, and you can sit and listen." Emma clapped a hand over her mouth. That sounded bossy. When would she learn to phrase things politely? Ever since Sam had encouraged her to start being herself, she found she spoke too quickly and said whatever was on her mind. "I mean, if you wouldn't mind, that is."

Sam chuckled briefly, and for a blessed moment, it felt

like old times. "If you don't mind, I think I need to weed too," he said quietly.

Sam knelt in the next row. Emma pulled several weeds with a vengeance, yanking them out of the ground the way she wished she could yank the past out of her life.

Then setting her jaw, she forced the first words from her lips. "I owe you an apology. Kyle was...well...I know what you saw, but the truth is there's nothing between us because, well..." No. She'd almost admitted that she had no feelings for Kyle because she was in love with Sam.

"What?" Sam's brows drew together. "But it looked like—" He sounded both uncertain and hopeful.

"I know what it looked like. You see, I knew Kyle before my accident." She stole a glance at him, saw that he sat frozen, waiting.

Waiting for the blow.

"But I'd forgotten all about him. The memories I lost? They included him. Lydia never told me about him. She hoped I'd never remember. But I did. Now I know things in my past that I'd forgotten. Things that will change what you think of me."

"Nothing can change that."

Don't be so sure, she almost blurted out. "We'll see." Emma took a deep breath, and the words tumbled out faster and faster, so fast that they almost blurred into one another. As each word left her mouth, it was as if she were tossing the weeds from her heart onto the growing pile by her side. Yank. Blurt. Yank. Blurt. Yank. Blurt. Until her story was finished.

Emma took a long, deep breath. She had one more thing to say. "When you saw us, Kyle was distraught about the baby, so I hugged him. He was crying, and I didn't know what else to do." She stumbled to a stop.

Only silence greeted her. Sam sat immobile, a weed dangling from his fingers. Emma had expected censure, disappointment, or rejection. But not silence. Maybe he was so upset, he'd never speak to her again.

She couldn't bear to stay around. She jumped to her feet and started toward the house.

"Emma, wait." Sam didn't look at her but held out a hand. "Please? This is a lot to process all at once."

"I know." Shame choked her, closed off her throat. Her eyes stung with unshed tears. At least she hadn't told him how she felt about him. That all her hopes and dreams for the future, for the two of them, had been dashed.

"At least give me until the end of the row." Sam's voice sounded odd, as if he were struggling to push his words out past a too-tight throat. He knelt and began to pull weeds methodically, mechanically.

Emma knelt in another row. She plucked and tossed, plucked and tossed. *Please finish, and let me go.* All she wanted was to escape. To run into the house and hide her face in her pillow. To hide her shame.

When he finished the row, Sam stood. Emma kept her head bent, turned away. What if he rejected her? She couldn't bear to see his face.

Sam came closer, stepping carefully over the plants. "Emma?" His voice was as gentle as when he was training Bolt.

So he planned to speak to her the way he did his dog. Tell her what she needed to do better next time. Only in this case there was no next time. Some things could never be fixed. Never be made right.

Sam knelt beside her, reached out a hand, and set it on her arm. Emma flinched as if burned but then forced herself to stay still. He hadn't run away, and he'd even kept his touch compassionate. She couldn't bear to look into his eyes and see the pity. He always championed the underdog.

Then he spoke.

"That took a lot of courage to tell me the truth. I've always known you were special, Emma, but this proves it."

What? Emma risked a glance at his face.

His eyes held only admiration and... what? A mix of sadness and—? "You've been through so much. Things that would have broken most people. And yet, in spite of it all, you kept your honesty, zest for life, and integrity. Before your accident, it sounds as if you'd decided to come back to the faith, but Kyle has no interest in becoming Amish?"

"I wish he did for Caleb's sake."

"But not for yours?"

Emma stole a glance at Sam's face. Did he think she should marry Kyle because of their past? "Of course, I'd like to see him join the church, but..."

"You don't love him?" Sam asked.

"No!" she cried. "I love—" She pressed her lips together before she blurted out her real feelings. Her cheeks heated under Sam's scrutiny, and she floundered for a way to finish her sentence that would be truthful. "I love... God and the church, and he doesn't."

"But you still care about him?"

"Oh, Sam, I feel so sorry for him. He blames himself for the accident, for what happened to me, for what happened to"—Emma squeezed her eyes shut—"the baby. He's carrying such a heavy load of guilt. That's why I hugged him. I wanted to comfort him and show him I forgave him."

A long silence stretched between them as she remembered that horrible moment—hugging Kyle, seeing Sam's shocked face. She shivered. "I'm sorry."

"Don't be sorry. Hugging Kyle shows what a forgiving, caring woman you are." Sam glanced off into the distance. "I only hope that someday I'll be worthy of one of those expressions of forgiveness."

Emma sat slack-jawed for a moment. "Why would I need to forgive you?" she asked.

"Because I thought the worst of you. That you had betrayed me with Kyle, just like Leah had cheated on me."

"Well, I did in a way..." She looked at him uncertainly. Did he mean that seeing her embracing Kyle had been worse than everything she'd just disclosed about her past?

"But you didn't. Not knowingly. Emma, I believe you're a different person than you were three years ago. Broken, yes. But stronger. More resolved. More faithful. Not rebellious or wild."

Did he mean what she thought he did? That he wouldn't hold her past against her?

"So you'll still be my friend?" she asked, her voice small and incredulous.

"Of course."

"We can still go on wagon rides and work together?" She dared not ask more. Not until he'd had time to absorb all she'd said. And not till she knew who she was—this new person, with a past.

"I'm here for you, Emma." He took her hand and pressed it reassuringly.

Misty-eyed, she squeezed his hand back. Never in a million years could she have predicted this...this grace. If Sam could give her grace, might not God too?

"Sam?" she asked in a small voice. "All the things I've done...Do you think God—?"

"Can forgive you?" His steady gaze revealed his understanding. "What do you say at every meal?"

Emma knew he was referring to the Lord's Prayer and God forgiving her as she forgave others.

"Didn't you say you forgave your *dat*? And Lydia and Caleb for not telling you about the past?"

"Of course."

"And Kyle?"

When Emma nodded, Sam said simply, "Then there's your answer. And remember, God's forgiveness is so much greater than ours."

Although Emma struggled to believe she was worthy of such grace, her soul whispered that Sam was right, and she thanked God that He had given her Sam as an example of His forgiveness here on earth.

Chapter Twenty-Eight

EMMA HURRIED INTO the house to start breakfast, her
heart lighter than it had been in ages. Sam and she
were friends again. She could hardly believe it; she'd
never dreamed of that possibility. She'd expected him to
reject her. Knowing Sam, she'd expected politeness, but not
this. If she weren't worried about waking the babies, she'd
burst into song. Instead she hummed quietly as she practically skipped around the kitchen.

Oh no. In all her excitement, she'd forgotten to get the
eggs. She'd have to collect them after breakfast. Caleb always
helped with the *bopplis'* morning feeding so he could spend
time with the twins, but he'd be down soon. She'd make
coffee soup, which he liked.

While the coffee brewed, she tore up a slice of stale bread
for each bowl. By the time Caleb entered the kitchen, she
was pouring coffee into the bowls and stirring in cream and
sugar.

"Wow, Emma, you look cheerful this morning," he said as
he sat at the table. "You're grinning ear to ear."

"I told Sam about my past."

"You did?" Caleb looked as if he'd been hit over the head
with a full feed sack. "How did he, um, take it?"

"Very well, actually. He still wants to be friends."

"Friends?"

"Yes, and he's still going to work with me." That was great news, but Emma had something else on her mind. The thought in the garden about God's forgiveness had brought to mind something she'd need to do, now that she could ride to church.

As Caleb sipped his coffee soup, Emma sat on the bench and propped her chin in her hands. "Now that I know about my past, I'd like to confess and join the church."

"That would be wonderful. Did you want to take baptismal classes here or in your home church?"

Here? Did that mean they were willing for her to stay until the fall? "I'd like to do it here, if it's all right with you and Lydia."

"We'd be happy to have you. Let's talk to the bishop."

Lydia was overjoyed when she heard, and so was Sam when she told him. So for the next eighteen weeks, she took classes, practiced riding with Sam, and even drove a short distance alone. The weeks flew by as she and Sam played volleyball and baseball with the other *youngie*, walked Bolt together every morning before Sam left for the fields, and weeded the garden together twice a week, joking and laughing about how they first met.

She might never be able to marry, but her friendship with Sam was a precious gift. So far he hadn't dated anyone in the *g'may*, and Emma couldn't bear the thought of him with someone else. For now, he seemed content helping her overcome her fears, encouraging her as she studied for baptismal classes, and helping her care for the babies.

The twins were beginning to sleep through the night, and Emma wondered if Lydia and Caleb would send her home soon. They'd at least wait until she was done with classes.

But as her baptismal day approached, Emma dreaded leaving Sam. They'd grown closer every day, and she could be herself around him, but she wished they could be more than friends.

On the day of Emma's last baptismal class Sam headed across the yard to the Millers' in the late afternoon. He wasn't sure if the flips in his stomach were from eating too much at the church meal earlier that day or his excitement at seeing Emma again.

When Emma answered the door, he had his answer. The summer heat had curled a few tendrils around her face that she was unsuccessfully smoothing back. He sucked in a breath. The flips in his stomach had turned into cartwheels, and when she smiled, a whole circus did acrobatics inside.

"Sam!" She pulled the door open wider. "Come in."

Seeing her standing there, the bright sun lighting her face, made Sam forget why he had come. He hemmed and hawed for a few seconds. Then he rushed out the words. "Would you like to go to the hymn sing with me tonight?" As he had done that long-ago day, he gestured toward his courting buggy in the driveway next door.

Emma hesitated and stared at the orange sun in the western sky, and his stomach plunged. He'd made a mistake. It had been several months since she'd ridden with him at night. One evening ride had not meant she was cured of her fears. He wished he'd made alternate plans.

Then Emma said in a soft, sweet voice, "I'd love to."

Sam couldn't resist teasing her. "I'm disappointed. I was expecting you to slam the door in my face."

A mischievous grin on her face, Emma grasped the door-knob. "I could do that if you'd like."

"You wouldn't."

"Try me."

Sam laughed. "I have no doubt you'd do it. But you already said yes, so I'm going to hold you to that."

"I think I can manage a ride when the sun's still pretty high in the sky. It's summer now; we might even get home before it sets completely."

Sam had no intention of hurrying home after the hymn sing. "What if we don't make it back until dark—would you still go?"

Without even the slightest hesitation, Emma said, "If I'm with you, I will. I'd go anywhere with you, anytime." Then her cheeks turned rosy, and she clapped a hand over her mouth and lowered her head.

Sam reached out and tilted her chin so he could look in her eyes. "Never be ashamed of saying what's in your heart when you're with me. I can't tell you how happy that made me to hear you say that."

"You don't know what a trial it is to always speak without thinking." Emma sighed. "I hoped it would get easier as I got older, but..."

"But don't ever change," Sam said. "I l–like you just the way you are."

Emma beamed. "Is it all right to say that I think the same about you?"

Sam laughed. "What about *hochmut*?"

Emma only giggled and then said, "I need to let Lydia and Caleb know."

When she returned, Sam helped her into the courting buggy and was overjoyed to watch her relax on the seat. It was hard to believe she'd once cowered in fear at the thought of even getting into a vehicle. He was so proud of her for all she'd accomplished, and getting over her fears was the least of it. Although he'd been stunned and pained by the revelation of her past, his first response had been right and true: she *was* a different person. She was stronger, wiser, committed to God, and committed to the church and its teachings. Everything he'd seen in the last few months had only confirmed what he'd known instinctively all along: she was a beautiful woman, full of warmth and feeling and courage.

Once they arrived at the hymn sing, Sam had difficulty keeping his mind on the music with Emma sitting across the table from him. Whenever their gazes met and she smiled at him, he forgot words to songs he'd known since he was a child. He tried concentrating on the hymnal, but his nerves were skittering so fast, he could barely sit still, let alone pay attention. Maybe going to the hymn sing that night hadn't been a wise idea.

Sam was relieved when the singing ended and couldn't wait to have some time alone with Emma. He took the long way home, until the sky darkened and one by one the stars came out overhead. He kept a close watch on her for any signs of fear, but she only squeezed his hand and breathed in the night air. When the sky overhead was spangled with stars, Sam pulled into a graveled area by the side of a deserted lane. He'd picked out this spot days ago because it was private and surrounded by trees.

The setting was the one he had dreamed of the first night he had kissed Emma. The beauty of God's creation all around them, the moon glowing overhead, and the most beautiful sight of all—Emma, her eyes lit with starlight and love—sitting beside him.

Sam slid across the bench and drew her into his arms. Her beauty dazzled him so much he could hardly speak, but he had a question he wanted to ask her. The most important question of his life.

"Emma, I love you with all my heart. Would you do me the honor of marrying me?"

Emma stilled in his arms and stared up at him, speechless. For the first time in her life, no words came to her lips. Because no words could express the joy overwhelming her.

Sam stared at her fearfully as if afraid she planned to say no, but she couldn't reassure him. She'd lost the power of speech.

He drew back a little and studied her face, pain in his eyes. He started to speak, but she laid a finger across his lips to keep him silent.

Before she could blink them back, tears rolled down her cheeks. She'd thought no man would ever want her, ever marry her, and there was Sam, the man she loved most in all the world, asking a question she'd never dreamed she would hear. Her heart had expanded so large, so full of wonder and gratitude, it filled every inch of her.

A tiny puff of air escaped her lips, a sigh from deep within. A sigh that expelled all her fears and expressed all her hopes for the future. A sigh that carried all her love.

His wary expression showed he'd misinterpreted her sigh. If words wouldn't come, she'd resort to actions. Emma threw her arms around him and pressed her lips to his. After she kissed him so thoroughly he sat there dazed, she rested her head against his chest and reveled in the rapid beating of his heart.

Sam cleared his throat. "I worried maybe you didn't feel the same way I did."

"Oh, Sam," she breathed. "I thought I showed you how I felt every time we met."

He chuckled. "Well, maybe you did, just a little." His sideways grin showed he'd noted both her expressiveness and her restraint, and he appreciated both.

He prodded her. "You never answered my question."

This time Emma wanted to shout her answer so the whole world could hear, but she managed a demure "Yes."

"You're sure?" Sam looked disappointed. "You don't sound very enthusiastic."

She batted her eyelashes at him. "I was trying to be ladylike. I didn't think you'd want me to knock you out of the wagon in my exuberance."

Sam laughed. "Actually I was kind of hoping for that kind of response."

Emma gazed into his eyes. "Do you want to know the truth?" When Sam nodded, she admitted, "I was so overwhelmed, I couldn't speak."

Sam's smile outshone the full moon. "I made you speechless?"

"Yes." Emma snuggled closer. "I think it's the first time in my life I've ever been at a loss for words."

"I hope I'll be able to make you speechless many times

throughout our married life." He looked down and flashed her a devilish grin. "Only in good ways, of course."

"I have no doubt you will." Then she reached up, drew his face down to hers, and kissed him until they were both speechless.

Amish Glossary

ach—oh

Ach, vell—Oh, well

aenti—aunt

Ausbund—Amish hymnal

boppli—baby

daadi—grandfather

daadi haus—small house attached to the main dwelling

danke—thank you

dat—dad

dummkopf—dummy

Englisch—non-Amish people

Englischer—a non-Amish person

ferhoodled—confused; perplexed

g'may—church district

Gott—God

Gott im Himmel—God in heaven (when *Dat* says this, he's praying)

grexy—whiny, out-of-sorts

grundsau—groundhog

gude mariye—good morning

gut—good

Gut-n-Owed—good evening

hochmut—pride

jah—yes

kapp—prayer bonnet

Kumm esse—Come eat.

mamm—mom

mammi—grandmother

onkel—uncle

Ordnung—unwritten rules that govern the church
district

redd—straighten up, clean

Rumschpringe—"running around time"; the period
before Amish teens join the church; some experiment
with *Englisch* ways

rutsched—wriggled

strubbly—disheveled, messy

U bent welkom.—You're welcome.

uffgevva—giving up, surrendering

verboten—forbidden

Wie gehts?—How are you?

wunderbar—wonderful

youngie—youth

Amish Recipes

By Maria Lebo

RED BEET EGGS

2 14.5-oz. cans red beets with juice
1 cup sugar
½ cup cider vinegar
12 eggs, hard-boiled and peeled
1 thinly sliced onion (optional)

Strain the red beet juice into a bowl, reserving beets. Add sugar and vinegar, and stir until sugar dissolves. Add the peeled eggs and onion to the bowl. Put the red beets on top to weigh down the eggs. Chill at least four hours in the refrigerator, or overnight for best flavor and color. Yield: 12 eggs.

LEMONADE ICE CREAM

3 cups whole milk
6 egg yolks
⅔ cup granulated sugar
1 tsp. lemon extract
Zest of 3 lemons
2 Tbsp. fresh lemon juice
⅓ cup undiluted frozen lemonade concentrate

Heat the milk to a boil in a heavy saucepan. Cover and remove from heat. Beat the egg yolks and sugar together in a bowl until light and thick. Slowly pour the hot milk into the egg mixture, whisking constantly. Put the mixture into the saucepan, and cook over low heat, stirring with a wooden spoon until it thickens slightly and coats the back of the spoon. Do not allow it to come to a boil, or it will curdle.

Add the lemon extract, zest, and lemon juice. Allow the mixture to cool to room temperature, and then refrigerate it, loosely covered with plastic wrap, until chilled (at least three hours). Freeze the mixture in an ice-cream maker. Once it starts to set and thicken, add lemonade concentrate and continue mixing until the mixture is set. Place it in the freezer to set it further. Yield: 1 quart.

CONNECT WITH US!

CHARISMA HOUSE

(Spiritual Growth)

f Facebook.com/CharismaHouse

y @CharismaHouse

O Instagram.com/CharismaHouse

SILOAM

(Health)

P Pinterest.com/CharismaHouse

MEV MODERN ENGLISH VERSION

(Bible)

www.mevbible.com